SCARLET DRAGONFLIES

SCARLET DRAGONFLIES

AND OTHER STORIES FROM THE SUNDERBANS

AMRITA NILANJANA

olive turtle

NIYOGI BOOKS

Published by
NIYOGI BOOKS
Block D, Building No. 77,
Okhla Industrial Area, Phase-I,
New Delhi-110 020, INDIA
Tel: 011-26818960, +91 7428978881
Email: niyogibooks@gmail.com
Website: www.niyogibooksindia.com

Editor: Anwesha Panda
Design: Nadeem Ahmed
Cover design: Pinaki De

ISBN: 978-81-990243-0-4
Publication: 2025

Printed at Niyogi Offset Pvt. Ltd., New Delhi, India

Dedicated to my late father,
Birendralal Mukherjee,
and my mother, Gita Mukherjee.

CONTENTS

PREFACE

When I had set out to write a collection of short stories three years ago, I didn't imagine making shocking discoveries about life stories that were untold, unheard of and distressing to the human mind, to the extent that they defied logic and reasoning. My quest for stories brought me in close contact with ordinary people and their extraordinary journeys. From the city of Kolkata to the Sunderbans and back, I travelled restlessly to hear the tales about the lives of these simple people that they chose to share with me. Initially, I found them reticent as they struggled with the idea of opening up their lives to a complete stranger. But with my continued persistence, they began to see me as someone who would not judge them, but rather someone willing to share meals with them, understand them and return to them bearing the same simplicity that characterised their lives.

This collection is largely inspired by real-life events. The stories push the borders of imagination as they narrate tales that are likely to shock, bewitch and spur the mind to discover some of life's intuitive battles and contrasts unbeknownst to humanity. From the wild backwaters of the Sunderbans to the cunning of urban existence, the diverse landscape of the narrative compels protagonists in each of the twelve stories to script turns of events that determine whether they live or die to be remembered or dismissed to unconsciousness. At the centre of the narrative arc is "Spellbound", the story of a young girl who becomes a tiger charmer in the mangroves to not only break the glass ceiling but also connect so deeply with the wild that tigers begin to speak to her silently.

While "Spellbound" is deeply rooted in the absolution the inhabitants of the Sunderbans islands seek from their ruling deity Bon Bibi, "A Boat too Far", based on a true event, embodies the eternal struggle between man and beast in the mangroves. The protagonist of the piece is a poor fisherman, who dares uncharted waters to find a rich haul that would help him free his house mortgaged to a sinister landlord. As he sets out to explore uncharted waters, he engages in a face-off with a tiger stalking him. But in his desperation to make more money out of fishing, he throws caution to the wind.

Four other stories: "Ninety-Eight", "Scarlet Dragonflies", "Unsold" and "Come No closer" also set in the backdrop of the Sunderbans offer tell-tale accounts of issues that people on the mangrove islands face every day. In "Ninety-Eight", a tribal woman leads her ilk to rally against deadly Sundari log smugglers, not knowing that her own estranged husband is a part of the mafia. In "Scarlet Dragonflies", a simple village girl is pitchforked into city life after marriage just when Kolkata was rebuilding itself from the after-effects of World War II. Though the city fascinates her deeply enough to weaken her memory of her home in the Sunderbans, an old family tragedy from decades ago brings her back to where her home was before Partition, reconnecting her with a forgotten sense of loss. The woman at the centre of the narrative is long gone now, but the words she had inscribed in my heart will forever remain indelible.

I was equally fascinated by the story of a simple village girl that culminates in "Unsold", in which a child metamorphoses into a lovely young woman years after being sold to human traffickers by her poverty-stricken mother. Rescued by the police, the child finds a new identity at a rehab centre and grows to become a doctor. But destiny brings her back to her village in the Sunderbans where a painful surprise awaits her.

Of all the Sunderbans stories, "Come No Closer" reveals a shocking truth about a woman who had spent six years with her twin daughters on an unnamed island in the Sunderbans, abandoned by both her in-laws and parents. Rescued by a forester, her new life in Kolkata becomes a battle of attrition with her wild past, and her disdain for men keeps tearing her apart in a near-relationship with her saviour. "Come No Closer" is based on a true story that was narrated to me by an old widow in Hasnabad in the North 24 Parganas of West Bengal. The story has been built with a fictionalised form.

The other five stories are set in different backdrops away from the Sunderbans. They speak of a hangman's cunning ("Hands of Silence"), a nude model's emotional emancipation in sculpture ("Scent of Clay"), a woman's battle with her shady past ("A Room to Forgive"), a raw village idiot picks up arms to call the bluff of a conceited sarpanch ("Paint it Red"), and a man with dreamy fancies courts a picture on the wall for deliverance ("Corsican Images"). "Paint it Red" had been published under the title of "Riparian" in *Indian Literature*, a quarterly published by Sahitya Akademi, in October 2018.

In this collection, I have strung together stories that I feel are a must-read for humanity, and I hope my readers would be as intrigued as I was when I chose to walk hand-in-hand with people on the soil upon which they were born, dismissed and resurrected by their own courage to live with pride. Thank you, dear reader, for coming along this journey.

AMRITA NILANJANA

A BOAT TOO FAR

This river is called Peechkhali, which is flanked by the tiny village of Jamespur and the Tiger Reserve. Even though the river flows gently and almost noiselessly, it is deceptive. The current it carries on its back and beneath can be treacherous to anyone not aware of the unpredictable moods of these backwaters of the Sunderbans. Big boats and skiffs never try to negotiate the waters sideways, what is called 'aarey' in the local dialect. Instead, boatmen either sail with the current or take the current head on. Many boats rest at the bottom of these rivers as a result of errors in judgement.

The Peechkhali shoots off from the Gumri that makes a sweeping turn from Sajnekhali before finding a new course towards Bangladesh. This is tiger country, where nothing is a given. Wildlife and humans jockey for space in disquieted co-existence along the creeks and rivers. The entire tiger reserve is surrounded by firm netting, mainly made of thick nylon cord. Steel meshes have also been put up by the Forest Department at places where nylon has proved to be weak. Long stretches of the netting cannot be seen as fast-growing wild vines have covered them. The deadly mangrove forest has to be cordoned off, as it is home to the Royal Bengal Tiger—a killer and a champion swimmer. On the other side of the Peechkhali, remote human habitats like Jamespur go to sleep knowing they are safe.

There used to be a time not too long ago when tigers would swim across the crocodile-infested waters of the Peechkhali to prey on human habitats. Too many human lives and livestock had been lost. The tigers of the Sunderbans have an uncanny ability to identify the weakest prey. Crouching on their padded paws, they would enter Jamespur late into the night, and wait behind the thick bushes for the last lamp to go out. In a flash, they would pluck an old woman, sometimes an old man or a child, out of bed, grabbing them by the jugular, and disappear without a trace as the rest of the family slept. The drops of blood that would lead away from the home towards the river bank would be the only evidence of someone having been taken.

But then, the hushed silence of Jamespur evenings is a thing of the past. Grandmothers can now sing bedtime songs to their grandchildren: *Nodir buke bhaishya jai jeler dol, dheuer dolai sundarban kore tolmol* (With distance in their eyes, the fishermen flow with the tides, and in the tunes the waves play, the Sunderbans softly sway), their voices wafting through the night like a ballad, and ever so slowly, fading into the moist air of the Sunderbans.

Yet, the trauma remains somewhere deep within, as people of Jamespur never let their guard down. In the back of their minds, they know these nettings can never keep a hungry tiger back.

Usually, they don't get to see tigers, though the felines seem to be watching them all the time. The forest often moves. The *jat baine*s, the *kalo baine*s or the *hental*s would suddenly rustle without any breeze. That's when people become alert. By living in the wild through generations, they have developed a keen sense of hearing, coupled with strong intuitions. But they know even if they see a tiger, it might be too late to carry home the excitement of spotting one. Jamespur has lived with the knowledge that every tiger in the Sunderbans is a born man-eater. But that fearful realisation hasn't stopped the people from venturing out in the mangroves.

The two main occupations of Jamespur are fishing and honey-collecting. The fishermen and honey-collectors, as they try to merge with the surroundings, know too well that being careless in these mangroves is death.

Yet, there is contentment and pride in what they do for a living—skills passed down from one generation to another.

Like Himu Naskar. A lanky man, lean but muscular, with tanned brown skin and hair brushed back, Himu was a fisherman with a small dinghy. Every day at four in the morning, he goes out fishing. There are some fishermen who move about in the creeks but Himu avoids these waterways. The creeks are like blind alleys and too narrow for safety. Himu prefers the wide open river where he can be safer and at the same time have a catch as rich and diverse as *Bhetkis*, *Faluis*, *Kholshes*, Mackarels and Catfish. And if he nets *Nona Tangras*, he considers himself very lucky. This fish is much sought-after in the town markets. Still, the perils of fishing in the Sunderbans are everywhere, every time. This has been all too evident to Himu.

Quite often, he has spotted a tiger next to a creek on the banks opposite Jamespur. An opening in the netting in that area didn't appear to have been cut with a knife or a pair of scissors. This is bad news for his village. If there is a tiger, free, the chances are that many others may follow. Himu feels a shiver running down his spine whenever he sees the tiger, which he calls Sultan because of the way he perches leisurely on the bank and moves his raised head in a slow arc scanning the surroundings, as if he is the crown, surveying his kingdom.

Himu knew not to take his boat too far across the river towards the mangroves. It offered little protection from a tiger attack. More of a skiff with room for just two, the boat is his lifeline. Lately, with Sultan invading his thoughts, Himu had become unmindful. The second tide of the day was set to come in. The current was getting stronger. Himu stood quietly, feeling the wetness of the damp wood of his boat and looked at the banks, squinting to focus on the wilderness.

Sultan was missing that day. The air was especially still. Himu held his breath; there were fresh pugmarks. A twig snapped somewhere in the thickets. A rustle of leaves followed. He could hear his heart pound. Himu needed to row back immediately. On top of it, any further delay would mean he would have to sail *aarey*. Pulling his net out of the water, he went to the rowing end of the boat, sat down, stretched his legs like a sculler, and clamped an iron loop attached to the side of his boat on the oar to secure it. The oar was heavy. Its handle was made of wood and the paddle, of iron. The paddle was thick at the top but had edges as sharp as a razor. This was his only defence against the unpredictable waters and the wild. He thrust the oar into the water and pulled with all his might but the boat didn't swivel as fast he wanted it to. He tried again. The boat moved a little bit to the left. Himu looked up. The small waves had begun to slap the banks and the wild growth behind was undulating like a Mexican wave. His mouth was dry. 'Come on! Move!' Himu said out loud.

And, the boat began to move faster, as if it had a soul, as if it could hear the voice of its creator.

Day after day, Himu would continue to cast his net in the middle of the river, ready to row his trusted boat back if he spotted danger on the bank. Just a fortnight ago, he had to retreat hastily as a tiger had suddenly walked up to the edge of the water. It was Sultan, the tiger he had grown familiar with—whose presence scared him, but whose absence left him with a sense of emptiness. Sultan could be easily identified. He had a black crescent-like mark on his forehead, a mark completely out of place in a crowd of stripes.

✣✣✣

Between the two high tides every river in the Sunderbans gets every day, Sultan leaves his mangrove fortress and comes out, hungry as always. His last meal was a small *langoor* which had fallen off its tree two days ago, stunned by Sultan's fearsome roar at the bottom of the trunk. He has since survived on large crabs. For months, Sultan has been perching himself on the bank to keep an eye on Himu, but outwitted by the human all the time. To get Himu, Sultan knew he had to employ an overdose of cunning. He needed to do something to get close to Himu or Himu closer to him. Dusk was descending on the mangroves and earthen lamps inside homes in Jamespur were being lit. They looked like dotted filigree on the border of a saree. The clotting darkness was being bejewelled. Sultan got up, stretched, yawned, brushed his very sensitive whiskers to rid them of small, nocturnal insects and walked back lazily into the darkness of the wild.

✣✣✣

On the other side of the river, Himu stepped into his house that was softly illuminated with light from two kerosene lamps. Their glow was being absorbed by the clay walls, turning them translucent. One lamp hung from a hook on the wall, next to a *swastika* mark in red that looked so alive in that magical light. The other was kept in the middle of the floor, diffusing soft light all around. The radiance inside the room was enveloping his wife Shuktara, who was hunching over a stove. Himu felt spent after a long day at the river. The hauls, the tension and the rowing were overpowering him. Yet, the joy of returning home to be with Shuktara, who would melt into his tired chest like a candle, touching him with comforting empathy, affection and love, would light up his mind once again, priming him to take on another day.

Himu had plucked Shuktara out of a village fair in Gosaba. Her parents had initially dithered to have her married off to Himu. But they consented realising Himu had no dependents. In other words, whatever he earned would be shared between only him and his wife. Four years along, they appeared a fairytale family of contrasts—Himu, the always outbound, weather beaten bread-earner and Shuktara, the docile and homely epicentre of their common and ordinary quests.

✣✣✣

One thing that gnawed Himu like a rodent was a brutal reality: the land on which he had established his home was mortgaged to Nitai Sardar. This man was a dreaded landlord of the mangroves. It was said that Nitai's tentacles spread wide and far beyond the backwaters of the Sunderbans. He was politically connected. He was also the kingpin of a group of smugglers and poachers who ferried logs from illegally felled trees, and tiger hides, to Bangladesh and Myanmar. These delta pirates used the waterways and channels that ran past Netidhopani before merging into the Bay of Bengal. Not even the police bothered Nitai; after all, he was their cash-cow. Surrounded most of the time by his bodyguards who carried guns, Nitai was said to be brutal and ruthless when it came to dealing with his unassuming beneficiaries. Not one defaulter had survived his wrath. There was another side to him. He was a stealthy womanizer.

Himu was already three months' behind in terms of paying his dues. Some of Nitai's men had arrived all of a sudden last week to remind him of exactly that.

He was aware that whatever cash he was fetching from his everyday catch wasn't enough for him to repay Nitai without defaulting. The content of the mortgage papers he had signed with an impression of his left thumb was skewed towards Nitai. If by any chance the deal went sour, Himu's side of the story would not hold in a court of law. The original papers were with Nitai who never gave Himu a copy.

Himu knew he had to do something to earn more money, not just to repay Nitai. He needed to give his house a makeover. The cracks on the walls were widening, turning them into a haven for insects. The *kuchha* floor also needed to be concretised as seepage owing to excessive monsoon was causing the precipice to weaken. And some of the wooden beams that held the thatched roof up were termite-stricken. Above all, Shuktara had just two sarees. One, a cotton saree with prints that she wore in the daytime while going through her chores. The other, also of cotton, was white with a red border that she wore with its tail covering her head in the evening while offering prayers at the *tulsitala* (a place in the courtyard of a Hindu home where *tulsi* plants are grown for worshipping) in the courtyard. Himu realised he was not being fair to Shuktara. A turnaround for the household was overdue. And to bring that about, it might take months, even years. The only way to speed up the process was to explore the depths of the unknown waters for more fish on the other side of the Peechkhali. But it was Sultan's territory.

He sighed, and stretched out on the bed. It was eight in the night. Tomorrow is another day. He turned towards Shuktara, trying to gauge her mind. Himu still couldn't make out what material this doe-eyed girl was made of.

'What's on your mind?' Shuktara was curious.

'Nothing, just looking at you.'

'I am sure something is eating you. Tell me, what is it?'

Himu gently held Shuktara's face between his palms like a feather, and looked into her eyes. 'If I die suddenly, do not hold on to this house. Go back to your parents.'

Shuktara's eyes stung. 'Why are you saying that?'

'I don't know why, but pray you don't have to see that day.'

Himu pulled Shuktara onto his left shoulder, disturbing the bun she had so carefully rolled. Her black, cascading hair formed a lattice on her face through which her coy eyes and trembling lips were willing to surrender to a gathering storm.

Jamespur always retired to early nights, leaving the long hours until dawn to the wild, inside homes and outside.

✣✣✣

Over the past week, Himu, while fishing, had found Sultan missing from the bank, again. He half-expected to spot Sultan every second day. He wondered what had happened to the tiger. Has he migrated to another island in search of prey? Neither could Himu spot fresh pugmarks. Sultan seemed to have vanished without a trace. He couldn't accept his disappearance but he had to remind himself that given a chance, the big cat would tear him apart like a rag doll. He hadn't seen anything more majestic than this tiger, burning bright on the otherwise dull landscape. Despite all the fear he felt, Himu was in awe of Sultan. The tiger's absence was leaving a canvas incomplete, so artfully created by nature. A sense of loss gripped him, and Himu just couldn't explain to himself why he felt the way he did.

Himu's mind was racing as he began to haul the net. He was in a dilemma. A part of him, the one which was in bondage to Nitai, was urging him to sail to the other side of the river. The other part, mortal, fearing and submitted to a life he so lovingly shared with Shuktara, was warning him not to. In between, Himu the fisherman stood on a narrow dinghy on a wide river that promised much.

When Himu returned home, he found Shuktara sitting on the verandah, sobbing uncontrollably. He rushed to her.

'What happened? Tell me what happened?' Placing a reassuring hand on Shuktara's head, Himu drew her close.

Shuktara told her that while he was away fishing, Nitai Sardar had come with his men. Nitai had pulled Shuktara by the hand before warning that if Himu failed to pay up next month, he would take away his land and every other thing that was in the house. 'He had winked at me when he said 'every other thing.' Fear and disgust were visible in her eyes.

Himu knew something needed to be done, and fast. The next morning, he went to the village chief and explained the situation to him. Himu wanted the chief, an old man of 70, to take action against Nitai even though he knew that complaining would be of little consequence. Nobody had the courage to stand up to Nitai. Just like he had assumed, the village chief surrendered to Himu saying he could do nothing because the land he lived upon belonged to Nitai, like so many others in the village. One cardinal truth was: Nitai could only be appeased with money and women.

As a parting advice, the village chief told him to send Shuktara back to her parents in Gosaba. Himu walked away, fuming and completely frustrated.

Come what may, he knew he had to dare the wild for Shuktara and himself to live with dignity.

✣✣✣

Himu and his dinghy remained immobile in the middle of the Peechkhali. A white-bellied eagle flapped its wings across the river in pursuit of a Mangrove Whistler, leaving in its wake the echo of its noisy flight, disturbing the silence. A monkey squeaked somewhere and a mother barking deer hooted, calling her fawns to a leafy meal. A red newt slithered out of its muddy burrow and crawled up the bank towards a deep pugmark inside which insects swam in accumulated rainwater. The many rewards of nature were unfolding into one magical system of life. A little later, an army of unseen crickets began stridulating, the well-orchestrated noise turning into a hypnotic drone, only to switch off all of a sudden. The jungle was shifting between life and silence at will.

Himu was scanning the bank on the other side. His trained eyes found nothing amiss. He held the oar in a vice-like grip, as if it was the source of all power that he needed at the moment, and began cutting across the current to the other side, his heart in his mouth. He stopped about thirty feet from the mangroves, a distance no tiger can leap across. Another five feet towards the bank, and Himu would have been within the reach of the canines that probably lurked in the deep mangroves. A strong wind was blowing from further down the river to his left. The wind was making the netting bulge in places, as if an invisible creature was trying to break through them. He closed his eyes and cast his net. He heard a splash. Alarmed, his heart skipping a few beats, Himu looked at the bank. Two sparring water monitors had rolled down into the waters. He heaved a sigh of relief. The day turned out to be rewarding for Himu. Fish was plenty on that side of the river. No other fisherman had ever sailed that distance for a catch. Himu was the first. All Himu required to do now was to hand over his catch to the ferry that would arrive in an hour to take the fish to town wholesalers. Before leaving for his side of the river, Himu joined his hands together, said a short prayer to *Bon Bibi*, the Mother Goddess of the Sundari jungle. Himu looked back at the bank one last time for the day.

✣✣✣

Surplus cash began to flow in for Himu. With a little more effort, he would now be able to settle his dues with Nitai. Yet, Shuktara would continue to warn her husband with a sense of trepidation. 'Do you really need to go that far out in the river? What if…?'

Himu did not want to ignore the warning but the other side of the river kept enticing him. 'Nothing will happen to me. You see, the tiger has left for another territory. I heard that most tigers are now being seen around the Dobanki island.'

Himu was not making this up. More than forty armed pirates from Bangladesh were trapped on the inhabitable Dobanki. The river police and the Border Security Force came to know of their presence after three of the pirates surrendered to a tourist boat. They didn't want to be eaten by tigers. The newspapers went to town. Himu came to know about it from the local priest whose daily chores included reading out from yesterday's newspapers to villagers.

Himu knew Sultan was not the only tiger ruling the wild of the Sunderbans. If that territory has truly been vacated by Sultan, it won't be long for another tiger to occupy it. Himu knew he had to be always careful. One weak link in his guard, and he would be an easy meal. And so, he continued to keep a safe distance from the banks. Still, he couldn't rule out the intuitive feeling of being watched, sized up and stalked by another. If need be, he knew his dinghy would be able to swiftly take him away from the danger zone, the way it has always reached him to safety like a true companion.

The next day, when Himu returned from the river, Shuktara told him that Nitai's men had come to collect cash. While doing so, they had said their boss would visit the house just to check on them. Himu knew Nitai never made courtesy calls. He was aware of why Nitai wanted to visit his house. In all probability, he would do so again when Shuktara would be alone. Himu was helpless. He could not give up fishing to protect Shuktara, whereas he needed to ward off this two-legged beast, constantly stalking, while there was time. Until then, his need for more fish would remain.

Himu had a plan. First, he would try and free himself from the mortgage as soon as possible. Then, he would sell off the land and shift to Shuktara's hometown Gosaba, where he would open a small shop of supplies. Himu would seek the help of Shuktara's father, who happened to be a person revered by locals because unlike many in the area, he could read English newspapers, even if haltingly. But it was still a long haul.

With wary optimism, Himu looked at the fading light being split into a billion glistening particles by the Peechkhali.

❖❖❖

Himu took his boat closer to the other side of the river. The haul was rich. Gleefully, he sailed back. If he could continue to fish like this for just six more months, he and Shuktara would be free from all the fears that had shackled their lives. He needed to get closer to the bank. Sultan definitely was gone. Or else, he would have, at least for once, come out from the deep forest. Neither has he heard a roar from the deep. It's been a month he has not been sighted. It was likely that he had found another territory to prey upon. Or maybe, he has proved to be too wily for Sultan. But it never crossed his mind that with his recklessness, he was causing the line that separated need and greed to blur. Every day, he would be promising himself that it would be one last time for him at the other side of Peechkhali, and the very next day, he would be back, throwing caution to the wind. Fish was important, but what became equally important was the daily dose of the high he was getting from fishing in forbidden waters. Challenging Sultan in his absence and returning home without a scratch felt like a pull of *afeem* (opium).

In the meantime, Shuktara had begun to accompany him. Himu didn't want to leave her alone any more at home while he went fishing. Besides, two nets were better than one. He was still a few thousand rupees short on the mortgage but he knew the day wasn't far when he would be able to clear all his dues.

With Shuktara joining him, Himu afforded himself breaks between hauls. Initially, Shuktara was clumsy with fishing. But she proved to be a fast learner, especially when her trainer was her husband. Their fishing duet continued without a hitch.

✣✣✣

One day, as they were casting their nets, Himu heard the foliage inside the mangrove rustle. He noticed a sudden gap in a growth of green and yellow leaves. That gap wasn't there just a moment ago. By now, he had subconsciously memorised the foliage patterns on Sultan's side of the river. Was there something behind the growth, something that had now moved? There was no sound except of the waters that flowed. He dismissed the thought and went back to fishing. He heard the rustling again. This time, when he looked up, he found the gap in the yellow-green growth wider than before. Possibly, a spotted deer was eating the leaves. And then, the silence became more overbearing than he ever remembered it to be.

Himu hid his nervousness beneath a smile as he told Shuktara that it was time to return. Just 10 feet from the bank, standing on the boat, Himu turned his back towards the mangroves and began hauling the net. He bent down to hold it firmly. The net was exceedingly heavy. It seemed another rich haul awaited him.

It was at that moment Shuktara screamed: 'Himuuuuu!!!'

It all happened in a flash. Himu took less than a second to turn and as he turned, subconsciously, he held the long wooden oar with his both hands. He could see the flash of a yellow thunder, dropping on him with unmatched ferocity.

It was Sultan, fangs and claws bared, and roaring.

Himu lifted the oar in a swift movement but Sultan was faster. The tiger wouldn't let go of his prey after months of stalking. With his right paw, Sultan swiped at Himu's left shoulder, taking off a thick slice of flesh. Rocking violently, the boat was dangerously close to overturning as it tilted heavily to the side Sultan attacked it from. Shuktara picked up a metal bucket from the bowels of the boat and hit the tiger hard on its head. But it wouldn't let him go. Himu could feel the warm and pungent breath of Sultan falling on him. He kicked the tiger with all his might in the belly. Sultan let loose a heavy grunt and recoiled, ready to pounce again. Himu knew he could never wrestle the tiger away. Sultan was preparing to launch his final attack. With each moment, Himu's strength was deserting him. His left shoulder was bleeding profusely from a gaping hole that exposed a part of his shoulder bone. As Sultan lunged at his throat, Himu let out a war cry with all his might and swung the oar, aiming at the tiger's rib-cage, catching him mid-air.

He gasped for breath and extended his right arm, looking for Shuktara. Through a thick layer of darkness that was descending on him, Himu could see a faint silhouette that looked like hers. He was falling fast like a burnt-out star. He could hear Shuktara's voice at a distance. What was she saying? Was it already dawn? Was she trying to wake him up so that he didn't miss fishing?

❖❖❖

Six days later, Himu opened his eyes. Still dazed, his eyes were trying to scout the surroundings. He couldn't make out where he was, or why he was surrounded by so many people. And then he recognised the red swastika sign on the wall and the lantern next to it. He could see the faces of the village chief and some neighbours, all looking at him smilingly. A soft hand touched his forehead. Himu tried to speak.

'Don't say anything now. You are all right,' Shuktara whispered into his ears, with her hand still touching the forehead of the man who was her sanctuary of everything she lived for.

It took Himu almost two months to be able to walk properly again. Every step of the way during his recovery, Shuktara was by his side. While Himu was convalescing, the village chief began visiting him frequently. During one of his visits, the chief narrated to him how an inexperienced Shuktara had rowed the boat back by the sheer dint of her willpower. She was screaming for help as her boat had moored at the jetty. It was right then the chief, who said he was out for a stroll at the waterfront, had heard her cry for help. Without wasting time, he had called the river clinic to treat Himu then and there. There was no time for him to be taken to a hospital in Kakdwip.

Himu, somewhat restored, wondered why the village chief was suddenly so fond of him until the old man explained.

'Himu, before you, nobody from Jamespur had ever survived a tiger attack. You beat back a tiger. This village needs brave people like you to show the way.'

From Gadkhali to Netidhopani, Himu quickly became an icon of courage for the people of the Sunderbans. His picture and story were published in the leading newspapers of West Bengal. People now listened to him, deferred to him. And Nitai Sardar, apprehending a popular revolt against him, took his business of sharking away from Jamespur. After all, Himu was the new panchayat chief with a strong following in the region. He was not to be messed with.

⁂

Himu is still fishing, but with more caution than ever. He now has a big motorised boat that helps him spread farther out on the Peechkhali. The old dinghy doesn't sail anymore. It sits in the courtyard of his house like a guarded treasure. Several fishermen in the locality wanted to buy it. But Himu just couldn't let go of his old and trusted companion.

Himu was sitting on the verandah that overlooked the courtyard. He was looking at the dinghy. Without it, he would not have seen daylight again. That dinghy was now a part of folklore.

Shuktara handed him a bowl of *Muri Makha*—puffed rice mixed with boiled green peas, diced onions, green chillies and a pinch of salt and pepper. Minding her bulge, she sat down slowly next to her husband, each bend of her body responding gingerly to the process of her sitting.

'Tell me, what would it be?' Shuktara quizzed Himu, her hands curled under her chin with lush femininity.

'How do I know?'

'If it's a girl, what name you have in mind for her?'

'Nayantara.'

'And if it's a boy?'

Himu didn't answer. He only lifted his face, his eyes and raised brows pointing to the far side of Peechkhali.

'Are you serious?'

Himu nodded. And then, they broke into a fond smile together to romance a past that was so exclusively theirs.

The golden light that was bouncing off Peechkhali had begun to dim and the herons flying low over the water had started homing. Darkness was descending slowly. It was time for the Sunderbans to return to its silence, into which would be sucked the many forms of nature that mesmerise life in the day.

'Go inside, Shuktara. And oh! Don't overcook the rice like yesterday.'

"That's not happening again. But what about you?'

'I will join you in a while.'

'All right.'

Himu kept standing in the courtyard, as if he was in a trance. His eyes were transfixed on the bushes just behind the fencing.

There was suddenly a gap in the green and yellow foliage, which was not there even some moments ago.

✣✣✣

COME NO CLOSER

Down by the river, a very young girl is racing a spotless white cormorant flying low on the backwaters. She knows she cannot outrun the bird, it is cutting through the salty air with ease. Yet, she continues with her breathless run, one hasty leap after another, every day along the river, racing birds that would be in whispering distance of her, only to fly away into a brilliant emptiness. Children of her age, in their early teens, follow her in the chase, flailing their arms and shouting with joy in gay abandon, as if they are being led by her into a dream of flying. She doesn't pause or even look back at them cock-a-hoop behind her. Overcome with a sense of being unchained, she keeps dashing towards the edge of the banks even though the bird has flown away. 'Hiba, don't go any farther. The jungle starts from there,' a young boy from behind screams a warning. And soon, the pack behind loses her to the forest-line, not knowing if she would ever emerge from there.

Neither does Hiba.

The jungle unfolds to her with a warring dance of demons and angels. The ungodly spirits begin rising from beneath its treacherous soil, breaking into wicked gyrations, and the angels start flying with ladybirds on drifting leaves. Hiba watches in awe as the moist air begins to circle her like a magnetic vortex, drawing her deeper and deeper into its depths. And then, it is neither light nor darkness, only a caress of electric white in which she appears as the cormorant that she could never defeat on the banks of the river.

Sweating and breathing heavily, Farida Khatun sat up on the bed in the middle of the night. This was not the first time she had this dream. And every time Farida did, she would listen to the silences she shared with Hiba, a girl she knew with her heart once upon a time. Farida's daughters, Rehana and Sultana, have seen their mother like this before, as a solitary pillar on ruins.

It is in this half-light, she is sometimes like soft footsteps parting magpie woods, sometimes like drowning paper boats, and some other times as wildly woven as the veins of wilderness.

✣✣✣

The breathing roots of the mangrove plants are nature's own defence system. If you invade, there will most likely be blood. These roots emerge in millions from the wet river banks of the Sunderbans islands. They look like reversed conical pegs, like the spiny back of a mythical dragon. They are spear-sharp at the top. Walking on them is impossible, let alone running, which one might have to do as danger is everywhere in these jungles. Many honey and wax collectors have slipped on the wet soil and fallen on these roots, impaling themselves.

One such island, near the mouth of Bay of Bengal, has remained untouched. That, however, doesn't make it any different from the rest of the islands in the Sunderbans, habited or uninhabited. It looks serene from a boat, and very, very quiet though inside its foliage, it is dangerously wild.

But the island is on the verge of losing its anonymity.

Senior forester Ramkumar Manna and his two colleagues are preparing to land on its soft soil today. There is no movement anywhere. The tree-line on the island is absolutely still in the sultry air of the day. It seems the island, like an undiscovered human tribe, is waiting curiously to find out the intentions of these invaders.

The Forest Department wants to set up an outpost on the island. From here, it will be convenient for the rangers to keep an eye on the riverine movements of poachers, smugglers and delta pirates. They come under the cover of darkness and leave before daybreak. These brigands have become a thorn in the side of the police. Equally disturbed is the Forest Department.

✣✣✣

A rifle hanging from his shoulder, Ramkumar walked down a sloping wooden plank that bridged the banks and his double-decker boat. His colleagues Sidhu and Charan, also armed, followed. Even though the water was knee-deep near the banks, they would not wade through it. Saltwater crocodiles would often wait unseen under moored big boats for anyone or anything that would dare to walk the shallows.

The three men began walking up the bank towards the forest-line laboriously. The surface was dry, but very moist beneath, almost like the heel of a soft loaf of bread. Every step they took, they felt as if their feet were kneading a mound of dough. Their thick gumboots were depressing the soil, leaving deep footprints behind them, probably the first-ever in the island's history.

Or, so it seemed.

Walking in a single file, they carefully wove their way through the breathing roots, the guns now in their hands, safety catches released.

'Sir, there's a clearing. We will get a clear view of the surroundings from there,' Sidhu told his boss, pointing to the right.

Ramkumar nodded as he stepped forward. He was taking one deliberate step after another, hunching his body a little, his gun leading the way. He was being careful as he knew anything could come out of the thickets without warning.

In his long career as a forester, Ramkumar had dealt with extra-ordinary situations, each trying his wisdom. He had taken women in labour from remote Sunderbans villages to town hospitals and rescued tiger attack victims. He had once joined the border police in chasing pirates on the water. He had pounded the waters from a boat with long wooden sticks to drive a pouncing tiger away. Ramkumar had prepared himself to expect anything, anytime in these deceptive jungles.

But nothing could explain the random human footprints on the wet soil. One pair belonged to an adult and the other footprints were tiny. Who on earth would want to be here, and that, too, along with children? Shocked, Ramkumar turned towards Sidhu and Charan. They were as nonplussed.

Crouching and holding their breath, Ramkumar and his team moved noiselessly towards the clearing, their guns at the ready. It was then they heard rustling of leaves in the thickets, as if something was being dragged through the bushes, sounding like a signature tiger kill being stashed away. Slowly he approached the bush, with the forefinger of his right hand and the trigger within teasing distance of each other. From his tracking experiences, he could make out that the undergrowth had been disturbed. The mesh of vines was twisted at places, as if something had torn through them. The Keora leaves littering the jungle floor appeared to have been trampled upon.

As they started moving deeper into the bushes, Ramkumar heard a shriek coming from behind. He swivelled swiftly, ready to fire. There was nothing there, nobody except his colleagues. Sidhu, eyes trained on the bushes, had been surprised by a passing Russell's Viper, whose tail was vanishing into the thickets.

'Sidhu, you should have been more careful. I don't have to tell you that we cannot give away our position to whatever that is out there,' Ramkumar whispered.

'Sorry, chief, I had almost stepped on it.'

The rustling returned, this time pronounced. Ramkumar did not wait any longer. It was not just his life, there were two others who were counting on his experience and expertise in these jungles. He fired a shot in the air, instead of into the bush, to scare away what he thought was definitely a tiger.

The gunshot rang out in the forest, slicing the silence. The noise triggered an echo that was taking too long to die down. A commotion broke out in the forest canopy. Startled monkeys began to squeak as they jumped from one branch to another with desperate leaps and a few birds broke into a sudden flight. The small birds flew low under the canopy to once again disappear among the leaves while a fishing eagle broke out into the open, flapping its wings across the waters.

That's when Ramkumar heard screams, unmistakably human, coming from behind a thick wall of the mangrove foliage.

Tension was palpable. Ramkumar could feel his heart beat too fast for his comfort. Cold sweat had broken out on the back of his neck. He noticed Charan pointing to a clearing in the foliage.

What they saw seemed to have jumped straight out of fiction, but unbelievably real. His twenty years in the forest had trained Ramkumar to steel his nerves no matter what he encountered in the wild of the Sunderbans. He was ready to accept what even fiction would dare to recreate from reality. But not this, definitely not this.

On this godforsaken island, a half-naked woman was standing in front of them, her modesty on the verge of surrendering to six pairs of eyes from civilisation. What she was wearing did not look like the remnants of a saree but a random piece of clothing that barely covered her body. It was soiled and tattered at places. Her hair was like an overgrown jungle, dropping from the crown of her head like the twisted long roots of an ancient banyan tree. Her bare legs were caked with dry mud up to the knees and her hands bore old and fresh marks of abrasions. She looked like an early human belonging to a hunter-gatherer tribe lost in a time-warp. Clinging to her were two children, maybe five or six years of age, looking as dishevelled as their mother. They wore a thin strip of cloth around their torsos like a short sarong, equally soiled. It was difficult to make out if they were boys or girls. Their knotty hair had grown up to their waist and patches of dirt covered their faces like clustered freckles. None of them looked human, though they were standing like humans.

Ramkumar kept his gun aimed at them. His mind was grappling with probabilities that might give him an idea about how the woman and her children had arrived on the island. Even one faint clue would be enough for him.

The three stood motionless, with the woman giving them a spiteful look, as if Ramkumar and his men were trespassing into her territory. Nobody spoke until Ramkumar raised his right hand and waved at the woman in an attempt to soothe her nerves, and his too. '*Bhoi peona, amra bon doftorer kormi. Tumi ke?* (Don't be afraid. We are foresters. Who are you?)' Ramkumar slowly lowered his gun to assure the woman that he meant no harm.

'*Tumi Bangla jano?* (Do you understand Bangla?)'

The woman nodded. Ramkumar took out a bottle of water from his rucksack and gave it to her. She hesitated, not sure if this was a genuine gesture of kindness or a deception. 'Take it, it's yours,' Ramkumar said reassuringly. She took one step forward. Her right hand began to reach out to the bottle, millimetre by millimetre. And then, with lightning speed, she snatched the bottle away from his hand. She backed down a few steps and passed it on to the two children who finished the bottle with quick gulps, as if they have not had water for long.

Charan took out his bottle of water and gave it to the woman. This time, the exchange was calm. She began to drink from it slowly, savouring every sip as if it was an exotic drink.

'Where do you stay?'

The woman pointed to the ground.

'You mean here?'

'Yes, I live in this jungle.' Her voice was coarse; her words, guttural and separated by monosyllables. It seemed she hadn't had human to human conversation for long.

Is she putting me on? Ramkumar was not sure because he still could not comprehend how a human could live in this part of the Sunderbans, where life could be snuffed out without warning. Nobody ever did, as far as he could recall.

Breathing laboriously in between speaking, the woman gave her name. She said they had been living in the jungle for such a long time that she didn't remember when she had arrived.

'But how did you arrive here?' Ramkumar asked, taking a step forward.

Without replying, the woman went back a few steps, dragging her children along with her, as if she couldn't trust the men or their intentions. She took out a rusty old machete that was tucked into her clothing. Raising the machete in the air, she stood there, appearing to Ramkumar like an unconquerable force. Her nostrils inflated, her eyes reflecting a fire that only fury can kindle, she hissed: 'Come no closer.'

And then, she turned and began running into the jungle, her children as swift as her.

All his life, Ramkumar had been travelling between the islands of the Sunderbans on various missions, of which rescue of both humans and snared or wounded animals was one. Though taken aback, he realised he now had one more mission to accomplish. He picked up his gun and ran after them, with Sidhu and Charan following.

Shortly after, the three men returned from inside the jungle with their guns trained on the woman who, along with the children, were being marched towards the river.

As the six of them made their way out of the jungle, the pilot of the Forest Department boat hooted thrice to signal that it was time to leave. The second ebb of the day was approaching. Nobody in the Sunderbans wanted a boat to get stuck in silt near the bank of a river. Tigers were known to have plucked crew out of boats that had failed to dodge the ebb.

'But, sir, what about the work we came for?' Sidhu asked.

'It can wait for the time being.'

The discovery needed to be reported. Ramkumar sat in the wireless room of the boat, leaving Sidhu and Charan to keep an eye on the woman on the lower deck. He raised the sub-divisional forest office in Namkhana on radio. Cellphones didn't work in these parts of the Sunderbans.

'This is Ramkumar Manna.'

The radio crackled to life as the operator in Namkhana came on line. 'Yes, Ramkumar?'

'We have passengers.'

✣✣✣

Farida spent a major part of her days at a shopping mall some five kilometres away from her house, where she worked as a sentry. She hated to be in her uniform. The blue saree made of artificial silk was unwieldy for her. Being used to cotton clothes all her life, she felt the saree stopped her skin from breathing. Her black leather pump shoes with one-and-half-inch heels caused her more dismay. But this was her uniform, this was her job. She knew she couldn't create a fuss over a saree or a pair of shoes. Her hours began at 9 in the morning and ended at 7 pm, with an hour's break for lunch between 1 pm and 2 pm. But often, the lunch break would be shortened because her reliever would not appear on time. 'This is becoming a regular affair,' she had muttered under her breath.

Farida always had a quick lunch as she ate little, and was frugal. So, her reliever arriving late wasn't really a problem. But what she did not like was, day after day her being taken for granted. Men, she concluded, would be men, as she shook her head, more in apparent disgust than with any sense of resignation. The watermark of distrust that lay indelible inside of her was a hex she would never be able to free herself from. Her calm countenance betrayed the tumult she was sheltering. She often saw herself as a jester feigning happiness to the world. She knew she had to live out the circus, like she had lived out rain, storm, thunder and peril in another time, in another realm.

❖❖❖

From birth, everybody called her 'Hiba', though her official name on the Panchayat rolls was Farida Khatun. She was born in a small village on the fringes of Jharkhali, situated along a waterway that connected two big rivers of the Sunderbans, the Matla and the Bidyadhari. Although being a waterway, that channel, called Matlakonya, was wide enough to be considered a river by the locals. These were the backwaters, full of saltwater crocodiles, small sharks locally known as *kamot*, tiger prawns, crabs and a variety of fish. Like most others, Farida's family, too, made a living out of fishing in these dangerous waters. More than the crocodiles, it was the *kamot*s that would cause grievous injuries to people, especially to audacious young boys and girls who would not know how far they should be from the banks in the shallows. But Farida didn't care.

At 16, she was already helping her mother with catching crabs and small fish near the banks. Their technique was common to all women who fished in the shallows of the Sunderbans. Her mother would throw a cotton saree with a loose weave into the waist-deep waters. The two corners of one end of the saree would be held by her and the other by Farida, making it hammock-like. Then they would pull it under water and drag it to the shores. More often than not, the make-shift net would produce small fish, crabs and small tiger prawns. One day, they even found a baby hammerhead shark thrashing about in the trap. Farida's mother had thrown it back into the waters.

Farida was fearless in a way. There were days when she would row away with her father's small fishing boat.

'Look Ma, I am rowing,' she would hoot from a distance, though not far from the banks.

'You terrible girl, come back right now, I say,' her mother would shout at her. This tug-of-war would continue between the daughter and the mother, until the latter would wave a stick to her from the banks.

Farida was a tomboy to the core. Her hair cut short up to the nape of her neck, and her lithe body, set her apart from the rest of the girls in the village. She could run faster than any girl, and would sometimes beat boys to the post in friendly races. She was more interested in playing games the boys in her village played than hopscotch like other girls. She would hold a dare by the scruff of its neck and complete it without batting an eyelid, even if it meant climbing the slippery and higher branches of trees to pick ripe *kalojams* (blackberries). Or being the only girl in a game of *pittu* (a local game), hers was a formidable presence. Farida could also use the catapult. Mark out a fruit or a bunch of small berries in the tree for her and she would shoot like a master marksman to bring them down with ease. She could go to any extent doing things 'ungirl'-like.

The girls were in awe of her. And the boys, though not comfortable with a girl gatecrashing their world, had to accept Farida as one of their own because of her spryness and daredevilry. But the elders in her village weren't approving of the way she was conducting herself, and neither were her parents. She was a girl and needed to behave like a girl.

Quite often her father Ripon Mollah would scold her, to rein in her boyish exuberance. 'Why do you have to play with Manu? He is a bad boy, already smokes bidis,' or 'Football is a man's game,'—suchlike sermons would be constant. For Ripon, Farida was a baggage in his struggling family. He and his wife Shamima Bibi would rather invest in their young son Momin. It was normal in these parts of the Sunderbans to see a boy as a future repository of fortunes. And Farida was topping their list of priorities for all the wrong reasons.

'It's time we got her married,' Ripon had said to his wife one day.

'You're right, she has become too wild. I shudder to think what she would be like when she grows up. Why don't you start looking for a groom for her? I am fed up with her antics,' Shamima complained.

Even though she was not of marriageable age, getting minor girls married off was a normal social affair in these parts. Ripon zeroed in on Mustafir, a young man who worked as a salesman at a small shopping mall that had come up in mainland Canning. Mustafir, who worked through the week at the mall, would return home in Pakhirala Island, at the mouth of the Tiger Reserve Project, on weekends.

Farida, who was still aiming the catapult at berries and blowing dandelions into the air, was married off before she could prepare her mind to accept a complete stranger as her husband. She was too young, too naïve and boundlessly sprightful for a regimen that awaited her in someone else's home. The idea of a marriage to her was more like vacationing with Mustafir in a town where she could have what she had only heard about—beautiful sarees, restaurant food and places to see. At the same time, she knew she would miss the daisies that crowded the pathway to her village home, or the dew-drop mornings spent picking ripe tomatoes from their kitchen garden. The games of hide-and-seek would no longer be the same without her. And Shaqueel Chacha would be sailing his boat past her home to take tourists back to the mainland, without having to wave at her anymore.

Obviously, Farida couldn't fit into her new home like duck to water. There were errands that crowded her days and nights. Aatifa Bibi had washed her hands of a majority of chores ever since her daughter-in-law had arrived. Farida endured the hardship without a whimper. Never for once could she leave the Pakhirala island to be with her husband in Canning. She was now Mustafir's weekend entertainment. Whenever Mustafir would be home, he would pound her body without any pangs of remorse while she would lay motionless like a cadaver, unable to participate in the most natural and romantic human act. Yet, the dream of having her own family one day kept her going. From being a bubbly young girl, she had quickly become a woman inured to prejudice.

One day a year later, Farida discovered that she had stopped menstruating. She had confided in her mother-in-law. Aatifa Bibi was quick to conclude.

So, this is how it happens, Farida thought as she looked out of the window at the waters that travelled towards Canning. It was a Saturday. She was waiting eagerly to break the news to Mustafir, hoping that having a child would probably bring her the dignity that she so deserved in that family.

'I hope it is a boy,' Mustafir said. Like most families in the region, Mustafir's too wanted a son. But all these thoughts never occurred to Farida as she was preparing herself to welcome motherhood.

Farida's lithe appearance was vanishing with each passing day. The contours of her body were changing, as if a sculptor was at work. The curves that were invisible to her own eyes were now emerging untamed, making her look so tender and wanted. A mother was being unveiled, slowly. The thought of a life growing within another kept her fascinated. And that also gave her the much-needed respite from household work as the ever-mounting errands suddenly diminished. Aatifa Bibi began lessening her daughter-in-law's burden by sharing the chores that she had stopped doing months ago. 'Our grandson is coming,' she went tom-toming in the neighbourhood. As the delivery date drew near, Farida could sense an air of excitement in the house. Yet, she was a tad upset. If a new baby was coming, so was a new mother, and that was what nobody cared about.

Farida delivered on time at a Gosaba hospital. She had given birth to twins, both girls. Overnight, the sudden care she was receiving during her pregnancy was replaced by barbed rebukes. A sense of gloom had engulfed the household.

'I knew this girl is a witch. She will devour my son and us, too. Who will now extend the lineage? Shame shame, two girls after all this?'

And the invectives continued remorselessly. Gritting her teeth, Farida held her ground in the hope that someday the family would realise that without women, there would be no humanity.

A deep sense of indignation that was filling her up was on the verge of spilling. Farida began seeking divine intervention. On most evenings when the microphonic call for Azaan would reach her home from a distant mosque, she would look up to the skies and pray. '*Allah, Ar koto din, ar koto din?* (O Allah! How long? For how long do I have to endure this?)'

She had decided to confront Mustafir. As another weekend arrived, she walked up to the pier. Mustafir was getting off the boat. Farida waited until Mustafir reached her end of the pier. Then she blocked his way.

'I want to know why I am being treated like a piece of garbage in your house?'

Mustafir looked uninterested.

'Is it because I gave birth to two girls? Aren't you ashamed of yourself? They are your children too. It has become impossible to stay in this house. Take me with you to Canning. Please.'

'No, you're not coming to Canning. You're going somewhere else.'

'What do you mean?'

'Almost every new wife in this village has had a son. Except you. Farida, you are a disgrace to our family. You are going back to your parents, and this is not a vacation. You are going there for good.'

'Are you giving me *talaq*?'

'I might.'

Two days later, they arrived in a small boat at the Jharkhali pier almost empty-handed. Her clothes, jewellery, and all her personal effects had been taken away from her by her mother-in-law. She hadn't spared even the kids.

From the moment Farida stepped into her parents' house, she could sense an uneasy calm taking over the household. A sense of relief was calming her to the shock of being shunned by her own husband. At her parents' house, she and her daughters would at least not be subjected to inhuman neglect and scorn. There were food, general talk and the usual work a family would have to live by every day. Still, that old bonding was missing, probably due to her long absence from home, she thought.

Concealed sparks of pique were emerging slowly, burning holes into her actuality. Not always in front of her, but there were talks about her and the twins when she was not in earshot. She was old enough to realise that her space in her parents' home was not forever.

If Ripon had his way, he would have turned Farida away from the jetty itself. But he didn't want to create a scene. To keep face, he had spread the word around that Farida was only visiting them for a while. 'After all, it's been two years she hasn't seen us.'

Her brother Momin, who had grown into a local tough, kept his distance from his sister. Farida could read disdain in his eyes. It was said that he was mingling with the underworld of the Sunderbans, which meant either smuggling of timber or poaching. Locals feared him and to a degree, Ripon, too. He was haughty, at home and outside. It was Momin who finally said what her parents had been trying to tell her all these days. Farida couldn't live in that house anymore. Her being rejected by Mustafir was hurting the family pride. Farida had to go. She had become an outcast.

'But where?'

'Anywhere but not in the Sunderbans. If I see you and the kids in this house after dusk tomorrow, I am going to throw all of you in the river.' Momin, drunk, was condemning her to peril while her parents stood in the doorway without uttering a word.

'But I have nowhere to go. Why are you doing this to me? We share the same blood, Momin,' she pleaded.

'You wretched girl, I am going to take you to a place where you deserve to stay in.'

For a girl who was just 18 and a mother of two, being dumped by her husband first and then by her parents would have led to catastrophic consequences in an area like the Sunderbans where home-grown dacoits, foreign pirates and the wild could prove to be lethal. But Farida was not scared and neither was she crying in despair. The font of her tears had long dried up.

Instead, she felt a surge of power, as if providential, run vertically through her body, steeling her for the uncertainties. The tomboy had returned, ready to beat the men at their own game.

After everybody in the house went to sleep that night, Farida began packing noiselessly. She tiptoed into the rice barn, picked up an empty sack and filled it with candles, matches, biscuits, four bottles of water, one blanket, two sarees for herself, spare flip-flops, a few extra clothes for her daughters and a machete that her mother used to break open dry coconuts. She stayed up the whole night, waiting for the darkness to thin. Just when she noticed a suggestion of a pink hue in the eastern sky, she slipped away, with her daughters in tow. Farida turned her head to take one last look at the house as if she felt a pull.

Farida was still hoping to live by a glimmer of hope. But it was all in her mind. She looked back. The overnight mist hadn't escaped into the dawn, obscuring the home she was once born into.

She kept on walking, towards the waterfront. Quietly, she unfastened her father's boat from the mooring, dumped the goods into the bowels of the boat, seated her daughters in the middle so that the dinghy didn't tilt, and started rowing. Farida knew everybody deserved a second shot at life, and that she had to earn it.

She had no idea for how long she had rowed. But it must have been hours, for she had left at dawn and now, the sun was right above their heads. The two girls were sleeping in the boat, hugging each other, their bodies rolling from side to side in rhythm with the unruly waves that had begun to break. Farida looked at her children, her eyes moist after a long, long time. They were sleeping so peacefully, abandoning their survival to their mother, like they had been doing since birth.

The first tide of the day was coming in. Not a good time to be in this small boat. All she could make out was the outlines of an island that was fast approaching. The banks and the tree-line could now be seen clearly. Another few strokes of the oar and she would be on land. Waking up the children, she rowed the boat with renewed vigour to the edge of the water. She had made it!

Not a soul was around; a perfect hideaway. After she got off and hauled the goods onto the banks, Farida tied the boat to the trunk of a Golpata tree with the rope she had pulled in from the moorings. She sat on the banks to regain her breath. A black-naped oriole streaked across, drawing a yellow and exuberant line in the free air. Two metres away from where she was sitting, a large crab with bulbous eyes peeped out of its burrow, scouted her and went back to the depths of its home. A monkey, invisible, squeaked. The forest had begun to watch them. Farida started walking towards the jungle, her children following. She found a small clearing to the right, next to which was a row of trees. *'This is going to be our home. God knows for how long!'* Another battle was set to unfold and she felt if she could defeat the heartless back at home, she would win this one, too.

Dark clouds from the Bay of Bengal began invading the sky above the Sunderbans, bringing a premature end to a sunny afternoon. Soon, the wind gathered speed, whistling through the forest like a locomotive, accompanied by hard rain. Farida and her children took shelter under a thick canopy. Still, they were wet as the spray from the lashing rain engulfed them like mist.

Their first night in the forest was spent without incident, except the occasional rustling in the thickets. Farida was prepared to dismiss the movements as a sign of carefree winds playing, just to reassure herself that they were safe. Yet, she knew the slightest sound in this forest could be the beginning of trouble.

The next morning, she went out to the banks to pull the boat ashore. She wanted to upturn the boat so that they could slide under it and use it as a roof above their heads. But the boat was missing. The strong winds and the driving rain had apparently yanked the boat off the Golpata tree. If that combination could create such a pull in the current of the waters to tear a boat away from its moorings, she wondered what chance a human would stand in a situation like this. She made a mental note—not to be in the waters when it rained, her first lesson in the wild.

Farida sat on the wet soil. The loss of the boat was weighing her down. But spending time on worrying would be luxury in these forests. She took a deep breath, hugged her children, mentally preparing herself to take on whatever dare life would throw at them henceforth.

✣✣✣

The candles lasted Farida less than two days. But the darkness didn't bother her. She had been through darker times among humans. The biscuits and the water had followed the candles quickly. Other than honey, there was nothing else to eat in that thick mangrove because no fruits, except wild berries, grew on that soil. To feed three hungry mouths, Farida had started drilling holes into the beehives to collect honey in the empty water bottles. But the bees would not let her go without punishment. Soon, the honey went off their diet, given the hazards associated with its collection. Farida needed to do something.

With each passing day, the struggle to gather food and stay sheltered intensified. She remembered Shaqeel Chacha telling her once: 'If you are lost in a forest, eat what monkeys eat.' The forest had an overdose of monkeys but they were so lightning fast in plucking wild fruits from trees or from the ground that it was difficult for Farida to make out which were the ones the primates had collected.

Initially, the monkeys were suspicious of them. They would keep distance from the humans. Farida, too, made it a point not to disturb them. But there was no stopping the children who were fascinated by the primates. To Rehana and Sultana, a new world was opening its many wonders to them and in turn, they were passing their innocence to the wild. The entire floor of the forest seemed to be their playground, like the canopies were for the monkeys.

✣✣✣

As Farida scouted the forest, not straying too deep into it, she one day discovered an abundance of Hingras, Dhundols and Choilas hanging from branches—all wild fruits. They were hanging too high for her to reach. That's when the idea struck her. She recalled the art she had perfected once. Farida took off her flip-flops and pulled out the rubber straps. Collecting a forked stick from the undergrowth, she tied the button-ends of the straps to its horns, turning it into a makeshift catapult. She realised she hadn't lost her aim as the fruits began to drop on the ground at will. She was happy, her children were happy and so were the pampered monkeys. In fact, the monkeys had gotten so familiar with her pursuits that they would follow her, expecting a treat, whenever she would explore the forest with the catapult in hand. To the monkeys, she was someone who meant no harm. And Farida looked with amazement at the way the wild was endearing itself to her, a family that she was building all over again, without distrust, without fear.

But berries weren't enough to satiate hunger. She took to fishing after a long, long time. 'Does my mother still fish?' She would look into the watery expanse and ask nobody in particular. She would not know when the unknown river flowing in front of her would transform into Matlakanya, whose every molten sunshine, twists and turns she knew by heart, whose quiet demeanour in the night she knew as a whispered story. She wanted to speak out to someone, or something and empty herself of the memories she was agonising for. She was trying to touch every chord with the forest and the lives that grew in it, to be the narrative in their merging existence.

And as the river rippled past without a name, she knew it was hers and hers alone, another offspring that flowed from her unexcavated tears. She went into the water, flinging her spare saree into the indomitable current, remembering to create a small hammock-like shape with it.

After repeated efforts, she caught some fish and a few small crabs. She wished she had the reflexes of the fishing cats that hunted so easily in the shallows. From a distance, she had spotted these shy animals at the waterfront.

The fish Farida caught that day went on the fire she had lit by lighting dry twigs with the matches. Fish was plenty, but not matchboxes. That's when she discovered the calling. The forest was slowly unfolding itself to Farida, making her understand that what seemed impossible wasn't actually so. And Farida had begun to return favours to the forest by being the kind of wild it wanted her to be.

They started to eat the fish raw when there were no more matchboxes. The children had begun to puke but Farida kept it down resolutely. There was no other way. Slowly, hunger defeated repulsion. Three humans, one forest and a million other lives or more in a disparate co-existence, into which Farida and her children kept returning to, day and night, without complaints.

✣✣✣

By now, Farida had come to know the forest like the lines on her palms. Still, she would slip up at times. She once had stepped on a small, curled up porcupine, mistaking it for a part of the undergrowth. A quill pierced her foot, though not so much as to impale her. The puncture wound began bleeding. Cuts and bruises, which she and her daughters would suffer because of walking through the thorny thickets, were covering their skins like tattoos. If one healed, another appeared too soon. But then, an injury inflicted by a porcupine quill was a different matter altogether. It was then that Farida had discovered a way to treat these wounds. As if it was a balm, Farida applied a layer of wet soil of the banks on the wound. Within minutes, the bleeding had stopped. The wound healed after a few days though she had to walk with a limp until it did. She was in awe of the healing power of the soil, so raw yet so life-giving. *What else did the forest have to offer in this symbiotic relationship?* Farida was still finding out in many ways, sometimes the hard way.

In the night, they would sleep at the base of a Garjan tree whose roots fanned around the trunk like an umbrella formation. One night, an unusually huge wild boar with sharp tusks curving out from either side of its mouth, came inspecting her abode. These tusks could rip apart a tiger's belly. Huddling, Farida and her daughters stayed as far as they could from the periphery of the umbrella formation. They dragged their legs up to their chest so that the hog, even if it somehow managed to squeeze its head in, wouldn't be able to reach them. The roots that night came in the way between likely death and life. Farida knew *garjan* in Bengali meant 'roar' but didn't know why a tree was named like that. Quite often, when a tigress gives birth to cubs, she and the litter take shelter at the base of a Garjan tree. It is just to save her tiny ones from their father, who is likely to kill the cubs. The tigress, which would lose considerable weight after giving birth, would easily pass through the gaps between the Garjan roots that prove to be too narrow for the healthier, larger male tiger. When the male fails to reach the female and the cubs, he circles the tree roaring in anger.

Time went by. One by one, the last of her belongings vanished. One of her two sarees was so badly torn that it couldn't be worn anymore. The other one, which she used for fishing, was in as bad a shape, with holes, big and small, everywhere. Similar was the condition of the clothes of her children. What remained intact were the machete, the catapult and the plastic water bottles. She was living off the land in the naked wild.

During the day, she and her daughters would squeeze out of their Garjan cage to explore the forest. They would, come what may, not venture out too far from the clearing she had created with her machete. There was just one nagging concern—where was the tiger in tiger country?

Even though she had heard tigers roar at a distance from time to time, not one beast had ever come close to them.

But how wrong she was! One day, she heard Rehana and Sultana giggle behind a bush. Farida reached them to find that the two were trying to fit in their tiny feet into huge pugmarks depressed deep into moist soil. *My God! A tiger was nearby!* Dragging her daughters by the hand, she quickly went back to her Garjan refuge.

❖❖❖

Farida had lost count of days and nights since the time she arrived in the jungle. How many years had it been since that dawn when she had slipped away from home? Rehana and Sultana had been growing fast. They were almost near her waist. Yet, she remembered the days and moments that had affected her life, in the cradle of her homes and away from them, especially that night of the storm.

A fierce cyclone had broken out, sweeping away everything in its path. Her island being near the bay, it bore the most severe brunt of the storm. Trees like Goran, Ora, Passur, Hental and Golpata started crashing all around them and the waters of the river rose too high and travelled too far inland to be at the feet of the forest. Farida's life in the forest had prepared her for eventualities. And though she tried to conquer fear but not always was she able to hold her nerves. So, when the Garjan tree under which she had built her leafy canopy had begun to sway uncontrollably, threatening to topple any moment, she was scared, truly scared. She was sweating, apprehending the worst. Farida was used to facing adversities but never before had she felt so small in front of nature.

The firm roots that stopped tigers held the trunk of the Garjan tree back. There was no noise, except of the gale force of the juggernaut and of trees collapsing. A fusillade of missiles crisscrossed the air as the storm picked up. Like Farida and her children, all life forms inside the forest fell silent. No tiger preyed, no deer barked, no monkey squeaked and no porcupine rattled its quills. The whole island seemed to be dangerously close to perishing.

After a long night of destruction, calm returned. The forest was mourning its dead in the morning as it stood still under a clear sky, hoping for signs of life. Farida went out to the banks, half of which was eaten away by the furious waters. Islands in these parts changed shape regularly. Scattered all around on the soil were dead egrets, barbets, sandpipers and bitterns, their nests blown away to smithereens. The entire waterfront was covered with logs, leaves, broken branches and sticks of all sizes and shapes. Amidst the ruins, Farida sat on the ground, legs splayed, stunned. Rehana and Sultana could not understand why their mother, who was standing ramrod straight just a while ago, had slumped to the ground. She sat there grieving the loss as much as the forest did. There was not a stich of fabric on her. The Sunderbans has a way with lives—it kills and then resurrects. Farida knew that she couldn't be killed anymore. And so, the starkness that she embodied as a human in the forest was her way of rising to the call of the wild.

She kept scanning the riverbank. It was then that Farida noticed an upturned boat stuck in the soil. It must have got detached from its moorings somewhere up the waterways and rode the retreating backwaters to finally rest on her island. Farida ran towards the boat. It had a tattered sail that had come off its mast. She crawled under the boat looking for anything that would sustain life, at least for some time. But there was only the sail to be had. She dragged the remains of the sail out of the boat and rolled it up. 'This would do, surely,' as she looked at the nakedness of her family.

Some weeks later, Farida and her children were searching for berries and edible shoots. That's when they heard a loud noise. Both her daughters had cried out in fear, and dashed for a clearing. But Farida reached them swiftly and held them close to her body. There were three men with guns, looking at them.

✣✣✣

The city of Kolkata offers a second chance to everyone. The city is ever willing to forgive, and even forget. Like many others, Farida too saw the human face of this bustling, overcrowded city up, close and personal. For her though, there was just one problem. Her life was being gatecrashed, something which she stopped tolerating years ago.

She had been rescued, if not resurrected, and sent for rehabilitation at a destitute centre in Kolkata. It was located on the road to Deganga, which shot off from Chinar Park near Salt Lake City. The process of bringing Farida and her daughters back into civilisation had its own rigours. First, it was Farida's feisty protests. She didn't want to leave the Sunderbans. And then, once she relented, she and the children had to be nursed back to health and then counselled. Farida had realised being in Kolkata was better than being 'thrown into a river'.

And Ramkumar, who felt an odd sense of ownership of Farida and her daughters, ended up being their de-facto guardian. He would be with them at every step of the way, building them from scratch. It was tough, very tough, to smoothen the anfractuous edges of their lives. Years of being in the wild on her own had already empowered Farida with a deep sense of liberation. Farida required to learn to listen. The layers of rawness that covered her dispensation had to be peeled carefully. Ramkumar was aware that harsh words or any rigid regimen would only spoil her rehab. Farida had to be dealt with like a small girl learning her first lessons in a school, gently admonished and forgiven as well for mistakes. Slowly, colour was returning to her cheeks and the disturbed, chafing skin was illustrating a feminine tinge it so deserved. A picture was being shaped by her mentor. Yet, her impatience of not being able to free herself from routine was telling on her mind.

'But for how long?' she had asked one day.

'Not for long, Farida. I have plans for you. I want you to work and earn a living.'

'But what work can I do?'

'Exactly, Farida, what work can you do?'

'Well, I can run barefoot, I can fish and I can bring down berries with a catapult.' As they started laughing together, Ramkumar discovered that there was, indeed, a jovial side to Farida. The bridge to her wasn't too rugged a cross, after all.

After a six-month crash course in industrial security, Ramkumar found Farida a job with a shopping mall as a sentry. Initially, Farida was uncomfortable in her modern uniform—a pair of trousers, shirt and shoes—feeling way too naked than her completely bare state in the wild. Yet, there was a sense of pride in what she did. Once upon a time, she had wanted to visit a shopping mall as a new bride. Today, she was deciding who went in and who stayed out.

The frequency of Ramkumar's visits to Farida's house had increased. In the beginning, when her rehab process had started, Ramkumar was careful not to encroach upon her private space. But as time went by, and as the line between the mentor and the protégé began to blur unobtrusively, that space was no longer only hers. In the interludes of their strivings, they had begun listening to each other's quietude.

Yet, Farida found herself caught between liking Ramkumar and the irritability of being with a man. The scars she was carrying would emerge like a spectre to haunt her peace, a hex she couldn't free herself from no matter how hard she tried. Farida was a captive of her chronic misandry. 'There has to be a way out of this,' she would say to herself in bouts of despair. She was grateful to Ramkumar for finding her a life without indignation and at the same time, she didn't want him to have false hopes about her. Inside her was building another storm, and this time, she didn't want it to devastate her again.

'Ramkumar babu, it's wonderful to have you around. But by being with us all the time, you are neglecting your work. I am so embarrassed,' she had said politely one day, but couldn't make out whether he could read the demurring tone in her voice. She was only trying to make Ramkumar understand that her own space taken by three gun-toting foresters on a dangerous island could never be surrendered. The blank easel that her life was had been filled up by the wild. She was not willing to let that easel be recreated with unfamiliar sensibilities.

Ramkumar was not a man who had blithe disregard for life's involute patterns. His time in the jungle had taught him to see that which was obvious wasn't necessarily true. He could sense that this woman, even though she seemed to be yielding to him in her new beginning, had a mind of her own that could probably be touched but not owned. He knew he had overstayed the invite. Ramkumar had spent most of his time on a motorised boat, scanning restless rivers and dangerous jungles. He understood the language of the wild. He could see the wild would never let Farida be free.

Farida stood in the doorway watching Ramkumar slowly disappear into the urban milieu, one last time. It was drizzling. She didn't know why her eyes were moist, whether it was for the clammy weather, or whether it was for him or for the price she was paying for her life to come full circle. She was on her own again, ready to walk the facile line she had so missed for a long time.

She looked at the sky. A Pariah Kite was streaking across the blue expanse. A smile broke out on her face as she whispered: 'Come, Hiba, let's race the kite.'

SPELLBOUND

He looked ghostly as he sat still in the courtyard. Breathtakingly out of place in a human homestead, he was seated like a marble statue, relentlessly drawing the moonlight into his wraithlike body, making it translucent in the pitch-dark night. Even the fireflies that usually filigreed the darkness were missing, leaving the night to survive the eerie hours alone. The pantheon of trees that overlooked the homestead stood paralysed, holding their breath in the spectral light that bounced off him. No birds shifted in their nests, no crickets stridulated, and no human voices could be heard. The Sunderbans didn't want to wake up, for they were afraid of stirring up the sleeping ghosts of their fables.

It seemed like Bela was the only human awake that night. She was startled when she felt a shaft of an unreal light illuminating her face through the partially opened window of her room. Her heart was pounding as she tiptoed to the window to find the source of that glow. As she flung open the window, her room was awash with an electric blue light, blinding her. Being a girl who was living on the razor's edge in the deadly Sunderbans, where she was snatching life from the jaws of death for herself and for those who believed in her every day, a sea of unworldly light at an unearthly hour wasn't a dare that would deter her. She squinted her eyes to look through the light at its source, and what she saw made the hair on her head stand up, not out of fear, not because she was alone. The sight, she felt, was too chimerical to be formed of real, human elements. Her mouth was agape and her eyes threatened to bulge beyond control, as Bela looked at him, awestruck by the resplendence of the moment. Bela couldn't recollect for how long she stood there possessed by the sight, but when she returned to her senses, he was gone. Was it a dream or was there really him in the forecourt of our house? She found no answers.

A disturbed earth brought Bela back to reality the next day. A terrible cyclone named Amphan swept across Dholkhali, causing livestock and human lives to perish. Her house was affected too. One half of the tinned roof had caved in, sparing the Gain family by the skin of its teeth.

The aftermath of the devastation rode the wind. Trees had collapsed, some of the mud houses were completely razed to the ground, dead life forms lay scattered everywhere, and the waters of the river lapped at the feet of homes. Two days later, she had confided in a man she knew from her profession. The man was quick to rubbish her claim of a 'vision'. But the image that had begun to nest in her mind would not leave.

✣✣✣

Bela had a mind of her own that she hardly allowed to be riddled with other people's opinions of her. Even though she enjoyed her girlhood to the hilt, she got tired of living the life of a teenager a little early than usual. One day when she had opened her mind to her father Sambhu Gain, which was about a year ago, he couldn't but vent his angst. Sambhu had vehemently disapproved of Bela's wishes to follow in his footsteps. 'What you want to be is not a matter of fancy or a hobby, Bela! Either you have a spiritual connect with the wild or when that connect is used for charming non-humans in the mangroves, can you rise to the calling you claim to be experiencing now? Just because you express a desire doesn't make you one like me.' Nobody knew it better than Sambhu.

Like most other villagers, Sambhu Gain was unlettered. He used to be a landless farmer. Producing *Chaiti moong*, a variety of green gram, and then handing the harvest over to the land owner for pittance was his only means to earn a living. He was an all-seasons man on the land he was born into. The elements dared him but he would succumb only to his will to feed two hungry mouths back home, his wife Kamala and Bela.

But that was two cyclones ago. The first cyclone had eroded the land into which Dholkhali was anchored. The second storm, more devastating, scythed through the village, leaving its fields of crops under saline water. Sambhu was even more landless upon the soil he was born. At night, he would sit on his bed, hour after hour, brooding. 'How to pull on now,' he would ask himself. Kamala, also awake and keeping herself shielded from Sambhu with a cover, would quietly wipe her moist eyes. Together, immersed in their silent yearnings, they knew there were just two fistfuls of rice at home to live another day.

Beyond the hardship was another world in which Sambhu had created his own alchemy with his surroundings. Leaning on spirituality, he was able to summon the strength to walk through struggle, at least in his mind. He believed that if called fervently, the universe would listen.

Even his younger days were characterised by such feelings. People who knew him would often reflect on what they thought were his special powers. From a very young age, when he was just a growing boy, Sambhu had become a leading topic of discussion among the villagers. They felt he had an uncanny ability to understand the language of the wild. He was their animal-whisperer, one who could cast a spell on anything that was not human. At least, that's what they understood from the day when he had looked into the eye of a snake from close and made it disappear from sight. 'Miracles' such as these gave him a distinct identity. People started to believe that he was a bewitcher. It was his deep belief in his own spiritual bent of mind that had, one day, led him to contemplate taking up another profession, which was not for the faint-hearted. He knew the land and the forest as much as he was aware about how humans sought a spiritual connect with beasts inside the deadly mangroves to live together undisturbed.

'I will try my hand at tiger-charming,' he had said one day to no one in particular, startling Kamala.

'No way,' Kamala said, warning, 'It's too risky. As it is, we are fighting to stay alive and on top of it, if something happens to you, do you have any idea where we will go? Not one person will stand by our side.'

Yet, Sambhu couldn't drive away the idea from his mind. He knew tiger charmers in the Sunderbans were paid in cash. Two fistfuls of rice might not become six overnight, but the aching for a better life would somewhat subside. And then, there was Bela standing in front of him, free as a skylark but ripening with each passing day without her own knowledge.

Every morning, fishermen would set off in their dinghy with Sambhu. It was in his hands they surrendered their fate.

He was their tiger charmer, the one who would use his special powers to keep them safe on the deadly riverbanks. Upon landing, Sambhu would chant *mantra*s to seek the blessings of the dominant deities of the Sunderbans. Before dusk, the boat would return to moor at the Dholkhali pier. Like this, Sambhu would return home every day to live the smiles of Kamala and Bela. But one day, he didn't.

'Gunin Gain has been attacked by a tiger,' the word went around Dholkhali like wildfire. 'How can a *gunin* be attacked by a tiger!' asked Kamala between intense bouts of sobbing. 'This is how it happens, Bhabi,' Dholkhali's eldest fishermen Mohiul tried to calm her down. 'If at all a tiger comes out of the woods, it is always the *gunin* who is its first prey, for he is the one who is pleading to the beasts to spare us.'

But, what exactly might have gone wrong for Sambhu? On that fateful day, Sambhu and the fishermen sailed the river in a manual boat. A soft cool breeze was coming in from the delta after a squall. Sambhu, though aware of his responsibilities, had loosened his mind to the restful calm of the morning, if not a tad unmindful. As the boat threw a line to anchor, Sambhu, as usual, was first to get off. After the customary rituals, he sat on the mudbank and waited for the fishermen to complete their haul. It was then they spotted him walking towards them at a leisurely pace, appearing all of a sudden out of a bend in the forested riverbank.

The tiger walked towards them with slow, deliberate strides, as if it had taken for granted that its prey was trapped. Two of the fishermen jumped off the boat in a flash to unfasten the line, while the two others readied their iron-edged wooden oars to scare the tiger off and pull away quickly for their lives. Sambhu had to wait no matter what, for he had to be the last to leave. It was then that the tiger increased its pace, shifting from its slow walk to a trot. Sambhu could see that the distance between him and the tiger was reducing fast. '*Uithya por, Sambhu, taratari noukai uithya por* (Get on the boat, Sambhu, quickly),' a fisherman shouted out to him.

Sambhu tried to break into a run towards the boat in a last-gasp attempt to board it but his feet got stuck in the gooey clay-loam surface. Even if he would have managed to extricate himself from the mud trap, he would still require to weave his run through the conical mangrove roots that sprouted on the bank at random like sharp spears. Even the tiger was having problems running fast on the mud because of its weight, but it was close, so close that Sambhu could get the pungent smell of its body. Panting, Sambhu summoned immense strength to get closer to the boat. Just a few more steps, and he would be on it. But then, the beast exploded from the mud with a demonic surge and leapt at Sambhu with such force that it overshot its quarry. As the tiger narrowly missed landing on Sambhu securely, it swiped at his head, taking with its open paws half of the left side of his face and skull. The tiger was in the river. The fishermen began beating the water with oars to scare it off. Daunted, it began to swim away. The men hauled Sambhu back onto the boat. By the time they could set off, Sambhu, bleeding profusely, was unconscious, with time running out on his life.

When Sambhu returned from the Bangur hospital in Kolkata two months later, he looked like an ogre. A part of his skin from the forehead had been pulled down by the surgeons at the hospital to cover the space where his left eye was. The left side of his skull, now without hair, bore the marks of innumerable stitches. His left ear, also missing, was a messed up mound of skin and flesh. He spoke with a garbled drawl. His speech was almost incoherent. He was no longer a *gunin*; just a victim of the wild. Nobody in the Sunderbans hired a fallen *gunin* again. The one who was supposed to protect them couldn't be trusted anymore, for his special powers had been proven to be vulnerable. And in the mutilated face of her father, Bela saw the reason all the more to follow her wishes with greater zeal.

❖❖❖

Parting the overnight rainclouds, the sun pinked the eastern sky over the Sunderbans, slowly diffusing a soft light to a half-awake Dholkhali. The wilderness surrounding the island was pandiculating, sending its sounds and signs of its many lives into the free air of the village. Bela woke up to the tweets of the birds and the susurration of the river that flowed by the island. The radiance of the morning stirred her into wakefulness. Each breaking dawn would pierce a hole in the miserable state of the household to remind her that she couldn't any longer wait; she needed to abandon the life of a teen that she had lived so far, out in the open, with her friends, wildflowers, dirt roads and meadows.

Bela had little idea about how the world was outside of the Sunderbans. The tales that fishermen would bring to Dholkhali from the mainland would fascinate Bela, but only for a while. Her universe was the soil she stood upon. The games of *pittu* she would play with other girls, her barefoot walks in the rain, her wide-eyed gaze at distant boats, or plucking at random flowers like *karanja*s and *kandelia*s, landscaped her days. She would breathlessly race the low-flying black-necked storks on the riverbank, or choke with laughter as curious mangrove whistlers and cinnamon bitterns would stop tweeting when she would try to mimic their calls. Small wishes illuminated her small face. In the deadly Sunderbans, these magnetisms left her unchained from a wrecked home. From inside the bubble that nested her, Bela was once oblivious to how the world changed every day. But all that were a thing of the past. The road ahead must not be a waste as his father's was.

From childhood, Bela shadowed her father to wherever he went in Dholkhali—she was so attached to him. She hardly spent time with her mother, which distanced Kamala from her daughter's way of life. It was an onerous task to keep her home. From a very young age, when she was ten or twelve, she would pray along with Sambhu, memorising each and every *panchali* (religious script) lines he would chant, even the incantations he would murmur during prayers. She had a keen ear and a sharp mind. By the age of fifteen, she could reel off the history of the deities of the Sunderbans at will. Many used to wonder how a girl so young could do this! She was precocious in a way, something which people, even Sambhu, failed to notice. Slowly, she grew up to be a replica of her father. That she could be equipped with special powers like him had dawned upon Sambhu but he didn't encourage her to use them. But then, the day Sambhu returned from hospital with half of his face missing, Bela felt it was time to walk in the shoes of her father and be the Shaman she wanted to be.

Initially, she had faced tremendous resistance from home as well as from the strictly-male bastion of tiger charmers. Kamala would throw a fit. 'You know what happened to your father,' she would warn. Then came barbs like 'this is not a woman's job' from other tiger charmers, who tried to stop her from breaking the glass ceiling. Even the local *panchayat* censured her, but Bela was hell bent on finding her own niche as a tiger charmer. So strong was her will that the opposition she faced at home and outside slowly faded.

Her first call as a *gunin* came from the wood-cutters, who were called *bawali*s locally. Bela still remembers the day of her opening sortie into the creeks of the mangrove.

The boat was cutting noiselessly through the first ebb of the day. The hot, humid overhang seemed to have stilled all life forms on either side of the river. Not a leaf was moving, not even a bird tweet or a monkey hoot. The mangroves were resting in their own shades. Bela was sitting cross-legged at the bow of the boat with her eyes closed. She wanted to be in communion with the unseen that lurked inside the mangroves. Bela could see the wild, hear them, feel them and talk to them in the language of the wild even when they remained out of sight. Sometimes the beasts listened to her and some other times, a few didn't. Bela's was only a silent voice that traversed the waters, the river banks, and the thick foliage to softly touch the heart of the wild in an attempt to separate life from death.

Yet, Bela was aware that the apparently becalmed forests that were watching them could jump to life with deadly intent any moment. The *bawali*s who sat behind her and oared the boat deeper into the creeks had dumped their mortal fears into her hands, believing she would be able to tell the beasts that they meant no harm.

Bela was the first to get off the boat, which was required of a tiger charmer. Breathing heavily while she scanned the forest-line, she placed a hand on the soil as part of the ritual. She then began chanting *mantra*s to invoke Bon Bibi and Dakshin Ray, the two ruling deities of the Sunderbans. In doing so, she was seeking to pacify the beasts. She then smeared herself with wet soil, weilding it like a charm as long as wood-cutting continued.

Dusk was close and they had to leave. Slowly, the forest was coming alive. The thickets began to rustle, signaling movement. It could be a monkey, a wild boar, a deer or 'him'. No one was sure and no one was willing to spend more time than was required. Bela looked at the forest. She felt it was advancing towards them, keeping pace with the approaching dusk, as if it had tolerated their presence for too long. The wet clay on her body was drying, beginning to flake off, leaving her with alarming goosebumps. '*Ami ar ei koboj ta re dhoira rakhti parsi ni* (I cannot hold onto this charm anymore)', she said nervously to the *bawali*s—a signal to leave. Her throat was dry as a horn. Before boarding the boat, she placed a hand on the soil again to break the spell. The boat began to row back as silently as it had arrived to end another day of good luck. From father to daughter, the inheritance was complete. Bela had made it.

Not once, not twice, but many a times Bela has looked death in the eye to live and tell the tale. Some tigers are rogue, she feels. They fight the spells she casts on the wild. Bela remembers how wrong she was once while she was leading a group of eight *mouli*s (honey collectors) into deep forest. Unlike fishermen and *bawali*s who work near the banks, *mouli*s are disadvantaged as they have to walk barefoot deeper into the forest to locate beehives. On one such foray, as she walked alongside the lead *mouli*, she felt unease. 'Have I brought them to the right place,' she mulled without making her feelings evident to others. Step by step, and crouching through the dense thickets, they moved deeper and deeper into the forest.

Suddenly, raising a hand, Bela stopped in her tracks and so did those who were following her. She put a finger on her lips to indicate that nobody should make any noise. And then she pointed to a long row of bushes that appeared to be parting. Something was coming at them. Except Bela, everybody began to step back slowly, warily. They stood in a single file twenty feet apart from each other, scouting the surroundings. And then a boar, foraging the forest floor, appeared from within the bushes. The team moved on as the boar dodged the humans to disappear into the forest. Another fifteen minutes, and they could see at a distance a hive that was hanging from a high branch of a tree. The lead Mouli made torches with twigs and dry leaves that would be used to smoke the honeycombs in order to drive the bees away. One by one, he started passing the torches to his team members. Suddenly, he froze in his steps. The last man in the formation was missing. A short distance behind them, where that man was supposed to be, was a trail of blood disappearing into the thickets that appeared to have been ploughed through. The man was never seen again. Something out there had not listened to Bela.

The vicissitudes of a tiger-charmer's life often affected the outcomes and earnings from their profession. Bela wasn't making enough money in that tense rush for livelihood, the kind she expected, to bring the desired ease into her family. Still, whatever she earned was keeping the earthen oven burning back home, assuring her mother that the hard days might be over soon.

So disturbed was Bela that night that she couldn't sleep. It was sultry and hot. To let some air in, Bela opened the window. That's when she saw him again, sitting quietly in the forecourt with his usual splendor. He was awash with moonlight, looking other-worldly in belief, real in plain sight. Unnerved, she quickly shut the window and jumped back. From an earthen pitcher, she gulped down water to calm her nerves. Why again? Am I hallucinating or is this real? On all fours, like a tigress, and holding her breath, Bela crossed the clay floor to open the window again. He was gone. Enough is enough, Bela thought. This puzzle had to be solved once and for all.

Two days later, she went to visit Basudev, the oldest man in Dholkhali. Basudev lived about three miles away from Bela's house. He was eighty. Basudev, it was said, knew the forest and its non-humans like the lines of his palms. Which snake was venomous, how stealthy the crocodiles were, how a tiger behaved in mating season, how far one can travel into the woods, or what are the signals of tiger presence—he had everything on his fingertips. He could identify birds even if they were in flight. He had seen life and death up, close and personal on the riverbanks. He used to be the Sunderbans' most well-known and revered tiger charmer. Never for once any kind of mishap had been reported on Basudev's trips by *bawali*s and moulis or fishermen with whom he had spent his lifetime as a *gunin*. Such was his following that until Basudev sought the permission from Bon Bibi and Dakshin Ray during local festivities, nobody dared to take home as blessings the propitious offerings of food to the deities. The legend still abounds that Basudev could get the scent of a tiger from miles away. These days, in effect, he is the head of the tiger charmers' association of the Sunderbans. People, particularly fellow-*gunin*s, come to him for advice from time to time, especially when narrow misses involving tigers would occur.

Basudev was not well. He was lying in the bed, with Bela sitting near his feet. 'How do you explain this, Dadu?'

she asked him. The old man smiled at her, as if he already knew the answer. 'They don't harm humans unless we show intent of harming them, Bela. But sometimes we do, when we become greedy and over-adventurous. That is the time when the forest punishes us in its own way.'

'But why am I having this vision?'

'It's a long story but let me make it as much short as possible for you. According to sayings, the Sunderbans used to be an uninhabited area. Nobody lived here, not even the tigers. We all migrated to this place. There is an enduring belief among us *gunin*s that the tigers too migrated to the mangroves from their natural habitats far away from this region. That's because they were being killed rampantly for their claws, fangs and bones that fetched high prices in certain markets. They are ground, dusted and used in quack medicines. Tigers know humans had migrated too owing to their own hardships. One migratory species doesn't harm another. That's what we believed in and that's why you and I are still alive despite our presence in a shared territory.'

Bela was dumbfounded. 'But then, why me?'

'Because you have become a tiger yourself, like I was back in the day. You know, whenever I used to land on the riverbanks, I would go down on all fours on the soil and sniff it like a tiger. Even if they were out of sight, I could still sense their presence and they, mine. Between the two of us would be peace because we understood each other. Believe me, I had even eaten raw meat to get a taste of it, one that drew them to prey. Treat the tiger as a friend, not a foe.'

'Can you, Bela?'

'I will try, Dadu. But have you ever had such a vision?'

'No, Bela.'

'What is so special about me then?'

Basudev closed his eyes, as if he had no answer. Then he began to speak. 'So far, only men have been tiger charmers. You are the first woman-*gunin*. And as we all know, tigers protect their females fiercely. Of course, the vision that you are having is not of a real tiger. It is only an image that is being flashed to you by tigers from inside the forest. They are trying to tell you something because they treat you as one of them. Nobody will believe this outside our own domain. There's too much of logic, reasoning and science that defy the beliefs our world of *gunin*s live for. Tell me something, have you noticed anything out of place lately?'

Lapsing into deep thought, she said she hadn't. And then it struck her! Goosebumps were rising on her skin that had been smoothened by smearing of clay on the riverbanks, day after day. Bela began to breathe heavily. She looked at Basudev with her mouth open in disbelief. She didn't know whether it was out of fear or excitement over a discovery. 'Yes, Dadu. The very next day after my first vision, this devastating storm came to damage our house. A portion of the roof came crashing down, narrowly missing all of us.'

'Ahh, I knew, there had to be something. When was the last time you had this vision?'

'Two days ago.'

The old man fell silent. Then he kept looking at the small idol of Dakshin Ray kept inside a niche in the wall. Bela could notice that Basudev was frowning as he began scanning her eyes. Almost inaudible, he said: 'Bela, rush home. Now.'

Bela didn't have to reach her house. From a furlong away, she could see people gathered in the courtyard. Bela could hear her mother and some women cry. Sambhu *Gunin* had suddenly died of a stroke. The tiger attack had left him in a vegetative state. Being unable to work, and unable to live like a worthy head of a family was having a telling effect on his body and mind. In the night of that day of death, Bela had kept her window open to find out what else fate had in store for her and her mother. But she could see only condensed darkness and the stars in the sky.

❖❖❖

Over centuries, the people of the Sunderbans have learnt to share land with the wild as much as they have gotten used to water salinity or loss of livelihood due to nature's vagaries.

Now, the islands are facing another mounting problem. Every now and then, young girls were either eloping or being trafficked, never to be seen again. Parents without livelihood are often falling prey to false promises by traffickers, who pose as grooms to take their daughters away to later engage them as sex workers. The Sunderbans are a sitting duck for human traffickers. The malaise hasn't spared Dholkhali either. Just the other day, Bela's childhood friend Rekha went missing. Some say that a young boy went missing too the day Rekha disappeared. Even though reports drift in saying the police have rescued girls from the clutches of flesh trade in places as distant as Delhi and Mumbai, and as close as Kolkata, homes on the islands still haven't fortified their defence against deviousness. For the daughters of the islands, the abominable spectre of being taken is slowly expanding. The fear constantly plays on Kamala's mind. At twenty-two, Bela fits the bill as a girl vulnerable to human cunning. Kamala is concerned. With Sambhu gone, the onus is on her to handfast Bela. But how? The savings make little sense even though Bela keeps her tiger-charming practice alive. A simple woman, Kamala doesn't have the wherewithal to even plan or think ahead. All she knows is that, with Sambhu, she had lived for the day; with Bela's earnings, she wishes to live for another day.

As Kamala swung between spending on Bela's marriage and needs—neither could be spared for the other—a young man named Arizul called on her one day. Arizul was quite up and about, and often travelled to the mainland. Nobody knew what he did for a living, but that he was the most well-off in the village was clearly evident. He owned an android mobile phone that nobody else had in Dholkhali. He wore expensive watches. Arijul's appearance smelt of urban opulence.

His arrival at the Gain house seemed nothing short of providential.

Without any preamble, Arizul went straight to the point, setting the tone of the conversation in no uncertain manner. He knew Kamala was way too gullible even by her own level of innocence. 'Kamala Bhabi, there's a nice young boy I know. His name is Nabin Mandal. He works as a security guard with a bank in Kolkata. Bela could be an ideal bride for him. What do you think?' Arizul looked at her expectantly.

Kamala was nonplussed. She didn't know Arizul well, but had heard of him. No matter what, she was aware that the youngman who stood in front of her might prove to be a messiah in disguise. 'How old is he?'

'He is thirty-five, Bhabi.'

'Isn't he too old for Bela?'

Displeased, Arizul asked her politely whether she was concerned more about the groom's age or with the prospects of settling Bela in a fluent home. 'What is the future of her tiger-charming, Bhabi?' To Kamala, Arizul made sense.

'But how, Arizul, how? We don't have that kind of money to spend on her marriage. Had your uncle been alive, we could have given it a serious thought. And why on earth a city boy would marry a *gunin* like Bela!'

'Bhabi, Nabin wants an ordinary girl who is not gawky. I thought Bela could be the right choice. By the way, the parents of this boy are long gone. He is on his own. So, it would be just the two of them. The boy doesn't have siblings either. Imagine, how happy they would be together! No in-law hassles, no nothing. Now it's up to you,' Arizul said as he began stepping out of the house, deliberately delaying the punchline to ace the conversation, for he could see apprehension and confusion.

'By the way, Bhabi, the groom's side will give you one lakh rupees as dowry.'

One lakh! Kamala's head was spinning. Never in her wildest dream, she had seen one lakh rupees. So many hurdles to cross and so much to live for! Her heart was racing. There was hope, after all. Bela was hardly available in the house. On the one hand, she was putting her life on the line every day to keep the home alive, and on the other was the bliss of life-long comfort.

'You know, Bhabi, there are so many marriageable girls in these parts. If not her, there will be someone else. But since I knew Sambhu Chacha well, I thought I will come to you first. Let me know. I will then ask this man, Nabin, to come and see you.' Arizul prepared to leave. 'Bhabi, please speak to your daughter. Her consent is also important.'

'Why do I need her consent? She will do what I ask her to do,' Kamala said curtly.

Subduing the smile that was emerging on his face, Arizul stepped out and called a Kolkata number.

'Yes, Arizul?'

'She has almost agreed.'

'Almost?'

'Yes, but if we make her an advance, I am sure she would fall in line.'

'How much have you quoted to her?'

'One lakh.'

'That's steep.'

'Think about it. A girl of twenty-two, virgin, raw and lithe. She would be a nice bride for you,' Arizul chuckled.

'All right, go ahead. Meet me at my Topsiya home tomorrow.'

✣✣✣

The day Nabin got off a ferryboat at the Dholkhali pier, almost the entire village had gathered on the forested bank. Hugging the Bangladesh border in the eastern part of the Indian Sunderbans, Dholkhali is remote, way too remote to be found on a map. The village rarely had visitors. So when the young man in rubber kitos, a red tee and a pair of jeans leapt onto the pier as a sharp contrast to the benighted soil of Dholkhali, he appeared almost like a *Banshi* in blood and flesh, a mythical musician locals believed lived deep in the forests. An advanced cellphone that he was gripping made him stand out from other visitors, who were usually fishermen plying their trade.

'Could you please show me the way to Kamala Gain's house,' Nabin asked an old man who stood at the forefront of the curious clutch of people.

'What business do you have with her,' the old man inquired. He wondered what an apparently city-bred *babu* had to do with an unassuming simple woman like Kamala.

'She is expecting me.'

❖❖❖

Standing in front of a narrow mirror with a diagonal crack, Bela is ornamenting herself today. A suggestion of kohl on her eyes, a red bindi on her forehead, and a nose ring glistening with light, and powdered cheeks – she is emerging in the mirror like someone she has never seen before. A tigress in the wild was beginning to look tamed, and that's what Bela was unable to come to terms with.

She felt uncomfortable wearing them but had to, at the behest of Kamala. The wet soil on deadly lands has been her brand of cosmetics all along. A thin necklace beaded with false stones that she had bought from a local fair dirt cheap adorns her neck. She draws a Dhoniakhali saree–the advance Kamala had received from Arizul made this possible–from the *alna* and begins to drape herself with it. Even though a little nervous, she looks with bewilderment at her own transformation, from a homespun girl in a wild place to a stranger in the mirror. She sat on the bed, wondering if she did the right thing to give her consent in marriage.

No matter the promise of comfort in a city she has never seen, the winding rivers she sailed every day, the songs of the oarsmen and the excitement of being in communion with the wild, could never be easily sent to history. The dirt road that so freely wound out of her heart towards the games she played with her friends, the storks she raced on the bank of a river, or the gay abandon with which she blended with her surroundings, were coming back to her. How would I leave all this in one stroke of fate? She had built her mangrove life, brick by brick, and now an unknown man was coming to take all that away.

In a flash she recalled an incident that remained as a cornerstone of her life as a *gunin*. On a day of fishing, she had just cast a spell on the land when a tiger walked out of the thickets. The oarsmen shouted out warnings to her, but she stood her ground in a face-off with the beast, in almost a situation her father had faced once. The striped pogrom of doom sniffed the air, growled and began to take one step forward at a time towards her. Bela's heart was in her mouth. She raised her hand, signaling to the fishermen to stay quiet. Her lips were moving. She was muttering the *pala gaan* from the *Bonbibi Panchali*. She hoped she was not erring while invoking the blessings of the deity.

She couldn't explain to herself why the tiger later backed down into the forest, but the oarsmen said later that the beast knew it wasn't dealing with a common human. Those moments had signaled her emancipation from the clutches of anonymity. The adrenaline flow she experienced that day became her addiction. One side of her wanted to stay wild, and the other left her torn between her mother's wishes and the man who was coming to see her. Bela felt abandoned to greed.

'Bela, what's taking you so long? The man would be here soon.'

'I am ready, Ma. But...'

'But what?'

'Ma, what will happen to you after I am married? Who will take care of you?' Her eyes were moist. She didn't know tigresses cried.

'Don't worry, Bela. They are giving me enough money. If something happens to me, there are neighbours who would take care of me, like they did when your father passed away. If ever I am too frail to take care of myself, I would go to you. Right?'

Someone knocked on the door. 'Come on Bela, he is here. Wipe your tears and get up quickly.' Kamala seemed a little harsh on her, and Bela didn't like it one bit. A girl being pitchforked into marriage needed time to ready herself for the first contact with the groom.

Bela liked what she saw. Polite in conversation, the young man in a red tee and jeans with sprightly steps looked able and enterprising to her. Bela found Nabin staring at her. There was something in his eyes, however, that Bela couldn't make out, a certain something that didn't befit the appearance of a man who was a groom-in-waiting. Greed? Lust? Or misplaced dignity? They began to talk, Bela demurely and Nabin with a tenor that intended to please her and her mother.

'Let us then fix a date, Baba,' Kamala said to Nabin.

'Yes, as early as possible. I have much work to do back in Kolkata.' Did Bela detect immoderate haste in his response?

That night, Bela was lying sleepless, tossing and turning in the bed. She believed her father was living in her, a tiger charmer who virtually gave his life taming the wild with his spirituality. She was his legacy. And that very tether was now set to be severed in the name of marriage. Bela wanted to walk away from it but the situations that preceded Nabin's arrival – Arizul's visit, offer of one lakh rupees and her mother accepting an advance–gave her little time to make up her mind. 'Isn't there anyone who can free me from all this,' Bela whispered to herself. It was then she felt a presence in the courtyard.

She opened the window. After almost a year, he was there, shining in the moonlight. This time, he was pacing under her window restlessly, as if he wanted to tell her something.

✣✣✣

NINETY-EIGHT

Armed to teeth, they ducked under the cover of darkness, the engines of their boat killed to evade attention. The boats had oared the last mile on the Gomdi River. Their greedy eyes were trained on Gorjontola, a hamlet of scrawny, malfed people in Satjelia, one of the Sunderbans' many island villages. One by one the boatmen disembarked, their laboured steps on the sticky bank leaving wicked footmarks in the mangrove mud. Readying his rifle to take on anything that might spring out of the darkness, the leader of the pack walked circumspectly towards the tree-line. Tonight, the mangrove forest would lose some of its lungs and shrink to avarice.

✣✣✣

Like an arced pantheon of Gods, the Sundari trees surrounded Gorjontola, a hamlet too tiny to be called a village, a settlement too out of place to be remembered. Forming a canopy, the trees, almost sixty-feet high, partially blocked the sun to keep Gorjontola somewhat cool in the unbearable heat of the summer. The shadow of the leaves drew random filigrees on dry soil, like a carefree work of art without a defined form. In the winter, the trees stood naked, gently pressing sunlight onto the soil of the village, needed to stay warm and produce livelihood. And when it rained, they would swing their heads in the air, as if waving goodbyes to passing boats. The rustling of their leaves, blending with the tweets of birds, or the howling noise they would make in a rising storm, seemed almost like music. The Sundaris that grew in abundance in the area meant life to Gorjontola where a clutch of homes have been holding onto the land since eons. The landscape was mostly flat, with undulations few and far between.

Dirt-roads, abutted by paddy fields, small betel-leaf plantations, and hyacinth covered ponds, made the solitudes that idled towards the Gomdi River. Boats waited twice a day—7 in the morning and 2 in the afternoon—to connect the hamlet to the small, local market on the other side. There were no roads connecting it to the mainland. Two rejected forest department jeeps with flatulent engines, parked at the local *thana*, were the only means to lend speed to emergencies for a fee. But then, the people of Gorjontola, comprising mostly Oraons and Mundas, have for centuries lived off the land, with no highway to hope. They are as old as Man. Or Woman.

Matangi Oraon sat in the forecourt of her house, weaving baskets from palm leaves. She had lost her husband several years ago to evanescence. Her husband, Soilo, had left home one day for Kolkata, where he was said to be working at a sawmill. He never came back. Over the past years, Matangi tried to establish his whereabouts by asking Kolkata-bound men from his village to investigate his disappearance, but nobody returned with any heart-warming news. Initially, she would cry alone in the night, her tears absorbed by the pillow. But as years went by, Matangi began to accept that she was saddled with a life nobody else would take care of, not her neighbours, not even her relatives. Deep inside, she had begun to harden, each layer of reality lending her the might that she never imagined acquiring.

She looked up to find a shaft of blinding sunlight falling on her face. Strange, she thought. *I sit here every day, weaving the baskets but never before the sun has fallen on my face when I am perched on this particular spot.* She used her palm to shade her forehead, squinted her eyes and looked at the Sundari trees. She discovered a gap in the treeline that never existed before.

'Kalki, Kalki.'

'Yes, Ma?' Kalki stepped out of the hut as she answered Matangi's call. She was used to her mother calling out for her every now and then. Her curvaceous body belied her 17 years of age, which had turned out to be a cause for concern for

Matangi. As a fast-growing teen, Kalki wanted to join other boys and girls in a game of kabaddi, or take afternoon dips together into a nearby pond. Her saree with nothing beneath accentuated her curves to a point that the boys would steal glances at her and some would begin to visually scan her wet body. This caused much discomfort to her and her mother and, at times, discomfiture. Matangi's frequent search for her wasn't for Kalki to join errands; it was more about finding out where the girl was. Alone? With a boy? At the river? So, when Kalki was walking towards her mother, she thought it was just another routine scrutiny call.

'What, Ma?'

'Look up there,' Matangi pointed to the gap in the Sundari canopy. 'Do you see a gap? Something was there until yesterday and is now missing.'

Kalki stood watching the Sundaris. She could notice a cleft near the top of the treeline. It seemed like a long-closed door had been suddenly opened. 'Yes, Ma, it doesn't look the same.'

Without a word, Matangi picked up a *hanshua* (sickle)—the *hanshua* had earned the infamy of being a deadly weapon when used for defending any attack, be it by a beast or a human. She signalled Kalki to follow her. Matangi would not dare to walk alone into the Sundari forest where tigers, hyenas, King Cobras and tusked wild boars had often been spotted. With the *hanshua* in Matangi's hand in a striking position, and a bamboo stick in Kalki's, the mother and the daughter crept into the forest. An eerie silence prevailed. Even the rustling of the Sundari leaves had stopped. The trees were standing still like dumbfounded actors who have forgotten their cue on the stage. The moist air was heavy. Not a leaf moved as Matangi and Kalki looked around, breathlessly.

'Look, look!' It was Kalki who broke the silence. Matangi found her daughter standing near what looked like stumps of trees. She rushed to the spot. It wasn't difficult for her to figure that a few Sundari trees had been neatly sawed off from their base.Who possibly could have done this? She looked around to find footmarks that led back to the river. It was easy for Matangi to make out that a group of people had entered the forest to leave it a few Sundaris fewer. Blinding rage began to replace the sense of shock. Her whole body was shaking in agitation. Her vision became so blurred that she could see nothing except the devastation that lay in front of her. The Sundari was one of the many gods the Oraons worshipped since they landed in the mangroves centuries ago as labourers, enslaved by the British with nowhere else to go. Through the passage of time, the Oraons have come to believe that the Sundaris have healing properties, often used in folk medicine to treat nagging ailments. Gods heal and it is the duty of the healed to guard the healer with life was the creed of the Oraons, at least for Matangi.

'Nobody can touch our Gods, nobody,' Matangi swore under her breath. She gripped the *hanshua* firmly in her right hand and blurted out a literal war cry.

'*Harami*! (Bastard!) If you are a true son of your mother, come and face me. I swear I will turn your torso into that stump you have left behind.' Fiery exhalation was escaping Matangi's swelled-up nostrils, her loose hair flew in every direction like a burning supernova. Her eyes looked like orbs that were trying to burst out of their astral course as she began to dash towards the edge of the forest with her *hanshua* poised to strike anything that would cross her path.

In complete bewilderment, Kalki looked at Matangi. She had never seen her mother in such uncurbed fury. She ran after her. Kalki tackled her mother from behind to cut off her run. Both fell to the ground, Kalki on top and Matangi beneath her. Kalki kept her mother pinned to the ground, preventing her every move to get up. She could feel the upheaval of Matangi's chest, like the bellow of an ironsmith. She kissed Matangi on her forehead, ran her fingers through her hair and whispered into her ears, 'Calm down, Ma, calm down. Whoever it was must have come well-equipped. You can't take all of them on by yourself.'

Slowly, Matangi's breathing eased as she looked at her daughter with a look of surprise. *When did this girl become a woman*?

Later that day, urged by Matangi, the entire hamlet gathered at the chief's house to discuss the disappearance of the Sundari trees. While everybody agreed with the strong likelihood of the Sundari forest being the target of timber smugglers, none displayed any gumption to help form a defence against the unknown, unseen invaders.

She was at a loss for words, numbed into silence by the sheer indifference of most villagers to the issue. She knew that the land they claimed to be their own would one day become too hostile to live in if the 'forest of Gods' was not protected from human greed. But how? Is there a way, she asked herself.

✣✣✣

Over a hundred kilometres away, in Kolkata, Bablu Sardar offloaded logs from his heavy-duty truck into a warehouse owned by a timber merchant. Bablu made it a point to let the owner of the warehouse know that the timber contained Sundari logs he had procured from a village. Sundari logs fetched a good price in the grey market. 'One cubic foot of Sundari timber can get you over four thousand rupees,' Bablu said with a roguish smile that spread on his face beneath a wicked wink.

'You have a Sundari here?' The timber merchant looked deeply interested in the haul.

'Yes, of course.'

'Where did you get it from? Sundaris are rare these days. You know, all that embargo and ban on felling of Sundari trees has been a thorn in my side.'

'I got it from a village called Gorjontola.'

'"From where?!'

'Gorjontola in the Sunderbans. There are lots of Sundari trees, unguarded.'

Soilo almost jumped from his seat. Yes, there were many Sundari trees and as many dumb people in Gorjontola, choosing to remain ensconced in their primitive way of life. Drawing upon memory, he could deduct that, between now and the point of time he had left Gorjontola, the Sundari trees must have grown in number in the village.

Always enticed by the stories of good money being made in Kolkata as told to him by boatmen, Soilo had distanced his mind from the back-of-beyond Gorjontola. He had taken a call—come what may, he would try to make a fortune in Kolkata, even if it meant abandoning his family. He hadn't let his tenure as a strong-arm labour at the saw mill go waste. Every day, he learnt something new about timber trade. By the fifth year of his stay in Kolkata, he had equipped himself with adequate knowledge to kick off his own timber trading firm, small yet bankable. Quick money had made Gorjontola bleak in his memory.

There had been no frantic letters from home—Matangi was not literate—and neither did he try to walk that extra mile for the upkeep of his family in the fear that if he did, once again, the rigours of poverty would come to bear upon him. Yet, he just couldn't summarily dismiss his daughter and wife from memory. It's not that he missed them dearly. The link had been stretched too thin, too far, but it still remained a tether, its time-weary threads notwithstanding. When under bouts of loneliness—he had no friends in Kolkata—he would wonder how they were, what they were doing. He also knew that his wife and child would find a way to fight his absence from home. Maybe, someday, he would return to his land to reclaim his family but he didn't know when. He was not ready either to bring them over to Kolkata. If he did, he would have to spare time for home, which was a luxury in the cut-throat timber trade, especially when a man like Bablu Sardar left him hamstrung.

Even though Soilo had managed to blend into urban life with ease, he still held some remnants of what he had come to the city with—his rusticity. Desires, and the craving for fulfilling them, would often interfere with his concentration, particularly in the night when he would toss and turn in the bed, seeking feminine touch. To satisfy his lust, he would visit sleazy whorehouses where he would mingle with criminals, adventurous students, police informers and pimps. He had met Bablu Sardar on one such visit to a red-light area. Soilo's constant hobnobbing with unscrupulous men had made him the weakest prey of avarice. He wished he could return to Gorjontola to chop off all the Sundari trees but he also knew that the village would not pardon him. He would probably be driven out by a kangaroo court. But he needed Sundaris desperately. An exporter of timber had promised Soilo good money for Sundaris. He was aware that for bridge-building, boat-building, joinery, electrical poles and tool handles, the Sundari timber was just the right fit across the world. More so, the Kourikhara village in the Nesarabad region of Bangladesh, was South Asia's epicentre for smuggled Sundaris.

The only way he could lay his hand on the Sundaris was through Bablu. If Bablu couldn't deliver, nobody else could. 'But will he do it for me, or should I take his help?' Soilo was cautioning himself for a reason.

Bablu belonged to the underground or the underground belonged to him. His all-pervading legend hadn't bypassed Soilo. Bablu didn't own any gang; all gangs were just happy to have not earned his wrath for any reason. Organising country-made bombs during elections, disturbing political rallies with violence, evicting tenants, assigning contract killers, smuggling firearms from Munger into the city and still managing to stay on the right side of the law were gifts

Bablu was endowed with. He never left any trail that could lead to him. Any one of his underworld associates who would dare to renege would never be found again. There was another plus to his profile—he never served time. The police had, from time to time, arrested Bablu but had to let him off due to lack of evidence. Bablu was clean on papers, vicious in private realm.

'Do you think you can get me more,' summoning courage, Soilo said to Bablu one day.

'Yes, but you know the price. It's not easy to fell trees in the middle of the night and lug them off before dawn.' Like most hardened smugglers, Bablu would keep the Sundari logs submerged with weight in remote creeks of the Sunderbans. Once the coast was clear, his boats would haul them towards their destination.

'All right, name your price.' Soilo was aware that he wasn't the only customer of Bablu. Soilo's fellow trader Kabir Seth, who operated out of a small facility just a block away, was an acquaintance of Bablu.

All his life, Soilo had been careful to keep off trouble because anything untoward involving him could be potentially insalubrious to his dreams of making it big in a city like Kolkata. He did fight his demons, but they always took place in his imagination where he saw himself as unbeatable. He had been slaying his competitors, Bablu Sardar and the diseased underworld in his dreams. Fantasising the unreal gave him a high but he knew the fantasies would not come to his aid when dealing with a scum like Bablu.

✣✣✣

A passel of wild boars was foraging the land. The alpha male was on guard, scanning the surroundings. Suddenly, his ears shot up and his eyes glowed like embers at night. Humans and quite a few of them! He and his herd had never had to worry about humans in the Sundari forest. Alarmed, the alpha male raised his neck in the air and grunted. The entire passel stopped grazing, waiting for a signal from its leader. Neither the alpha, nor the rest of the passel was ready for any confrontation with humans. It's not that the boars hadn't spotted a human before. But they had always chosen to keep off conflict even though, if provoked, they could be a ferocious adversary.

Fifty meters away, Gansha whispered, 'Sardar, boars!'

'Don't make noise. They have spotted us. Give some time and they will leave.' This was not the first time Bablu Sardar was in an unknown jungle, hunting for fortunes. He had always drawn on his faculties to slip out of danger. He knew this was one more occasion that required him and his men to endure the tension arising from the locked bellicose between man and beast. Years ago, he had faced a similar situation in the

Sunderbans while smuggling Sundari logs. He knew being anonymous was critical to survival in the deadly wild of the mangroves. Without moving, Bablu and his men stood their ground while the boars turned antsy, grunting and kicking into the soil. Slowly, the fidgeting boars began to disappear into the darkness as silently as they had appeared, convinced the humans didn't have any design for them.

'Now, get to work. Find trees that are nearest to the bank so that we can carry them off without fuss. Cut the boat lights. Light up your halogen lamps. Take out the saws. And, no matter what, leave no personal bearings behind. Come on, we don't have much time. Don't forget to deep-etch some other adult trees with your knives. We would take them away the next time we come here.' Bablu spewed out his orders, went to the boat, picked up a long-muzzle rifle from the pilot's cabin, and walked up towards the trees.

The wind, blowing hard, was tunnelling through the Sundari forest, passing the trunks of the trees like a whistling, weaving train, to burst out in the open near the Gorjontola that lay just behind. Then it thinned into a pleasant wave, drifting into homes.

Kalki wasn't getting any sleep that night due to the heat and humidity. She let the sudden gust of wind caress her body. Thirsty, she got up to get water from the earthen pot lying near the foot of her bed. That's when she heard the sound.

It was coming from the forest side. It seemed like a hum, steady but distanced. It was too mechanical to be dismissed as a night-time occurrence of strange sounds that a forest can create.

'Ma, Ma, wake up.' She shook her mother firmly by the shoulder.

Awakened and alarmed, Matangi shot up in the bed. 'What happened?'

'Listen carefully, Ma. A strange sound is coming out of the forest.'

Matangi grabbed her *hanshua* and stepped out to the courtyard, with Kalki behind her. After a while, she turned towards Kalki, 'Don't you have anything else to do so late in the night than waking me up? That must be some birds or the wind. Haven't you gotten used to these sounds? Let me sleep now.' Kalki knew protesting would be futile. Her mother was not willing to sacrifice sleep for some strange noise. After all, she did work hard through the day, every day. She deserved the rest to recoup for the next twenty-four hours. It would be inhuman to keep her awake as a nocturnal listening post. Kalki went back to bed.

Inevitably, Matangi and Kalki went into the forest the next day to discover that a few more trees had been felled and taken away. 'You were right, Kalki. I should have listened more carefully last night.'

'But Ma, what possibly could you have done alone? You would be killed if you confront these people. If they are coming in the night to cut trees, they must be well-armed.'

'I know, Kalki, I know. But I just cannot bear it anymore.' Matangi leaned on a Sundari tree and looked around. Some of these Sundari trees had been saplings when she was a child. They grew up together like siblings. Matangi considered the trees as her bloodline, a part of her life. With each felling, she felt as if a limb had been torn off her body.

'We have to do something, and fast. This cannot go on.'

Back in the village, Matangi went straight to the chief's house to let him know it was time the matter was reported to the police. The village chief was middle-aged. He had nothing else to do than asking her daughter-in-law to frequently prepare the hookah so that he could get his own highs. And then, he would pass it around among his sycophants who visited him at odd hours only to complain about neighbours. He told Matangi that asking the law to interfere would be useless.

'Why so?' Matangi was losing her temper.

'Ask yourself. We went to the police to report about Soilo's disappearance. Did they help? No. Did they come to the village even once to investigate? No. Have we heard from them again about Soilo? No. So how do you expect the police to take action just because a few trees in a Sundari forest have been felled? No, Matangi. We're barking up the wrong tree.

Go home, eat something and take rest. You are worrying more than you should.'

Matangi felt crippled. She was trapped between despair and desperation. She was hell bent on preventing the timber mafia from denuding the forest any further than it already had. But the trees kept falling one by one. Emboldened by any lack of protest or defence, the invaders had thrown caution to the wind, so much so that the raids on the forest were taking place even in broad daylight. Bablu Sardar had begun to deploy heavy machinery and armed men to carry out his brazen heist. From a distance, the Oraons, including Matangi, would watch as one Sundari tree after another got loaded onto boats that would sail away before nightfall. A clearing in the woods had formed. The forest line had begun to recede fast, so rapidly that the sphere the Sundari forest had formed around the hamlet had begun to expand in diameter, slowly making Gorjontola look like a dot in the middle of a huge, blank circle.

✣✣✣

The area had little governance. Even then, the lie of the land needed to be governed by law, like any other place. But the nearest police station was six miles away where station officer Bankim Babu sat in his dirty khaki uniform and wore a tobacco-stained toothy smile as he talked to someone on his cell phone.

'No problem, Bablu babu. Isn't nature supposed to support our existence? If we can pluck coconuts and fruits from a tree for sustenance, why can't we take a whole tree home to make things out of it for human use? But there's something I need to tell you. If for some reason the villagers fight back, I don't know you, and you don't know me.' He put the phone down and began counting the wad of notes Bablu Sardar had left for him last night. It contained twenty five-hundred rupee notes. He would need the money for his son's admission into a Kolkata college. It didn't occur to him that he just sold a forest for a mere ten-thousand rupees.

He called out for his assistant, who happened to be a lean, docile man from a nearby village, 'Manuaaaaa…'

'Yes, babu.'

'Where the hell had you been since the morning?'

'Babu, my wife is pregnant again. I was looking after her. She is about to go into labour.'

'Another child? *Shaala*, you guys not just know how to fuck, but you fuck your work too.'

Manua stood with his head in his hand, appearing like a low-life in front of an imperious, corrupt man.

'Fill up the bank forms and deposit this money in Canning today.'

'Babu, today is Sunday. The banks are closed.'

Bankim Babu dismissed Manua with a nonchalant wave of his hand. He lapsed into deep thought. Sunday meant a holiday for Bablu Sardar too. He made a point to call Bablu Sardar on Monday as he suddenly remembered that his daughter's wedding was just around the corner.

✣✣✣

It hadn't taken long for Matangi to figure out that the timber mafia took its day off on Sundays. She had a plan but to make it work, much needed to be done. Over the past few days, she had managed to galvanise some women in the village into seeing her point that the Sundari forest needed to be saved from the unscrupulous traders. Murku, the woman next door, Yamuna, the daughter-in-law of the village chief, Roma, a boatman's wife and several others of their ilk had listened aptly to a fiery speech Matangi had delivered at a thin gathering.

All these women had defied the sermons of their men to fall in line with Matangi. She had to knock on every door to tear each woman away from the clutches of the patriarchs and their biased conventions.

'The crisis that is facing us will one day destroy all of us. This land, where we were born and are destined to die, is our home. The pillars of our homes are the Sundari trees that we worship. These Gods are watching us closely. I know for a fact that no man in this village will ever step out of his home to protect the forest. But then, someone has to fight back. The women of this village are now the warriors. Wasn't Goddess Durga, who had saved us from peril, a woman? What are you waiting for? Today, they are cutting the Sundari trees. Tomorrow, they will enter our homes. Are you waiting for the day when, like the Sundari trees, our daughters too would disappear from homes, taken away by pimps and greedy men? No, we cannot let that happen. The advance of the devil must be stopped. To the last woman standing, we will protect the forests and fight, we shall.'

'Yes!' the women roared in unison while raising their *hanshuas* in the air to express complete solidarity with Matangi. Their eyes, burning like pits of coal, the women belted out a loud, collective voice that portended revenge, 'Jai Ma Durga, Jai Bon Bibi!' rent the air. The font of eternal power was once again rising, this time in a village that had refused to wake up to reality.

'Ma, I am afraid,' Kalki whispered.

'Don't worry, Kalki. When Gods declare war, no force can hope to win,' Matangi had kept a reassuring hand on her daughter's head.

Matangi and her squad spent the Sunday counting the number of Sundari trees that were left. 'We have ninety-eight of them.' Murku spelled out the count to Matangi.

'And how many have been felled so far?'

'Seventy.'

Matangi was crestfallen. How could people do this to a land that gifted humans permanence? Weren't they ashamed of themselves? Wasn't there anyone among that timber mafia who would refuse to join the rampant rape of the forest? Matangi knew each one of these men was readying for the next sally on Monday, which was less than twenty-four hours away.

'Matangi, do you think we can defend with just *hanshuas*? I am sure these men are well armed.'

'Yamuna, I really do not know whether we would succeed or not. If it comes to shedding blood, ours or theirs, it would happen.' She paused for thought. *A message had to go out to everyone*. She instructed, 'Call everyone to my house.'

⁜⁜⁜

Before the stroke of dawn, Kalki slipped out of her house, carrying a conch shell with her. She made her way through the bushes towards a particular Sundari that had climbed too high in the air, wildly insolent and rising above the forest line with a clear view of the Gomdi. She was extra-careful to keep herself unsighted by men who had the habit of using the fields early in the day for ablutions.

The women didn't want their men to throw a spanner in the works. Kalki climbed the tree and perched herself on a thick, leafy branch that hid her from open sight. She was required to blow the conch shell the moment she would notice Bablu and his men approach the village. Her heart was in her mouth but when she remembered that her mother was risking her own life by being in the forefront of the turnaround, Kalki felt better. She took out a fistful of *muri* from a small side bag that slung from her left shoulder and began to chew on them to stay awake.One mistake and the whole plan would collapse like a house of cards although her mother did not share with her what exactly she had in mind.

Matangi, too, left her house as unobtrusively, a few minutes after Kalki had disappeared into the slate-grey darkness. She was feeling sorry for her daughter. After all, Kalki was only a child who had no clue to the events that were to unfold in a few hours inside the Sundari forest. Matangi arrived at the edge of the forest to find that her squad had already gathered there, each armed with a sickle.

'If anyone has second thoughts, raise your hand. Nobody will be forced to join this movement.' Nobody did. Matangi could feel the adrenaline rushing. Like Matangi, all the other women didn't know what to anticipate but were sure that this cause couldn't be fought for without bloodshed. Matangi walked up to a point from where the cluster of houses could be seen. Not one door was open, as if households had been caged into a fearful ghetto that no man wanted to free.

They sat down on the damp soil in separate huddles and talked about cooking, weaving and their everyday chores. The women looked immune to the palpable tension that was in the air but deep inside, they were preparing to ride their fear to glory. 'If you aren't afraid, then you are not normal, fear will be the key to our success,' Matangi had said to them a few days ago.

Matangi looked at the sky. Between the balls of dark clouds was the first glimmer of light. Dawn was breaking.

It was then that they heard the sound of a conch shell.

'The devils are coming. Take position.'

With their sickles drawn like a sabre, the women stood ten feet apart from each other, forming an arc and shielding the forest. Matangi looked at the tall Sundari, but Kalki had already slipped down the trunk and disappeared into the surrounding bushes.

Mechanised saws, axes, mud pumps and armed men got off the two trawlers that had sailed down the Gomdi, making their way on the muddy bank towards the Sundari forest silently.

⁂

Gansha raised a set of binoculars to his eyes. 'Sardar, trouble.'

'What trouble?' Bablu snatched the binocular from Gansha. What he saw made his hair stand up on his head. Scores of women, with sickles, were standing in front of the forest, obviously to prevent his men and machines from entering it.

'What the hell! Where did they come from?'

'Why are you asking me, Sardar? I am as nonplussed as you are.'

Bablu looked at Gansha, 'That bastard Bankim babu must have double-crossed us. We will take care of him later. But first, the women.'

As they reached the edge of the forest, Bablu walked straight up to Matangi, who was standing ahead of the arc, about fifty metres in front of the forest. 'Get out of the way. Your army of women will not be able to stop us. Go home, cook and bear children. That's what all of you are meant for,' he chided her. Matangi locked her eyes with Bablu's. She didn't speak a word. Instead, she raised her *hanshua* even higher to indicate that her battle was just beginning.

'What's your name?'

'My parents called me Matangi. Matangi is long gone. I am now the species that life is born of.'

Bablu laughed out loudly, apparently at the stupidity of her being on the wrong side in a disparate war, 'All right then. If this is what you want, so be it.' Bablu turned towards his men, pulled a pistol out of a holster that was hidden under his shirt and fired in the air. That was meant as a signal for his men to advance and the women to retreat. The machines that had come to a halt began to be hauled again as they resumed their advance towards the forest which was still some distance away. The men, armed with *lathi*s and machetes, began to walk towards the trees, led by Bablu.

The women, including Matangi, stood their ground, ready to strike at the slightest hint of assault.

Bablu's mind was racing. All his life, he was used to seeing men and women cowering before him. Compelling his most stiff opposition into subservience has been the hallmark of his rule. Even the drawing of his gun didn't seem to deter Matangi and her women. He knew for sure that any confrontation with the women in that heightened tension wouldn't be bloodless. And Bablu didn't want any trail of blood to lead up to him.

He called a number from his cell phone.

'Yes?' The voice on the other side was keen.

'We have a situation here.'

'What happened?'

'An armed group of women is blocking our path. I spoke to their leader but they won't budge.'

'Who's their leader?'

'A woman named Matangi.'

The cell phone almost fell from Soilo's hand. *Matangi? What was she doing there*? He recalled Matangi as a docile woman who had never raised her voice, literally, and didn't know what defiance was. But then, Soilo was in a fix. On the other side of the phone was a dangerous man he saw quite frequently and in front of the man was a resolute woman he hadn't seen for ages, a woman he thought about from time to time. In the history of mankind, reality has always emerged from the realms of the unreal, which was what he was trying to come to terms to.

'Wait it out, Bablu, even if it means you have to park yourself and your men for a night near the forest. Don't get into a fight right now. They will disappear gradually if you stay put. Meanwhile, let me figure this out. Under any circumstances, do not open fire.' No matter his business acumen or greed, Soilo knew the difference between felling a tree and felling a human being.

✣✣✣

Shadows were drawing long into Gorjontola. The war of attrition had consumed one whole day. Matangi stood looking at the other women. They had decided to stay near the forest. She wondered what had made the men fall back and set up makeshift camps about 500 metres away from the forest all of a sudden. Is this a ploy? Are these men waiting for the women to tire out so that they can enter the forest effortlessly? Alarmed, she looked at the other women. They looked tired as they sat on their haunches on the wet soil in separate clutches. Matangi hissed, 'Nobody sleeps tonight, nobody.' They lit torches made of hay and cow-dung to not only ward off beasts but also to keep the vigil burning with heightened resolve.

❖❖❖

The dark sky was beginning to transform into a soft pink expanse. Dawn was breaking. One whole day was begetting another. The first tweets of egrets and cinnamon bitters, unspotted, had begun to drift through the air. Every specimen of hopeful life forms had a day to look forward to, unlike Matangi and Bablu Sardar who stood on the either side of the battle-line, unsure of how the coming hours would play out. Bablu looked at his cell phone. No call from Soilo. Raring to go, he was restless, while Matangi waited with an odd confidence, neither willing to allow the other any leeway.

Suddenly, they spotted a trail of dust billowing out at a distance, following a dot that grew bigger in size every moment to finally take the shape of a speeding Jeep, one of the forest department rejects. Bablu Sardar held the butt of his gun sleeping snugly in a chamois-leather holster strapped to his waist. Maybe, a posse of policemen was pouncing on them. Bankim Babu must have been singing like a canary. 'Watch out and wait for my command,' Bablu shouted out an order to his still sleepy-eyed men.

From near the forest, Matangi kept her eyes on the vehicle. It was heading straight for them. The vehicle stopped fifty metres from her. A man jumped out of the driver's seat. Who's that man? What does he want with us? And then, her whole world began to spin around her in chaos that could only be likened to a kaleidoscope gone rogue.

'O my God!' She screamed. The man who was walking towards her with wary steps appeared to be emerging from among the dead, from a past that she had so painstakingly kept quelled in memory. It was Soilo, her husband. A sudden calmness cascaded down Matangi's face and the fire that was raging in her eyes seemed to be dying down. Yet, the grit with which she had triggered the awakening among the women in her attempt to save the forest did not leave her.

'Why are you adamant, Matangi? Let the men do what they have come for. They are working for me. Remember, I am still your husband.'

'Maybe. But I will accept no sermons from you. My feelings for you are long dead. I feel for what that grows on its own soil, like the Sundari trees. I don't love anything that defiles the very soil it was born on.'

Soilo smiled, 'I accept that I had deserted you and our daughter. But the point is, if I hadn't remembered you, I wouldn't have appeared here today to interfere. Matangi, I do not want anyone to get hurt.'

'What do you mean? These Sundaris are our life, our souls. You want to hurt them.' She made it quite clear to Soilo that she would defend the forest come hell or high water, even if it meant going against her own husband. He pleaded with her, saying these were dangerous men who would brook no answer and would go to any length to get the trees. But Matangi would have none of it.

'If you ever loved me and our daughter, if you ever loved this soil, ask these men to go back where they came from.'

Without speaking another word, Soilo began walking towards Bablu Sardar and his men.

'Bablu, let's call it off. I don't need bloodshed.'

'What do you mean? You have already spent so much. We are so close to the forest and you want us to go back?'

'Yes, Bablu, that's what I want you to do now.'

Bablu looked at him without batting an eyelid. It was impossible for Soilo to tell what was going on in the depths of his amoral mind at that moment. His eyes looked morbid as they locked stares. Taming Bablu wasn't a task any sane human being would want to try. The pique of the situation was overbearing for him. On the one hand, his wife stood at a distance near the thickets, expecting him, Bablu and his men to leave the Sundaris to their sylvan abandon. On the other, the one who wanted to decimate his family stood in front of him, motionless, without remorse and with a sinister reason.

'Bablu, let's go back. We can find Sundari forests elsewhere. Can't you see that only blood and gore are awaiting us here?'

'No, we can't. If you are not interested, you leave. But me and my men will complete the job that we came for.'

'But who would buy those Sundaris from you?'

'Kabir Seth.' Bablu smiled for the first time in many hours.

Soilo realised that Bablu had used his cunning to outthink him. As he felt short-changed, an uncontrollable sense of fury began to spiral up his body. The soil beneath his feet seemed to be boiling. The blood that ran in Soilo's veins was still wildly tribal.

'All right then, do what you have to do.' Soilo began to move away from Bablu Sardar.

'Where are you going, Soilo Babu?'

'To join them,' Soilo pointed at the women guarding the forest. He began to walk. The fantasies he had been living with had now been shed. For the first time in his life, Soilo was stepping into a real battle. There were ninety-eight causes to fight for.

SCARLET DRAGONFLIES

The huge toy shot past her house pompously, creating a whirlwind behind. Dipali ran after it like a child, wanting to grasp it with all her might. It's been such a long time that she had been running after the toy. She was stumbling, faltering and panting. It was not an easy pursuit. The space between her and the toy had rivers, forests, beasts and a time that was hers and hers alone. And then, there was a tree that stood in between. Its branches were racing towards her. A demon was rising, warning her to be where she belonged. Sweating, Dipali woke up from her shut-eye she was affording herself every afternoon. This was a dream she didn't want to have but it kept returning to her with vengeance, turning her life into a shattered mirror of reflections. She drank water from a glass to calm her nerves and walked up to the window that overlooked a busy street of Kolkata. She looked out. Nothing has changed, nothing ever will. Dipali was no sleeping princess.

Dipali could still clearly picture how Kolkata looked when she had first stepped onto the disordered soil of a city desperate to shake off the after-effects of a war. The city had an intrigue about it that could invoke yearnings for even the most indolent and the nonchalant, to peel back its many layers to reach its heart. To Dipali, who grew up fed by curiosity, Kolkata did not need to send a calling card. The city lay there in front of her eyes, inviting and enticing like a bonny toy, as she stood on the threshold of new discoveries. That was over half-a-century ago, a long time to make memory bleak. But then, she lived inconspicuously in the two halves of her life—Kolkata into which she was pitchforked and Bhojdanga, an unknown village that stayed crystalised in the amber of her heart. Often, her mind would saunter in search of unaffected simplicity she used to be surrounded by, back home in Bhojdanga, in the undivided Sunderbans. Though Kolkata would remorselessly continue to beguile her, she wouldn't surrender the raw narrative of the mangroves to transience.

Dipali became addicted to watching the busy streets for long hours from the first floor of her house. Kolkata was a wonderment.

'What do you keep looking at every day, hour after hour?' Dipali's husband Amulya couldn't resist asking her. He was trying to figure out the reason for her fixation with the city.

The din, the grime and the tedium of noise down below captivated her. The hurried movements of people going about their work, the meaningless yelling by angry bus drivers, the occasional streetcar that would slow traffic down, policemen in white uniform and high Jodhpurs, and the sea of humanity that meandered through clogged streets were a bouquet of sights that greeted her every day. 'What I was and what I have become,' she would speak to herself smilingly.

She would immerse herself in the stories she heard from her husband. 'You know, zebras once pulled fancy carts on the Red Road.'

'Really? Or are you just putting me on?' Bewildered, Dipali would want to know.

'No, I am not kidding, Dipali. That really used to happen once,' Amulya reassured her.

Not just that, the anglicised Bengali gentry moving about in spacious Studebaker taxis fascinated her as much as people walking languidly on crowded streets, discussing food or Partition.

Like a kaleidoscope, the city kept changing its motifs in front of her eyes every day in the years that went by. The only thing that had remained through the times was the double-decker bus. 'O my God!' Overawed, she had exclaimed at the humongous presence of these buses that dwarfed everything around them. She had jumped in glee upon seeing them for the first time.

'What are you doing?' Her husband Amulya tried to throw a ring of caution around her excitement. 'Please, Dipali. There are people around in this house who would not approve of your loud elations.' On and off, he kept reminding Dipali that in her new home, she had to act as an ever-compliant daughter-in-law. To obey and deliver was the norm those days. As a 17-year-old bride, what else Dipali could have done? She could only hurdle towards transformation, learning fast at every stumble.

Over time, she and Amulya set up their family, brick by brick, making it almost flawless, like a master architect's blueprint. Their son Samar, a bundle of joy that arrived soon after their marriage, grew up to be a young man of virtues. They had been particular in shaping their son's life with care and circumspection. That was a time when the winds of the hippie movement had started to blow over Kolkata, like it did across the world. Both Dipali and Amulya didn't want their son to ape anything that wasn't at the root of their identities. The Haldar household was steeped in its own morality of convention.

Dipali walked away from the window and sat on her four-poster bed. From there, she could see herself in a life-size antiquated mirror that had probably been hinged into the wall years before she had arrived as a new bride. Her hair had greyed but the hairline hadn't surrendered to age. Her long nose—the bridge was a little dented due to years of spectacles use—was perfectly balancing out her high cheekbones. The eyes, though surrounded by a suggestion of crow's feet, had remained intense and inquisitive. They swept the room, from the ceiling to the floor and from wall to wall, looking for disorder.

There was nothing to be flustered about, but for the letter from Bhojdanga that had arrived in the morning mail seven days late.

✣✣✣

Bhojdanga is a black-hole standing out of time, silently consuming that which strays into its path and spewing out what it finds unpleasing. It tries human endurance and imprisons ingenuous people in its fief. Bhojdanga doesn't allow escape from its meshy tentacles that spread far and wide to enslave anyone or anything that even taunts its realm. In this small village of the Sunderbans, there are no free respites, or no time to be at ease even in sleep and dreams. Every breath taken is like an overdraft that one has to pay back in a lifetime, through blood and sweat. Every stride taken is bridled by two steps taken backward in these mangrove forests where hope is its inhabitants' greatest invention.

If dared, Bhojdanga shall return in some spiteful form or other to unfailingly punish lives. But young Dipali is untouched by the fall-outs of this disparate war between the wild and man. Hers is a life immersed in fantasies that she plucks fistfuls of from the free, blue sky over the mangroves whenever she stands on the western bank of the Shibsha river that flows by Bhojdanga. The egrets and the whistling teals that crisscrosses the air, the monkeys that watch her from the dense canopy, or the fishing skiffs that cut through the deceptive surface of the Shibsha to disappear into the creeks, are her universe. Even common flowers like Karanja Bain and Jhamti Goran that emerge from the overnight mist to bedeck the vast sweep of the forest are strokes of dulcet tones in her wide-eyed drapery.

Dipali didn't go to school. There were no schools in that area, barring a local *pathshala* too far away for her to dare the wild and reach it all by herself. Neither was it possible for her parents to escort her. The grocery shop that her father Bishwambhar owned demanded time of him, and so did little Shanta, Dipali's younger sister. Instead, Biswambhar Bairy, who had been to the same *pathshala*, tutored Dipali at home, teaching her how to read and write under a lit lantern in the evening. Crickets stridulated from the woods and trees like Sundari, Gewa, Goran, Bain, and Golpata swept the mangroves with their rustling, turning the dark darker with their whispered chorus. Dipali would go to sleep in the cradle of awakened silence, knowing there would be another day of runaway fantasies—a young girl living her girlhood like it should be.

But then, in what seemed like just two days, Dipali's parents turned her into a woman from a girl. She was only seventeen when the news was broken to her by her mother Nalini, 'You're getting married the next *purnima* (full-moon night).'

'Married?' Dipali had little clue to what her mother was telling her but she was old enough to be impacted by the decision of her parents. The look in her eyes was one of bewilderment.

'Yes, my dear,' Nalini was gently trying to assuage the air of tension that suddenly seemed to be invading the room. Nalini knew Dipali needed to be carefully drafted into womanhood, but the time she had on her hand wasn't enough to prepare her for the marriage, at least mentally. 'Everything will be all right, trust me,' Nalini was saying to her. As always, Dipali wasn't willing to disturb the fate her parents had chosen for her. That was the only relief Nalini banked upon as she laid out the marriage plans. The girl had never contested her parents' decisions since she was a child.

After Nalini left the room, Dipali sat next to the window that looked out to a fenced opening in front of the house. Her big eyes under fluttering long eyelashes betrayed all emotions she might have been experiencing at that moment. She was slender, taller than her mother at five feet four inches, her height accentuated by a long fall of black, curly hair. The news of her marriage had started to sink into her slowly.

Accepting inevitabilities was her staple diet of obedience at home. The only sign of rebellion that emerged inside her head was a question she couldn't stop asking herself: *why the haste*?

'Listen, don't go out in the sun. Stay indoors. You need to look good,' Nalini blurted out the command before disappearing into the kitchen.

The announcement was too brusque for Dipali to stomach. She wasn't old enough to realise the portents of marriage or what it actually held for her. But to visualise herself as a bride, waiting for a stranger to be accepted as her life-partner, was a thought too jarring for her tender mind.

'My marriage?' She whispered to herself. *So, that's the reason why Baba had taken me to a photo studio in the Paikgacha town a month ago, and probably for the same reason, the aunts and uncles, whom I hardly see had started to drop by.*

Dipali ran after her mother. Walking into the kitchen, she squatted on the floor next to the earthen oven on which rice was boiling.

'Ma, what will happen on the *Purnima* night?'

'What do you mean by that? It's your wedding.'

She knew the finality with which she was informed of her marriage couldn't be reversed. 'Who will be my husband?'

'The groom is a fine young man. His name is Amulya, Amulya Haldar. He works with a *firangi* bank in Kolkata.' Nalini raised folded palms to her forehead in a prayer. 'It's the almighty's blessings that we have got a groom like him.'

'Kolkata?'

'Yes. What's wrong with that?'

'It's so far away, Ma. I heard it takes more than a day to travel to Kolkata from our village.'

'So what? Your husband and his father will take care of that journey. You need not worry.'

Her mind immediately lapsed into a series of possibilities. *Do I have to cook like you and run household errands*? Nalini tried to soothe her daughter's nerves by saying that she shouldn't be unduly perturbed because Amulya's family was well-off enough to employ housemaids and cooks. Dipali looked at her mother's sweating face which reflected the heat from the oven. She was aware that the hot, iron ladle that was stirring food on the flames was being held by a wife.

'I will feel lonely there, Ma. Won't you and Baba come to see me?'

Nalini realised that Dipali needed to be told how helpless her parents were in those matters. 'How can we unless invited? You would be going to a new home, which will be yours forever. Instead, you and Amulya can come and visit us from time to time. I am sure he will bring you here whenever you wish to.'

'Ma?'

'Yes, Dipu?'

'You are trying to dismiss me, too, from memory.'

'What do you mean by saying me too?'

'You know what I am saying, Ma.'

Nalini sat benumbed on the floor, looking at Dipali. A storm that she had walked into many years ago had begun to rise again within her. She didn't want to revisit the tempest in the fear that she would not be able to bear its wrath anymore. She realised that the reminiscence of that storm was now in front of her, in the form of Dipali.

✣✣✣

Six-year-old Shanta went with Dipali to the banks of the Shibsha one morning. That's where she discovered dragonflies.

Dipali, who was then eleven years old, had seen dragonflies before but the excitement in seeing them every time she went to the river continued to stay with her. Dragonflies never ceased to leave her in awe of their flying manoeuvres. One moment, they would cut through the air with supersonic speed. The very next moment, they would come to a standstill, hovering above a flower or a leaf of grass, like a helicopter on a rescue mission. Standing beneath them, Dipali could almost hear the drone of their trembling wings. She had once tied a dragonfly to a thread, held the thread in hand, and let it fly like a kite. But the tethered dragonfly, struggling to free itself, had dropped to the ground, exhausted. It broke its wings and died after some time. Crying, Dipali had dug a small hole on the banks and buried the dragonfly. She had then placed a tender hand on the flattened soil on the hole and had promised not to do that again.

'Didi, let's go to the river.' That morning, Shanta, tired of being confined to the house due to incessant rainfall in Bhojdanga over the past three days, had been craving to go out. They couldn't even step onto the forecourt of their house because it was already under one foot of water. All they could do was to sit on the verandah and watch the rain pound the earth remorselessly. The only time they would manage to escape from the monotony of the deluge was when their father, Biswambhar Bairy, would wade through the accumulated rainwater on the forecourt after returning home from the local market. Watching him part water with labored yet steady steps lent the two sisters some excitement in that dull weather.

'Baba, why can't you swim back to the house?' Biswambhar had looked up at Dipali, who was perched on the verandah. He had begun to laugh. Dipali had joined his father in the laughter, while Shanta had stared at both of them wondering what was so funny about the conversation.

The general mood in the household was looking up that morning owing to a welcome let-up in the rains. Shanta couldn't hold back her glee. 'Come on Didi, let's go to the river.' She was jumping with joy, sensing freedom.

'If I go, I will get a spanking.'

'Nothing will happen, Didi. The water on the forecourt has also receded.'

Nalini, occupied in the kitchen situated to the right of the verandah, had overheard the conversation. 'No, none of you would go out in this weather.'

'But Ma, it's not raining now.' Shanta was adamant. She held her elder sister by the hand, looking antsy. Biswambhar sensed that Shanta was close to throwing a fit, which was usually uncontrollable until she was given what she wanted. Being the youngest in a family of four, Shanta always had her way. All the more so, because she could sing so well for her age, which was her license for everything that she wished for. She was quick to pick up songs and its tunes, even the intricate ones.

Whether she sang well or not, Nalini wasn't always prepared to approve of Shanta's tantrums and her husband's leniency with her.

'You are spoiling her.'

'Come on, Nalini, she is only a child. If not now, when again would she enjoy such freedom?'

'Maybe, but you need to draw a line somewhere. All parents do. I don't understand why you melt like a candle in front of her. You didn't do that with Dipu, did you?'

Dipali did not require pampering when she was younger because she was never skittish or demanding like her sister was. She kept to herself, preferring to speak only when spoken to, and doing what she liked, quietly, without raising the hackles of her parents. Quite often, she would sit next to the window, look at the skies, and see patterns in accumulating clouds. What she never asked from her parents was delivered by her mind that she would let loose at will. Some cloud formations would appear to her like a distant land full of bulging trees. And then, there would be those fading clouds in the evening that would seem like the tail of her mother's crimson saree, particularly during the sunset. Even the flat dirt road in front of her house held imaginings for her.

Dipali and Shanta had vastly different childhoods. She was fond of solitude, while Shanta screamed for attention, so much so that at times, Biswambhar and Nalini would have serious differences over the manner in which she needed to be raised.

But then, Shanta's singing had a magical effect on household arguments. She was like a Small Minivet that was abundant in the Sunderbans. The tweeting of the bird almost resembled the squeaky mellifluous voice of Shanta. Every time she would sing a song, the rest of the household would join in—Nalini from the kitchen, Biswambhar from his room and Dipali from her study table. Shanta's songs held the family together in mellifluous harmony, with or without her antics. Nobody knew how and when she had learned the songs from Bhojdanga's only radio owned by the village chief. Every Sunday, lanterns would be lit in an arc on a clearing near the bank, inside which sat people to listen to news, followed by songs of Rabindranath Tagore. That would be the only time she would be calm, absorbing the tunes in silence, to return home and sing them in a manner as if she had practiced the songs. Precocious, people saw her as.

Neighbours, both Hindus and Muslims, would drop by once in a while to hear her sing. And for that, advise for Biswambhar was dime-a-dozen—'You should let her be trained by a music tutor' or 'her talent is being wasted' became the refrain of the neighbours. In a pre-dominantly Muslim area, a Hindu family had become an unavoidable waystation for almost everyone who passed the house of the Bairys, all because of one little girl blessed with a sublime singing voice. And Biswambhar prided himself for being the father of that girl, which often reflected in the way he dealt with her.

'Nalini, let them go. It's not raining now. I will ask them not to spend too long on the bank.'

'All right, Dipu. You two can go but come back soon. You can see the sky is not yet clear. It might rain again and anytime soon.' Nalini relented as she did not wish to be drawn into an argument at a time when the day's chores were just beginning.

Biswambhar lifted his face from a three-day-old newspaper—it took about seventy-two hours for the *Ananda*

Bazaar Patrika to reach Bhojdanga from Kolkata those days—and watched her daughters hold hands as they hopscotched away, onto the road in front of his house. He wondered how so strikingly different the two girls could be in their nature. Biswambhar was aware that those who didn't know him closely would see bias in his behavior towards Shanta. And those who did knew how much he adored both. As he watched the two girls disappear down the road, he made it a point that henceforth, he needed to be a little strict about Dipali's movements. Her body had started to develop curves that separated a girl from a child. Seventy-three years ago in undivided Bengal, an eleven-year-old Dipu needed to be treated like a girl in advanced teens.

Fed by the monsoon waters, the mighty Shibsha was swelling. The otherwise idyllic river was suddenly looking like a beast, with its waves rising and falling, curling one after another as they raced towards the Bay of Bengal. Over centuries, the Shibsha has devoured hundreds of fishermen, country boats and steamers. It is said that a keen ear on the banks of the Shibsha can hear ballads rising from its depths, sung by the fishermen the river had consumed.

Dipali and Shanta stood on the bank, watching the Shibsha roar past them at a safe distance. And then, without any warning, Shanta broke into a run, apparently in pursuit of something. Dipali ran after her.

'Didi, look!'

Dipali looked at Shanta. Her eyes shifted to what Shanta was pointing at. It was a dragonfly that was trying to balance itself on a tall, swaying leaf of grass. Its long body, like a woman's finger, was shimmering in light.

'What is it, Didi?'

'That's a dragonfly.'

'Have you ever chased one?'

'Yes, I have.'

Then there were several others, pirouetting above them. Shanta had never seen a dragonfly before. She stepped closer to the one that was sitting on the grass. She sat cross-legged on the ground, closely observing the four-winged creature. But the ones that swooped down to fly in circles near the ground wouldn't let her. Soon, she was running after the dragonflies that so easily left her behind in their wake.

'Shanta, stop! We have to go back home.' Dipali could sense that Shanta needed to be reined in but the little girl was already quite ahead of her. She could see that Shanta was racing towards a small Gewa tree into which the dragonflies were disappearing. It was then she heard a deafening roar. The ground beneath her was shaking. It seemed so unreal. The Gewa tree that stood some distance away just a moment ago was tilting precariously and craning its branches towards the river. The soil around the trunk of the tree was giving away. Dipali could see wide cracks appearing on the soft soil, one crevassing into another rapidly. The Shibsha was spreading without warning. Dumbfounded, she stood where she was and watched Shanta break into a sprightly run towards the tree, unmindful of the disorder that was unfolding around it.

Inch by inch, the soil broke off from near the base of the tree and started to slip away from beneath the tiny feet of Shanta.

Shanta fell down. 'Didiiiiii…,' she screamed. Dipali, paralysed with fear, knew she couldn't go anywhere near the collapsing mounds of soil that were crashing into the river. Within seconds, the Gewa tree was sucked in by the rogue waters. Frozen in her steps, Dipali kept staring at the perilous spectacle. She saw Shanta caught knee-deep in disturbed earth. Flailing her arms, Shanta tried to free herself but got drawn further into the mudslide. Chocking on her breath, Dipali kept watching. She could see the wet earth rise up to Shanta's chest. By the time Dipali called out her name at the top of her voice, just one arm was sticking out of the mud. In a flash, Shanta was gone.

Two hours later, Biswambhar found Dipali unconscious on the banks of the river.

An effervescent home had suddenly fallen silent, like a song incomplete after falsetto. Nalini was particularly affected, which showed on her deteriorating health. She lost sleep and appetite. She would leave her bed, walk up to the bamboo fencing of the courtyard, and cast a blank stare on the road that ran towards the Shibsha, night after night.

Biswambhar tried to share his wife's agony. In doing so, he had to painfully withstand his memories of Shanta. To stay sane proved to be a struggle. But he knew surrendering to trauma would ruin the family. Worse was, neither he nor Nalini could get a glimpse of what exactly was going on in the mind of their elder daughter, who had sewed herself up even more than before. Dipu was grieving and would continue to grieve for the rest of her life. The deep sense of loss was consuming her, more so because she kept berating herself for not being able to save her little sister. Yet, she knew that she had to bring her everyday back into her life, to be the only succor for her parents. There was just one thing, however, that she vowed not to do again—chase a dragonfly.

The Bairy family was struggling to overcome the debilitating blow. Though Biswambhar and Nalini hid behind a charade and went about their lives, as if they had moved on from the tragedy, both were hurting deeply with their silent remembrances. Shanta remained as a watermark in their minds.

'I cannot leave her to memory,' Biswambhar had confided in Nalini one night. 'I need her to be in front of our eyes, every day.' Nalini raised her head towards Biswambhar, her eyes under a thin film of tears, tantalizingly close to spilling. Biswambhar had already made up his mind.

A few months later, he built a small temple in front of his house, where the road curved towards the Shibsha, in memory of Shanta.

The temple became a refuge for Nalini. Every day, she would leave Shanta's favourite food at the temple, which would later be fed to cows and birds. Neighbours too began flocking to the temple to remember a child they all loved.

❖❖❖

The heartbreak that had left the Bairy family in complete disarray was slowly getting healed with the passage of time. A sense of relief from ache and agony had begun to settle on the household. Biswambhar was keeping his shop open, Nalini continued her uninterrupted visits to the temple, Dipali wrote one letter every month from Kolkata to Bhojdanga and the *Ananda Bazar Patrika* became a more interesting read than before. Change was in the air.

'But this is not the change we wanted, Nalini.' News had reached Biswambhar that the Indian landmass was on the threshold of being divided by the British who were pulling out of their disobedient colony. Nalini wasn't visibly bothered about change, disobedience or division. She knew she would follow her husband wherever he went, the way she did to hell and back.

As if that was not enough, some of the Muslims who used to pause at the 'Shanta Temple' every day to remember their 'own girl' suddenly stopped using the curved road in front of Biswambhar's house. The final blow was delivered by Nasir Ahmed, one that could destroy the very precipice on which Biswambhar's and his wife's life stood. Nasir, a known sympathiser of Muslim League, had flashed chewy smiles at Biswambhar, pausing between sentences. The Muslims were not anymore accepting a Hindu temple on their own land that would be renamed East Pakistan.

'What are you saying?' More than being astonished, Biswambhar felt shocked. He wouldn't have minded if after so many years, Shanta was fading in public memory, for that was the human wont. But attempts to erase the memories of a six-year-old girl in the garb of religion were preposterous.

'How could you?' Biswambhar was fumbling for the right words.

'That's what we have decided, Biswambhar babu. The temple has to go.'

Outnumbered in a land Biswambhar realised could never be his, he struggled between relenting and defying. He knew he could only rave and rant at home, in front of his wife who since Shanta's death was consigned to accepting anything and everything as God's will. Biswambhar was cross with himself for not being able to tell Nasir off but he also knew that dismissing him would invite troubles that he wouldn't be able to contain. Something needed to be done, and fast.

He visited the village chief, a seventy-year-old man called Idris Mian. 'Idris Mian, how could this be possible? Shanta was and even now, is a child of this very village where you and I have been born and have grown up.'

'Biswambhar, I have no idea about this. But who said this to you?'

'Nasir Ahmed.'

Two days later, a small meeting, with representations from both Hindu and Muslim communities, took place in the forecourt of Biswambhar's house, headed by Idris Mian. The old village chief looked at Biswambhar with kind eyes and smiled.

'Biswambhar, as long as I am alive, there isn't anyone who can take Shanta's memories away from us. A child has no religion. And I am saying it now, the temple stays. Yes, the temple stays.'

Why didn't they have men like Idris Mian to decide the fate of this huge landmass, Bishwambhar thought.

Nasir Ahmed never visited Biswambhar again. He was wise enough to understand that religious zealotry could never defeat the collective will of humanity.

✣✣✣

Dipali was lying on the banks of the Shibsha, her ears pressed to the ground. Her grey hair lay scattered over the damp soil like disobedient rivulets. It was a clear day. The sky above Bhojdanga was flawless. At first, there was the sound of a breakaway wave that quickly settled into the surface of the river. And then, she could hear the concert of the ripples, a harmony that only she could sense. The last ballads of the fishermen taken by the Shibsha were finally breaching the surface for her to hear. They were singing in chorus, talking about their lives and times. So, this is true. *The tales weren't really a work of fiction*, she thought. *Or am I losing my sanity*, Dipali wondered.

She got up and prepared to leave for the town. As she began to step away, she felt a tug at the tail of her saree. Startled, she swiveled around. There was nobody. She shrugged and began to walk away. The tug came again, as if someone was really standing behind her, asking her to stay back.

Just when she had consigned herself to the improbability of anyone following her, she thought she heard a whisper that spooked her all ends up.

Goosebumps began to rise on her whole body. Dipali turned towards the river, her heart in her mouth. She walked up to the edge of the bank, her eyes piercing the surface and reaching the unknown depths of the river.

And then, the silence returned. Nobody whispered anymore. *I am getting too old, I guess*, Dipali inferred as she walked towards the private taxi that awaited her a short distance away from the banks. She had a pilgrimage to make.

Dipali sat on the steps of the temple that was absolutely dilapidated due to years of neglect, looking exactly like what the letter said.

A month ago, Dipali had received a letter at her house in Kolkata. It was written by Idris Mian's eldest son, Abu. He had written that most of the Hindus who once cared for the 'Shanta temple' had either passed away or had left for Kolkata after Partition. The new-generation of Muslims and Hindus, who had no idea about local history, were not concerned about its upkeep. The temple was crumbling due to neglect. It might be demolished since the local administration wanted to widen a concrete road on the curved path in front of her ancestral home. But without her consent, the temple couldn't be done away with, as had been decreed by her late father. 'I am sure if your parents had been alive, I would not have needed to write to you,' the letter had concluded.

Dipali walked up to the back wall of the temple where Shanta's picture used to hang from. The picture was long gone but the frame had left an indelible rectangular mark on the wall, as though Shanta was still waiting for Bhojdanga to fill up the blank space on the crumbling surface with remembrances. On the other side of the temple, Dipali could only see a road. The house she was born into was gone. There weren't even ruins to be preserved.

Even after Partition, her parents had refused to leave the property behind, like many other Hindus did. With Shanta just around the corner, the temple was their last bastion of any meaningful existence. But after their death, the house was taken over by the local municipality because of the absence of any claimants. The entire area was now covered by a concrete road. Dipali felt her childhood had vanished into her own absence.

She thrust the forefinger of her right hand into vacant space. 'This is where the gate used to be and about thirty feet behind was the verandah. And can you see that road sign? That's where the kitchen was.' Dipali's hand was outlining an invisible house for his son. On this trip back to Bhojdanga, Samar was accompanying her. He had unsuccessfully tried to convince his mother of the futility of returning to the Sunderbans after so many decades. But she refused to listen.

Dipali went around the temple with a lamp in her hand, lit for the memory of a sister whose face she had almost forgotten. Yet, somewhere deep down, she could feel a storm rising, as though strong winds were playing a thousand pipes, connecting her to a time that was solely hers and Shanta's. It was then she noticed that a huge red-cotton tree had come up just behind the temple. The tree was in full-bloom. There was a scarlet explosion on the branches. So brilliant were the flowers that they made even the sun pale in comparison.

She closed her eyes and leaned on the trunk of the tree. A sudden gust of wind came in from the Shibsha. The branches began to sway merrily, as if dancing in step with the rhythms of songs someone had shared with her a long time ago. She picked a stanza from her own intimate history and began humming a tune. Tears were welling up in her eyes. Dipali knew that which went around would never come around, at least for her. Yet, unlike the Bhojdanga village, she would not be able to eliminate her forever sense of loss, the last twitches of which were still pulsating inside her, silently.

Dipali paused as she felt something land on her right foot. She opened her eyes.

It was a dragonfly. She shook her foot and it took off, flying towards the red-cotton tree. Dipali began going after it on her wobbly old-age knees. There was no Shibsha, no Gewa tree, no river in front of her.

Dipali was only breaking a promise she had made to herself years ago.

PAINT IT RED

A flat and wide stretch of lemon-green land, occasionally dotted by stubborn shrubs, marked the river-end of Tikarampur. It is a mustard field in blossom. The lush expanse contrasts sharply with the brown and dusty embankment that runs along the village. Manmade furrows crisscross the field in carefully crafted geometrical patterns. They help keep farmers their respective tilled lands to themselves. Each plot of land has a unique scarecrow. If one has a tattered football jersey draped over a cross made with bamboo sticks with a painted clay pot faking a human head at the top, another will have an old saree wrapped around a similar crucifix. Its head would be made of hay, and eyes, of broken bangles. The furrows, watered, are home to toads that croak tirelessly in the night when hungry serpents slither out from their many dug-outs looking for a meal. In daytime, the sun plays on the mustard stalks that sway with the river breeze, creating waves, as if a yellow sea is waltzing to a harmony only it can feel and hear. Quite often, grasshoppers will lay motionless on the mustard leaves, moving with the stems that tilt from one side to the other in that brilliant upheaval. Right above the plants, in a close-knit constellation, dragonflies pirouette. Sometimes the mustard field stands still in leeward somnolence when the wind finds a sudden new course.

At the end of the field, the Ganges flows in rippled symphony, circumventing an island of silt that had surfaced one day, many years ago. Today, that island is home to coconut trees and wild boars that often fall prey to hungry local inhabitants. Once in a while, river porpoises will surface only to disappear into the unknown depths of the Ganges, lending a final touch to a canvas the multi-tasking nature has created.

It is in these fields Lakhan used to spend most of his time in the day with his friend Tilu. They were both seven years old and lived in houses situated next to each other's. But these days, Lakhan sits on the high embankment, his chin cradled in his palms, and looks vacantly at the field. He misses Tilu, who has not returned from wherever his family had taken him six months ago. Their riparian friendship had come to an end, as suddenly as it had begun three years ago over a game of marbles.

❖❖❖

Tikarampur has no history, like a man without memory. Nobody can recall when it had come up on the banks of the Ganges in the eastern state of Bihar, or for that matter, who were its early inhabitants. But Tikarampur doesn't complain. It has held on to obscurity without fuss, and with a certain degree of nonchalance. Like most other villages in the region, social recognition or the lack of it plays a major role in deciding the course of life in Tikarampur. The law of the land here is unshared, intransigent and, at times, brutal. Semi-concrete houses and mud huts lend the landscape a heterogeneous look. In that disparate demography, people like Ram Singh have managed to muscle their way into gaining an unfair share of the village's way of life. Everybody listens to them, heeds them and is afraid of them. Well, almost.

Tilu's father Budhia too listens more and speaks little, but that is not his weakness. He is a landless farmer with a minuscule share of voice in village matters. Budhia keeps to himself because he knows the fire in him can be disobedient; can invite disaster for his family if not contained. Budhia's background is as obscure as Tikarampur's. In fact, he does not know what he is. All he understands is that the landed men don't like him as a neighbour. He is the village-imbecile to them. More often than not, most other villagers, even those only moderately well-off, make him feel like an outcast—after all, he does not own land like them or cows and water buffaloes.

He is just a pitiable version of a human being, as they see him. But Budhia does not let their reproach affect him.

✣✣✣

Five feet from Budhia was his wife Sita, who was making flat, hand-baked bread from pearl millet, or bajra, that grew in abundance in the region. Measured doses of bajra bread, dal and pickled juliennes of raw mango dominated their everyday meal. He had to be cautiously thrifty because what he harvested wasn't enough to bring ease to the family. The frugal meals weren't his concerns. At that moment, what raked his mind were the waters of the Ganges. The river, which had begun to bloat since the skies had opened up a week ago, had started to flirt dangerously with the banks. Monsoon always kept its date with Tikarampur but never before had the village witnessed so much rain. Budhia knew the land he had taken on loan to produce mustard seeds might be inundated soon. He looked out into the black emptiness, at the river. It was pitch dark outside.

'Can you hear the river roar?' Budhia looked at his diminutive wife, his rhetorical question made Sita press her left ear into the air, as if to make sense out of the unfamiliar sound of the waves. The river had always moved like music, from one ripple to another in transcending symphonies, as if serenading the village like a suitor. But over the past two days, the Ganges had begun to misbehave, thrashing around like a trapped beast to shake off the land that abutted it.

'There's not much time,' Budhia, a man of few words, mumbled.

'Time for what?' Sita raised her eyebrows inquisitively. He kept staring into the darkness as a sense of unease settled on the small mud-hut. Sita had never seen her husband bear troubled looks. At the same time, his words were like God's own to her. That night, Budhia appeared tense for her comfort. Sita pressed her palms together, placed them on her forehead and turned bowing towards the small idol of Goddess Tara kept in a niche on the wall. There were other idols too, but Tara was the presiding deity of the house.

The next morning, Budhia found water already at the foot of the embankment. He stood watching the advancing waters, holding an umbrella on his head. In just seven hours of darkness, the river had overflowed. Its waters were slithering out like a preying serpent, uncoiling slowly towards the village, inch by inch. The Ganges was preparing to devour all that would come in her way. From experience, Budhia knew that a hungry river's appetite could be insatiable.

When Budhia was very young, he had witnessed the marauding waters of the Ganges invade the village where he was born, sweeping away everything in their path. Their house near the banks had crumbled. His mother and his elder brother were taken away by the surging waters as the river reclaimed space that once belonged to it. For many years after the deluge, Budhia would wake up in the middle of the night. He could still hear the screams and see the drowning arms with fists clasping the air in a last-gasp attempt to hold on to life. He remembered how his father, howling dolefully, had carried him on his shoulder through neck-deep water to the safety of a tree on a high patch of land near the village. Even after so many years, the demons of his past had not been exorcised. The memories of that fateful day remained in his subconscious, often emerging in staccato throwbacks. That night, when Sita said prayers to Tara, those phantoms inside his head began to rise like wisps of smoke from stoked embers.

✣✣✣

The only person in the entire village, who knew about Budhia's childhood tragedy, was Kanhaiya. Although Kanhaiya belonged to an upper-caste family, he was as poor as Budhia, and their poverty became a common thread of friendship. Budhia was always private about his woes or even about his otherwise rare moments of happiness. But he had opened himself like a book to Kanhaiya as he found in him a commiserating man, one who was unassuming and willing to listen without prejudice.

In spite of their friendship, Kanhaiya avoided being seen in the company of Budhia too often in daytime. His family chided him for his association with Budhia, whom they saw as an unacceptable acquaintance. Even some village elders had warned Kanhaiya to keep off him. Yet, Kanhaiya couldn't summarily dismiss Budhia from his life. He would come to visit Budhia after dusk, using the cover of darkness to surreptitiously enter his friend's house to pass on village vibes and receive unadulterated straight talk.

'Budhia, this is not your place. These people are not going to let you live with dignity. Why don't you find a new life somewhere else?' Kanhaiya would often tell Budhia.

'And do what?' Budhia would unfailingly answer. Kanhaiya knew Budhia would live and die in Tikarampur, tilling his borrowed land forever as he wasn't equipped with any other skills to discover a new living. As for Budhia, he accepted Kanhaiya as the one with whom he could be both banal and genuine without a motive in their innocuous conversations.

Just a couple of days back, Budhia had wanted Kanhaiya to accompany him to the waterfront.

'But why, Budhia?'

'I have an ominous feeling. The waters are venting their intentions.'

'Come on, you are unduly worried.' Kanhaiya, who hardly went to the river as he was a daily-wager at a brick kiln nearby, tried to assuage Budhia's fears.

✣✣✣

Budhia turned back from the embankment and began walking towards the centre of the village where a huge banyan tree stood. Myth had it that the tree was a thousand years old. It was under the tree the influential and the elders were supposed to meet everyone.

A crowd was seated on the wet ground in an arc, appearing like a class-room, facing the tree. The men who decided Tikarampur's fate sat smoking hookahs on a coir mat with their back towards the trunk. Budhia stood behind the arc, his hands on his waist, the stance subtly portraying defiance. He refused to cower to the weight of his poverty, no matter how unbearable the burden of living was, and that's what the men with power just didn't like. His direful nature was the scorn of the landed and the moneyed. But, much as they wished to, they wouldn't openly try and subdue him in fear of reprisals. From what the men said, it was clear that the village required to be evacuated as soon as possible because there was no let-up in the rains. Everyone under the tree agreed that the furious river couldn't be appeased, not even by incessant praying to the many Gods inside village homes.

Ram Singh, the richest man in the village, was as vainglorious as he could be in conducting the village meeting. He enjoyed being the cynosure of all eyes in public. His clout undermined reason and logic, even if he would come up with most outrageous solutions to other peoples' problems. The people knew what they were fated for but couldn't take a call on their own until Singh chose their destinies. That had been the norm in Tikarampur, even in the face of calamities. Budhia was the last to be addressed, as always.

'What about you, Budhia? Even though you have nothing to lose except whatever little brains you have, you have to get out soon. I suggest you leave at the break of dawn tomorrow to a safer place.' Singh chuckled conceitedly as he pointed at Budhia.

A pit of fire was burning inside Budhia's head. The very sight of Ram Singh and his self-assumed leadership had ignited it. But Budhia knew that was not the time to go off the handle. He stood ramrod straight and unruffled. 'Yes, sir, I will do something.' Budhia knew Singh, like many of his neighbours in the village, might not come to his aid should the time come to leave. But could everyone shun a fellow human being completely? No way, Budhia thought even though his wife, who was not from that village, would often whisper to him in private that the entire village was probably waiting to see them leave. The Budhias of the village were only sharecroppers—illiterate, poor and with nowhere to go. They were a blotch the village could ill-afford.

That night, the embankment collapsed. The gurgling waters first began to fill all cavities in the village before striking courtyards of mud-homes. The concrete houses were not spared either. Some were still holding their ground in a disparate conflict between man and nature, unlike Budhia's house whose weak precipice was beginning to surrender. The village was falling apart house by house as human resolve began to weaken rapidly in the face of inevitability. At the crack of dawn, Budhia, Sita and Tilu took a bullock-cart out of the village, joining scores of others who were fleeing like them. As the caravan began to pull away from the village, towards high land near the railway tracks, the juggernaut behind launched its final putsch. They stopped for a moment to look back and see the village vanish from the face of the earth. A collective mournful cry rent the air. Large whirlpools behind them were overrunning what were once homes. Only the canopies of tall trees jutted from the surface, looking like pompoms. Even they would go under when nature would land its final bite, which was going to be anytime soon.

Tikarampuar slowly walked towards dislocation. The people would be able to return only when the water subsided, and that meant probably several months, if not more.

✣✣✣

Two months later, Budhia called Ram Singh from a PCO.

Budhia's uncle, Vikas, who made a living by painting cars at a garage in Patna, had offered shelter to his nephew and his family, as the floods were ravaging many villages of the state. They had arrived in Patna like carpet-baggers, knowing not where their next meal would come from or how long the borrowed roof above their head would remain. Even Vikas knew that his nephew's stay had to end at some point. He didn't earn enough to keep his own family in shape, and now Budhia, Sita and Tilu! Vikas had been brutally frank with Budhia, 'Look, you can stay here for the time being, but you have to earn a living. I cannot feed you for free. I can ask the garage owner to hire you as a car painter and cleaner. I can only do so much. Is that okay with you?' Budhia, in low spirits and with no idea about how to regain his life, had little choice.

Engrossed in thoughts, with his mind travelling in different directions of possibilities, Budhia waited for Ram Singh to answer the call.

'Babu ji, I am Budhia.' He was speaking loudly in apparent delight, which was understandable because he was connecting with someone from Tikarampur after a long time. Budhia felt home was just a phone call away.

'Oh, yes, Budhia. How are you?'

'I am all right, Babu ji. I am safe with my uncle. What's the news about the village?'

'Nothing much, Budhia. It continues to be under water. It's still raining in Tikarampur. Call me after a month. I hope I shall be able to bring you some good news then.' Ram Singh disconnected the line abruptly.

How long does it take for the flood waters to return to the mother lode? Sixty days? Seventy days? Ninety days? Budhia wondered. He had no clue. His life in Patna had reduced him to a piece of refuse. He felt imprisoned in the squalor that surrounded him inside the garage. Besides, the obvious frictions he was having with his uncle's family—he, Sita and Tilu were surviving almost on pity—were another cause for concern. Budhia knew he had to return to his village sooner or later. From time to time, tempers flared—sometimes between him and his uncle, other times between Sita and his aunt. It was clear to Budhia that he and his family were an extra baggage for his uncle, no matter the fact that they shared the same bloodline. He had a premonition that the sporadic discord would surely expand into an uncontrollable explosion someday in that cramped house. And if that happened, he would have no other option but to beg, borrow or steal. He wasn't familiar with any of them.

In the evening, on the tiny verandah they called home then, Budhia looked at Sita. She was cooking. He sat with his legs splayed on the floor, and holding his head in his hands, almost. He was chastising himself for being a complete failure;

for bringing his family into the plight that it didn't deserve. He looked at the sham calmness that masked Sita's face. Yet, beneath that façade, Budhia could sense that her wife's eyes were agonized. Once in a while, Budhia had caught Sita off-guard, with tears welling up at the corners of her beautiful, gazelle-like eyes. But, like a true and committed partner in life, Sita never cried in the fear that any display of weakness on her part could push her husband into irretrievable depression. She didn't want Budhia to do something outrageous out of frustration.

Budhia also had concerns about raising Tilu. He felt that without the conveniences Tilu deserved as a child, his son might grow like a bent tree, twisted near the base of the stem at the sapling stage. Tilu was missing Lakhan. In that tiny house in Patna, and the small verandah on which they were being consumed by the ordeal of living, celebrating childhood was a calling the little boy could not discover. For the sake of Tilu, for the sake of Sita, Budhia had to go back to the mustard fields; to the free air that no machinations would ever dare to malign with motives; to the unforgiving, free-flowing river that he was willing to pardon. Being poor in your own home was markedly different from being poorer in someone else's.

Budhia called Ram Singh again. It was almost three months he had left his village. No pleasantries were exchanged as Ram Singh appeared overtly eager to quit the conversation as soon as possible. He regretted that the village was still not ready for habitation. The world around Budhia was cracking up like a fragile box of gifts being carelessly moved around by those who didn't own it. He wondered how much more time he needed to regain a semblance of life.

The urge to call Ram Singh again was testing his patience. For a man who had grown out of raw soil like its offspring, the life in a noisy car repairs shop was ruining Budhia's resolve to live another day. Budhia struggled to accept the irony of not being able to fix his own life while he hammered dented fenders back into shape. It had almost been a fortnight he had last called Ram Singh. Budhia walked hastily out of the workshop, towards the PCO down the road.

Singh couldn't bring fresh hopes to Budhia. The village was still under water. He called Ram Singh the next day, and the next day and the day after. The calls continued but Singh's cell phone was unreachable. As he walked back to the garage, Budhia looked up at the sky. In his struggle, he had kept himself insulated from the outside world for too long and had not been able to even figure out how everything around him looked like. The sky was royal blue, with white balls of clouds flitting like truant sheep, refusing to be shepherded. Sunlight fell on his creased forehead. He had forgotten to take a clear look at light after working long hours in a dark entrapment called an automobile workshop. All these days, he had been crouching over fenders and trunks of cars that needed to be repaired or painted. 'Oh my God, the weather is so clear now. It must be as sunny in Tikarampur.' Sunny? Then how come Ram Singh had continued to paint a picture of gloom, saying the flood waters hadn't receded and that the skies above the village were still heavily overcast?

Two days later, Budhia and his family left for Tikarampur. Budhia knew he had to till the field back to fertility. But then, he was now equipped with another set of skills, for which he could only thank his uncle no matter how unpleasant his stay was at his house in Patna. Should there be trouble farming, he could try and find a job in the nearby town, Munger.

Budhia, Sita and Tilu got off a bullock-cart near the entrance of his village just before noon, expecting to see nobody, since Ram Singh had said Tikarampur was still not habitable. The approach road to the village didn't appear barren. The slush that had dried up bore signs of human movement, resembling fossilised caveman footprints. He could feel butterflies in his tummy as they walked in, step by step, into the bowels of the village. Budhia froze.

The village was bustling with usual activity. Jeevan Narayan was walking out of his house carrying a jerrycan of milk, Lochan was returning from the fields bearing a plough on his shoulder, Parvati was slamming cow-dung cakes on a wall and the smell of meals simmering on clay ovens was emitting from inside of homes. Almost everybody was going about their chores, as if nothing had happened. Life was unfolding in front of Budhia's eyes the same way it did before the floods. He was perplexed. What did it mean? On one hand, Ram Singh had been rather insisting that the flood waters hadn't receded. On the other, he found the village populated, as usual, throbbing with daylight activity.

Budhia increased his pace and as he did, he could see people whom he knew so well were looking at him with wary eyes. He began to run towards his house. But his house wasn't there anymore. In its place, a two-storey brick building had come up. Budhia couldn't believe his eyes. He looked around despairingly. The landscape of the village appeared exactly the way he had left it. Nothing had changed except that a brick house stood where his home once was. A crowd had gathered around Budhia, following his every move, trying to anticipate his actions. He turned his head towards them and saw Kanhayia with an axe in one hand and firewood in the other, among the people. Kanhayia put the firewood down on the ground, stepped out of the crowd, nodded at Budhia and walked up to him. He placed a hand on Budhia's shoulder and whispered to him: 'This is not your house anymore. This has been built by Ram Singh for his son-in-law.'

'But where is my house?'

'Your house has fallen to design that you couldn't see or read.'

Kanhaiya turned his head away, struggling to avoid looking into his best friend's eyes. Budhia felt his body was being drained of all its strength. The bundle he held in his hand slipped to the ground, as if his whole being was surrendering to an apocalypse. The hammering he felt inside his chest seemed portentous. Breathing heavily, his turbulent eyes were looking at the scarred soil of Tikarampur, as if he was invoking fire from the core of the Earth. Kanhaiya knew his friend too well—he must rein in Budhia, at least for the time being.

Slowly, the entire story began to unfold at Kanhaiya's place, where Budhia and his family were taken for a meal. Budhia, being illiterate, uncouth, insolent and poor, was the most unwanted in Tikarampur ruled by Ram Singh. He and his cohorts had hatched a plan. The flood waters had receded 20 days after the deluge and by the 30th day, people had started returning to rebuild their homes. The opportunity that Ram Singh needed was provided by the floods. He knew, although Budhia had a rebellious trait in him, he would never be able to square off with him. Besides, Ram Singh had his followers whom he kept happy with occasional doles. He also knew that not a soul would dare to question him for his actions as long as he stayed rich and powerful. So, every time Budhia called from Patna, he would ward him off by saying that the village was still inundated. Ram Singh was only delaying Budhia's return by those many days that he needed to grab his land, demolish the hut and build a brick house in double-quick time for his daughter Vimla and son-in-law Shiv.

Budhia looked at his friend, his eyes piercing into Kanhaiya's soul. The questions in Budhia's eyes were scimitaring him. 'I didn't know how to contact you. Believe me, I was desperate to let you know what was happening here with your house.'

'I know, Kanhaiya. I had been a fool. Now I need to do something and soon.' Budhia's eyes were brimming with fire.

'Sure. You can rebuild your life by taking up work in a garage in Munger town. Didn't you say just a while ago that you were painting used cars back there in Patna?'

'Yes, I did.'

'So, what would you do now?'

Budhia stood up, leaving his meal half-eaten. Then he bent down, picked up Kanhaiya's axe from the forecourt and walked up to the exit. He stood there for a while, took a deep breath, and turned slowly towards his friend.

'I am going to paint this village red.'

CORSICAN IMAGES

An old man, with untamed white hair curling back from the top of his forehead, like smoke from a locomotive racing the wind, was trying to sell Tathagata a waistcoat. The man claimed the apparel was once worn by Richard Nixon. He pulled the waistcoat's lining inside out to flash him a label with an emblem of the White House. Behind thin-rimmed glasses, his pallid eyes belied the art of swindle he had likely mastered while hawking at the flea sales for eons. The locals called it the *Chor Bazaar*, or the market of the thieves, and Tathagata saw it as a logical imperfection at the chaotic Kidderpore waterfront in Kolkata. Every shop owner at the market was adept at inventing, and the former American President, Tathagata thought, was undeniably another fiction in a long heritage of fakes at the Chor Bazaar. From vintage copper coins to luminescent wristwatches, this was the epicentre of counterfeiters. It is in this spurious atmosphere, the seemingly unreal became the actuality of Tathagata's life one day.

Tathagata was an undemanding man who loaned himself wilfully to his family, friends and strangers to be experimented with. His thick glasses, side-parted hair with streaks of grey, and a height that neither towered over people nor dwarfed him in public, made him the ideal candidate who would fit perfectly into the shoes of a John Doe. He never shared his middle-age blues with anyone, the least with his middle-aged wife and their rebellious teenage daughter. He kept himself as a flat reading on an electrocardiogram that characterised his ordinary world where he could be killed, revived, dissected and rebuilt with ease by anybody. But far from his apparently enervated existence, he preserved the oscillations for another realm where he wished to remain unread. Deep inside, he was an inveterate romantic in search of soulful epiphanies.

Even the work he did offered little excitement. From across the table, he either gave help or refused it depending on his ability to tell truths from lies—he was a realty loan officer with a bank. Tathagata had made decent money from his job to build his own house that was equipped with fulfilled needs, just not always his. He owned a small car that he used on weekends or on bank holidays. He ate what was kept on the table, hot or cold, watched popular Hollywood on the TV and often kept the faucet running after brushing his teeth.

Tathagata was not a poet, not a writer, not an artist, not a singer, and definitely not someone you would remember for more than 24 hours if you met him. He would drive his tiny compact to multiplexes on Sundays with family and fight middle-class battles with the parking attendant. He would sit in an air-conditioned movie theatre to watch love stories and thrillers, and wonder why popcorns needed to be buttered. He would also find it impossible to leave his seat for the bathroom when the vamp would win the drunken hero over temporarily in the presence of a weeping heroine. Back home, he would catch the 10 pm newscast on the TV, remind his wife of north-bound prices of commodities, and turn in for the day without a whimper.

Tathagata was an inexpensive game everybody could play with ease. His wife Atmadeepa often wondered what made him so predictable. His daughter would bind conjectures to conclude her father looked like her high-school routine. His boss wondered what made him so artless.

'Every time I look at you, it seems I am watching a robot moving about inside the house,' Atmadeepa had blurted out one day, without being prompted by any precursive thought.

'Throw the remote out of the window, Deepa,' he replied without taking his eyes off the TV, his repartee catching her completely by surprise. Atmadeepa had stomped out of the living room, leaving her husband to the dregs of a late newscast.

Despite the uninterrupted stream of taunts at home, Tathagata knew where he stood in life. He often compared himself with modern Türkiye, which had one foot in Europe and the other in Asia. He had a parallel world in which he thrived as an entity that would be completely out of place in the real one. It was in this world he grew his fancies like a gardener would nurse his saplings, and his family had no idea that it existed. This was where he would be the uncrowned king of phantasmagoria. And he knew how to balance both. Or else, Atmadeepa would hire an insanity-manager for her husband.

One day, his wife and daughter left in the morning for a relative's wedding. They were not expected back in the next two days. Excusing himself from work rather early in the day, Tathagata hit the streets, walking languidly. But he knew where he wanted to go. It was the local flea market that had always fascinated him. That place looked like a *bazaar* in Zanzibar, straight out of the Arabian Nights. As he walked the narrow lanes to sink into the madness of hawking—merchants were selling everything, from old Grandfather clocks to stolen shoes—something caught his attention. It was a portrait of a woman, in black and white, held in an old mahogany frame, hanging from a side wall of a make-shift shop. The face in that work of art, he thought, probably belonged to someone who was no more. It was just a picture that hadn't been dusted for long. Whether it was a print or an original he couldn't make out but what had drawn him to the picture were the eyes that were lent life by its painter with extraordinary artistry. He made up his mind. Over the next 10 minutes, he won an intense bout of bargaining, which he was an exponent of, and began walking back to his car triumphantly, as if he had invoked a loyal genie out of a magical lamp.

Once home, he hammered a hook into the blank wall of his living room and left the picture hanging from it. His wife or daughter would never ask where he got the picture from and why. They never raised such questions as they knew he was a miser with answers when it came to his selections being questioned. It was not the first time he was crowding the home with his *Chor Bazaar* victories. A broken-nose Buddha bust sat on a book shelf as a false antique, and a Conway Stewart fountain pen had stopped writing when its legendary nib broke two days after it was bought.

A little later, he used the phone to order a double-decker chicken burger with a liberal dose of cheese and a large French-fries from a local takeaway, gorged like a glutton and then lit a cigarette. He kept looking at the picture, training his eyes on hers, wanting to see how far each pair would be able to pierce the other. But there were only balls of cigarette smoke spoiling the romanticism with a heavy overlaying smell of burnt tobacco.

Dehydrated by the greasy meal, Tathagata woke up in the middle of the night to drink water. He walked through the dark living room towards the kitchen to fetch a jug. He knew he would need to drink more water later in the night. Usually, his daughter Shivani lucubrated with a lamp on to finish her homework and because of that, light would be diffused onto the passage that connected his bedroom with the kitchen. But that night, he was all alone at home. Whatever little light that fell on the walls inside the flat came through the windowpanes from the moonlit night, carrying in its beams silhouettes of trees that looked so spectral. And every time the trees swayed in the breeze, the shadows became shrouded human figures dancing to bring the walls alive with a spine-chilling, other-worldly exhibition. It was then he heard someone whispering to him, in a woman's voice.

Tathagata froze in his steps. It took him a few moments to realise that apart from him, there was nobody at home. I must have been imagining things, he thought. He returned to his bedroom, drank water, and tried to get back to sleep.

Tathagata heard the whispers again.

He had goose-bumps all over his body. He didn't believe in ghosts but there was no reason why he shouldn't be alert about burglars. Getting off the bed, he went to the living room and switched the lights on. There was nobody. The shadows on the wall disappeared with a flick of the switch. He was convinced that someone was at the door, who was not diurnal, playing tricks on him to find a weak link in his defence of the empty house. He tiptoed to the door with a kitchen knife in the hand, ready to turn any intrusion into a misadventure. He opened the door with lightning speed. A cold foul-smelling breeze came in from the streets. The hair on his neck stood up. There was no sound of frantic footsteps running away from the door. But there had to be somebody or something that knew he was alone at home. Breathless, he shut the door and began tip-toeing through the living room towards his bed.

'I can see you now, Tathagata.'

He turned around to face the picture, focusing on the face of the woman in the frame. His mortal fear told him the voice had come from outside of the closed door but his rationale answered otherwise—how could that be possible? A picture might be full of life in venting human expressions but it was still an inanimate object. As he mulled possibilities, the Cimmerian shadows had returned on the wall to resume their spooky dance. And the eyes in the picture seemed to be following his every movement, as if they were trying his power of reasoning, or the lack of it.

'Why are you talking to me, what do you want from me? You are only a picture, an artistic progeny of the human kind.' Tathgata could barely hear himself speak.

'Come closer and look into my eyes. What do you see?'

'A picture and nothing else.'

'You are so grossly mistaken. I am not a picture. I am you.'

'How could…just how could a woman be me,' his slow words disordered themselves into a chaotic denial, wafting almost inaudibly towards the picture.

'You'll find out. You will.'

He wondered whether the pressure of juxtaposing improbabilities and likelihoods to keep his family undisturbed, like a gambit on a chessboard, was getting the better of him.

✣✣✣

This would be one weekend Tathagata would not be able to take his family out for its regular dose of Sunday entertainment. He had meetings lined up with outstation clients from Monday, which would keep him away from home for at least four days. The week had been hectic for him as one meeting after another took place with realtors who looked like fiends straight out of a horror story. Exhausted after these meetings, he trudged back to his hotel. He did not complain as it was routine work for him, yet the constant speaking and sparring with recalcitrant clients had sapped his energy. While in bed, he looked back at the previous week and wondered what had gone wrong with him. How could a picture speak to him? Was he slipping? His tired mind could no longer think. For a change, he went into deep sleep, with no man or woman whispering to him in that hotel.

Tathagata was not keeping well. The area he was visiting to meet clients was experiencing a cold wave, one that he was not accustomed to in Kolkata. Initially, he had minor fever which, with each passing hour, grew. He decided to return home, leaving behind work half-done.

❖❖❖

His fever, under control after his four days in bed upon returning home, was subsiding. His wife and daughter were next to him, administering medicines on time.

'Your fever was so high that you were in a delirium,' Atmadeepa had said the day Tathagata took his first proper meal after falling sick.

'Did I say anything unintelligible or nonsense while I was out of circulation, or did you hear anybody call out for me?'

'No, you didn't say a thing. Neither was there any visitor for you who pressed the doorbell, expecting you to answer it. You are so unsocial. Has there ever been any?'

But there was, he knew, there had to be, even if he was in a state of unconsciousness.

He left his bed and went straight to the picture on the wall. The eyes of the woman, always so keen and deep, clearly had a swelling around them.

Tathagata threw a fit as he splintered himself like a loose cannon firing aimlessly at his family, wanting to know who had tampered with the picture on the wall while he was away. He wanted to convince his wife and daughter that someone, while he was away, had indeed tried to re-draw the eyes, in the process trashing their appeal that made the whole image a real work of art. 'Come and see it for yourself.' And Atmadeepa sparred to argue her point home that nobody had the time or the inclination to re-touch a nameless face in a picture. Neither could she notice any change in the image. She walked up to the picture, scrutinising every detail, hell-bent on freeing herself from the ire of her unsettled husband. The picture had stayed exactly the way it had arrived, and had remained as yet another testimony to Tathagata's addiction for extravaganza.

'Yes, my eyes have changed.' The picture spoke to Tathagata that night, the first time since his return.

'But why?'

'I had fever. I needed your care but you were away.' The words drifted into his ears as he lay on the bed. The communion had started to cover distance.

He lay benumbed on the bed, not sure what had caused him to be stupefied–weird reality or an invincible unreal?

His head was telling him to destroy the image from his subconscious but his heart wanted him to understand that enough might not always be enough.

When the whole city had gone to sleep and Tathagata's ghosts began their demonic waltz with the soft-blue moonbeam on the wall, he slipped out of bed and stepped into the living room.

'Who are you? Why are you here?' Tathagata stood in front of the picture, breathing heavily, his eyes burning the very fossil he had excavated from the market of thieves.

The face in the picture looked like a dying star, consuming its own circle of aura, as if it was being sucked in by an event-horizon. His own face was trapped in ungainly contours. He was balancing himself on the unsteady line that swung between him and the picture in a dangerous act of trapeze. This was the world he had chosen to create for himself, away from the one he lived in physically. 'So, why am I afraid?'

But what surprised Tathagata was the ease with which 'picture' had breached the fortification of his parallel world where he allowed nothing or nobody. 'Or is it the very parallel world itself, awakening me with its bursts of distant signals, asking me to be its permanent storyteller?' He was seeking answers but there was none, not even the 'picture' was yielding. As he was turning away from the wall, preparing to leave for the bedroom, the face began to re-surface—a Supernova was emerging with gifts from the unknown once again. He was covered by a faint light, almost ethereal. He could see his veins, translucent in that light, pulsating to the touch of the re-energised aura. He could see his heart, a giant muscle throbbing furiously, as his whole being stood in front of him like his alter-ego, transparent like space, daring him, laughing at him and pitying him.

✣✣✣

Tathagata disappeared thereafter.

What remained of him was bionic—a half-terrestrial human form and a machine programmed to play the dual roles of a husband and a father. Two entities, holding hands, sharing stories and making love—him and the face—voyaged into their wildfires that nobody else could feel or extinguish.

There were days when Tathagata would stand in front of the picture to share both his woes and happiness. It would listen, smile, cry or hurt in tandem with his own feelings. Like conjoined at birth, they were inseparable, even though one held out ostensibly from the realms of the unreal and the other, from the mechanical confines of artificial reality.

His family discovered no change in him. Once in a while, his wife would notice him stand in front of the picture on the wall, mumbling. She chose to ignore because she knew probing would invite silence and consequently unease she could ill-afford in an already decaying home. They were sleeping in separate rooms.

Atmadeepa was aware that her husband had become a piece of ageing furniture in the house, and extinct as the human being she knew once, weathered as unused wisdom. His beard had turned white and his hair gained an overdose of salt-and-pepper with time.

Indeed, Tathagata had completed many laps of his life. He had slackened after touchdown. He knew the countdown had begun. He was only living for 'picture'. Between him and her was his lifetime, held so dearly in the few inches that he would stand away from the wall, once at least every day.

One evening, Tathagata stood in front of the picture and found her to be too silent for his comfort. He noticed an amazing change in her countenance. Her face looked younger and the laugh lines on her cheeks had disappeared. 'What has happened to you? Please speak to me. I am not well and I need to hear your voice.'

'Picture' laughed out. Then it began to speak. 'Go back to your bed. We will talk later.' Obediently, Tathagata returned to his bedroom, took two spoons of a red-coloured syrup to ease the wheezing he had been experiencing for about a month, and lapsed into his surreal dreams.

Over the next few days, in spite of his illness, Tathagata became a permanent feature in the living room, standing in front of 'Picture' between chores. To his amazement, he realised that she was appearing younger by the day. In the back of his mind, Benjamin Button began to make disturbing appearances. The kind of rewind fictional character Benjamin Button went through was possible only in a movie. But how could 'Picture', without the support of technology or artistic re-touches, do a repeat? Was he hallucinating or was he completely out of his mind? The more he thought about it, the greater was his predicament in fathoming the changes that were happening in front of his eyes.

Tathagata's health condition became worse. As he could no longer move out of his bed—even the slightest of movements were discomforting him—he had 'Picture' removed to his bedroom. She had stopped speaking for long. But, like a child fascinated by the changing colours and shapes of a kaleidoscope, he would watch 'Picture' become younger and younger.

Surrounded by family and acquaintances, who made it a point to visit him every day, he went into a state of oblivion, at least that's what everybody thought. In fact, he was still walking the pastures of his parallel world, rediscovering its many charms. On his diluted pupils nestled 'Picture' like a baby. He was talking in his own realm. 'You look so cute now. You are almost a baby. But why?'

For the first time in many months, the infant spoke, this time in a squeaky voice and giggling. 'Tatha, to be born again, you need to arrive as a baby. We are going to another time together.'

Tathagata began to walk. Held up by her, a brilliant light was beckoning him.

✣✣✣

Although Atmadeepa realised that the chasm between her and Tathagata had grown too wide to be bridged, she still could not come to terms with the way he passed away almost a year ago. He was drawing himself deeper into a world she knew nothing of but, at the same time, he was present in flesh and blood in front of her as a being, looking after her and their daughter like a responsible head of a family. She would often wonder what was so wrong with him that he had to go even though the doctors treating him had opined that nothing was serious about his health condition?

She felt she was being sucked into the void he had left behind—I should have tried to listen to his heart—as a sense of guilt began to weigh her down. So that his impression did not fade from her mind, Atmadeepa had moved into the room again where they once shared a bed, even if silently. She had even shifted the broken-nose Buddha half-bust and the picture into that bedroom to preserve her memories of her misjudged husband.

One night, as Atmadeepa was turning in for the day—she herself was ageing and needed early pack-up—she took a random look at the picture in a bout of introspection. She had no qualms in accepting after so many years that the woman's portrait was truly a craft of the highest order. It was then a surge of electric shock ran through her body. The lips of the woman seemed moving, as if she was trying to tell her something.

Atmadeepa smiled, shaking her head from side to side in denial.

The next morning, she woke up feeling a little weakened by a mild fever.

✣✣✣

HANDS OF SILENCE

Two burly men walked down the ill-lit corridor, the sound of their footsteps growing louder with every step they were taking. Even the stars on the flaps of their shirts refused to sparkle as they walked under each light muffled behind a cloudy celluloid cover. The cold walls that abutted the corridor held foul moisture gathered from confined air which smelt of wasted ammonia. Time and neglect scythed cracks along the old, concrete ceiling and the walls that hid squalor from the outside world. The uninterrupted overnight drizzle was letting in drops of rainwater, which created tiny pools on the corridor. They stopped in front of a man sitting on the floor in a corner with his head buried between his knees.

'It's time,' one of the two men said in a voice that had a peculiar combination of being both terse and polite. Still, the man on the floor did not raise his head, appearing oblivious to their presence. They lifted the man firmly by the shoulder and began dragging him towards the exit at the mouth of the corridor, a quarry set to become a trophy. The man tried to say something. Only a guttural sound came out of his mouth. He was crawling on his knees as his limp legs refused to carry his weight. He screamed and bit into the hand of one of the two men, drawing blood. The man winched in pain but did not let go of his firm grip. They were used to withstanding unruly outbursts of emoted human desperation.

A cold breeze was blowing in. Nebulised raindrops swung in the air like a thin curtain. The underfoot conditions at the mossy opening were treacherous. Rarely did people visit this zone. Holding umbrellas above their heads, they stood like machines, watching the dazed look in his eyes. Two huge arc lights were switched on for clear visibility. The drying rivulets of tears on his cheeks were glistening in the light. The man looked at Tarapada Das, surrendering his fate to his workman hands. His muted pleas bounced off Tarapada's stony countenance. Tarapada was not new to waiting at the end of the last mile for unwilling walkers. He had met their anguished looks with untouched calm that was required of him during break-heart moments such as these. He waited perfunctorily for the signal. As it came, he pulled the lever with practised detachment, sending the man into the unforgiving darkness of depth in the blink of an eye. The thick rope stirred, a throbbing vein trying to defy a hastened denouement, and then went still, swinging with the gentle breeze of a day that was breaking.

Tarapada was never told and neither did he want to know the history of those who had vanished into the rectangular opening. The rights and wrongs weren't for him to decide whenever he happened to stand on that concrete platform at the break of dawn. He was just someone who figured as an abrupt full-stop in the manuscript of lifetimes.

Once back home, Tarapada took out an ageing notebook, breaking off around the corners, and made an entry. 'How many?' Shanti asked as she fed her grand-son milk from a nursing bottle, the same way her mother used to feed her grandson Krishnapada. 'Four so far in twenty-two years,' Tarapada said to his wife without taking his eyes off the notebook. The Das family believed in tradition–from family names and feeding a child from a bottle with a teat to hanging humans.

✣✣✣

Tarapada was almost six feet. And the muscular architecture of his body made him look imposing. With his closely cropped hair, thick brows, a shock of hair like an eagle's nest and cold eyes, his presence could drive fear into the hearts of weaker mortals. But his deportment was of little use to his profession. Tarapada was a master executioner who drew strength from the knowledge passed on to him by his father Ramapada. He, too, was a hangman at a time when the British were preparing to leave India's destiny in the hands of Indians. A few years after India's independence, Ramapada died knowing his knotty craft was in the right hands.

'You know Tara, bringing a life to an instantaneous end by using a rope is not easy. It is a craft, no matter how morbid it is,' from time to time, Ramapada would remind his son. Tarapada, who had no misgivings about his father's profession or its accompanying unwholesomeness, was a keen learner. He believed that comeuppance by way of hanging was not murder.

'You have to assist me. I am getting old,' Ramapada would keep telling his son. Tarapada couldn't make up his mind. On the one hand, he had received little formal education to find meaningful work. On the other, he was not mentally prepared to inherit the skills from his father. It was one thing to do his homework on hanging, but a completely different proposition to practice it. 'Tara, the pay is good and you would stay enrolled for the rest of your life. There's a lifelong stipend to be had,' Ramapada would try to make his son see sense.

Tarapada yielded. It wasn't long before the father and the son became a team, with Tarapada becoming a willing apprentice. But what mattered most to him was for how long they could keep their skills a closely guarded secret.

'Does anyone know you're a hangman?'

'Yes, your mother and some other people,' Ramapada said nonchalantly. 'Who are these "some other" people?' Curiosity was killing Tarapada but the ageing executioner only whetted his son's appetite, 'You would know when the time comes for you to be summoned. As of now, practise the noose, the intricacies of the knot and how exactly you need to apply them.'

Today, after so many years, those words of his father were rushing back to him, reminding him all over again that his special skills were too private in their discharge and irretrievably extreme in their outcomes. The perplexing twists and turns that made an innocuous rope metamorphose into a prelude to fright might have been understood by Tarapada. Yet, the learning curve for him was still in transit between expertise and excellence. But that would do, at least for the time being. He had a ready-reckoner, which he had inherited from his father. It was just a small notebook Ramapada had left behind for his son, populated by words written by hand, addressed to him in simple Bangla. They were not hymns, prayers or family secrets. When he had read them first, he felt outraged as a life-form. But there was no escaping the grisly lessons. They were intrinsic to his trade. The more he immersed himself into the words, the greater was the impact his father's wisdom left on him. How could a man who never went to school acquire this knowledge?

'Remember, never use the traditional position for placing the knot. This may not cause instantaneous death. To be an expert executioner, you be aware of all this. The traditional position, just below the ear, squashes the arteries in the neck, cutting off blood supply to the brain. This, of course, delivers the result but not the desired one and this process doesn't bring death quicker than the one I use. So what must you do? Place the knot below the left jaw, exactly beneath where it begins to curve. In this method, when the drop is complete, the thickly coiled knot, coupled with the tightening noose, sends the jaw and the head savagely to the right. This process causes the vertebrae in the upper neck to break. The end is quick.'

Tarapada used common sense to deduct that this particular method couldn't have been invented by his father. In the realms of medical science and human anatomy, the hangman's knot was already there as a grim lesson. It was likely that his father must have heard about it from someone and perfected it with practice, in real as well with dummy runs.

Yet, Tarapada's exclusivity remained uncompromised, camouflaged in a forest of words and sentences between the jacket of that notebook, in which he was making an entry. In doing so, the attendant irony was not lost on him—to save this notebook, he could even give his life. The notebook contained an innovation whose architect was his father. He prided himself on being probably one of the very few hangmen in the entire country who had this secret up his sleeve for the perfect execution.

❖❖❖

Tarapada's was a typically desolate existence of a hangman. He felt debarred from the normal way of life, ostracized to say the least. He would recall occasionally the words of his father. Ramapada had said only a few people like jailors and 'some other' prison officials would be aware of his profession. But neither his father nor he could prevent anonymous leaks that had laid him bare in the eyes of the public. Somebody or the other was always willing to sing, selectively.

Going out for a walk or to a shop would turn into personal debacles for him. Nobody shook his hand, nor did anybody demonstrate any affection for him. At shops where cast, creed, religion and profession weren't supposed to affect transaction of business, he would always be the last to be served, or ignored completely. Even if a transaction took place, those selling would treat him like a contagion, delivering him goods with unspoken derision.

Awakening came to him one evening without any announcement. Lost in thoughts, he was walking down a neighbourhood lane on a wind-blown evening when he suddenly crossed paths with a young woman carrying a baby boy in her lap. Her disquietude upon seeing him unnerved Tarapada. There was fear in her eyes, a kind he had only noticed in condemned people. To reassure the woman that he meant no harm, Tarapada had extended his right hand, attempting to fondly touch the tousled hair of the baby. 'Don't touch my son!,' she hissed under her breath, her scorn raging through his every vein like a curse. The woman had stepped back hurriedly, creating an untouchable distance between her and him. Tarapada tried to reason but the woman had already dodged him and begun hastening her strides, as if she was running away from impending ruination. Inside the walls of a prison, condemned men awaited him. Outside, in the free world, he himself was the condemned.

That evening, Tarapada left one half of him slayed on the neighbor street and brought the other half to a futile act of reconciliation. 'Am I a sinner?'

Shanti knew all along a day would come when her husband would seek answers, from within himself, from her. But when the moment of truth had arrived, neither she nor he could comprehend the enormity of the question. Shanti could make out that her husband was groveling at the feet of conscience, one that was beginning to stir. The man who stood in front of her had fortified his mind with his own die-hard perspectives on life and death. Still, the defence had a weak link, and she could notice it too clearly.

Tarapada's quest for answers had commenced many years ago. Worded differently, he himself was asked the same question by a man whom he thought he would never meet again.

✣✣✣

Niladri Biswas was an astute police officer with the detective department at the Lalbazar. His uncanny ability to retrieve that which appeared implausible was looked up to by his colleagues and as much dreaded by those he used it against.

'You are making it difficult for us, Niladri,' his colleagues would say in a lighter vein. 'It is because of you the criminals are becoming exceedingly cunning.'

'How come?' Niladri was curious.

'It's simple. What we tend to ignore are basically clues. You find them with such ease. Obviously, criminals are now trying to possess a slice of your mind. So, they are planning perfect murders.'

Niladri would tell them there were no perfect murders. 'No matter what they do or don't do to keep off the radar of law, they would be found out, if not today, tomorrow.'

It was all in his head, in which the terms extrapolation and logic were in a never-ending pirouette, to be constantly redefined. He would reopen cases that were like cul-de-sac, abandoned and left to decay in thick files at his department. 'I do not know how he does it, but Niladri is perhaps the best friend of justice,' the Commissioner of Police had said once about his colleague. And Niladri believed he was only bringing undiscovered wrongs to their logical conclusions.

Inside one such closed file, a man had been hiding beneath unbreakable alibis for many years. Niladri had reopened the case at the bidding of the aggrieved family. The crime was heinous and its perpetrator definitely a depraved killer. Not only was a sixteen-year-old girl murdered but her lifeless body was subjected to necrophilia by her killer. It was left to Niladri to bring the criminal to justice when everybody else in the detective department had given up on finding the apparently traceless culprit.

That was the time when Niladri had come in contact with Tarapada. The man he had wrenched out of a maze of confusing leads and alibis was being hanged by the law. And Tarapada had been summoned to complete the process of justice.

❖❖❖

A week before the hanging, Niladri met Tarapada at the jailor's office in a high-security prison to understand the procedure. Despite being a man whose reputation preceded him, Niladri found it awkward to be shaking hands with an executioner. Like most people, Niladri too recoiled after the handshake felt like the palm of his right hand was being devoured by the jaws of an abominable creature. And the very next moment, Niladri chided himself for finding Tarapada loathsome. Of course, his slovenly appearance had added to his repulsion initially. But soon he realised that Tarapada was actually serving the law of the land in doing what he did—a job few wanted to take up fearing social retribution.

'Mister Das, I am here to know about how you want to set everything up. You should know that I am directly involved with the case,' Niladri said in a self-assertive manner.

Tarapada cringed. Nobody ever placed a 'Mister' as an honorific before his name, and standing in front of him was a legendary police officer who chose to do exactly that. 'You should come into my room, Sir, before I can tell you anything.'

'How do I start?'

'Start with where you live,' Niladri said in a matter of fact manner.

'Why do you want to know that, Sir?'

'That's because your background will help me figure out how you think.'

'Well, Sir, I live in Majhipatti.'

Niladri was getting increasingly fascinated with the life-story of Tarapada. The executioner was bringing the detective up to speed on how much time and planning were involved in the run-up to a hanging. Tarapada was not a good speaker.

'For how long do you need to prepare for a hanging?'

'A lot of time.' Tarapada was speaking almost in monosyllables, still not clear about the purpose of Niladri's visit. And Niladri, despite his exceptionally sharp sense of perception, wrestled to bind together the granular details coming from a man who lived in silence to deliver silence.

'How do you accept the reality of being an executioner?' Niladri had asked, trying to excavate what lay in the deepest recess of the hangman's mind. Tarapada squinted his eyes. A deep furrow appeared between his brows. His mind seemed stumbling for an answer, with his face contorting into minute curves of anguish. Either this man was a stone wall when it came to answering personal questions or his practice had left his mind scarred permanently, Niladri surmised. At the same time, he regretted asking that question because he did not want Tarapada disordered just the day before the hanging.

But Tarapada began to open up slowly. He could sense that the man in front of him had no nefarious purpose.

'Let me tell you, Sir. If I say I like this job, I would be lying. In reality, I belong to a profession where its outcomes have been decreed and set by law.'

'If you don't like it, why do you do it?'

'Sir, you must understand that it is a job few would want to do. If not me, they will somehow find someone else to do it, but hangmen are few and far between. Anyway, had I not inherited this job from my father, I probably would have been a porter at railway station, carrying on my head the baggage of others. I have no other qualification.'

A question almost escaped Niladri's mouth—don't you think there's a dreadful baggage you are carrying anyway–but he restrained himself from asking. This was not a philosophy class. He needed to know some basic facts and that's what he was there for.

'Never mind. Let's get down to brass-tacks.' Niladri wanted to end the soft-pedaling.

'Yes Sir,' the stoic hangman was quick to return to his elements.

Niladri paused, framed the question in his mind and then shot it out. 'I heard the rope needs to be lubricated so that it doesn't jam during the drop. What do you use, beef tallow or some solutions?' Niladri was as curious as he always was about the unknown, which was his finest facility for solving cases.

The question, all too sudden, threw Tarapada off. He was alarmed. He looked askance at Niladri but quickly regained his composure. 'I am a Hindu and so, beef is out of the question.'

'What then?' Niladri pressed for an answer.

This man, Tarapada realised, was too sharp, too demanding and obviously too superior to be wished away with silence.

The secret that lay in the crypt of his notebook untouched for years now needed to be dusted out as the detective appeared set on prying answers out of Tarapada. The hangman insisted that whatever he was going to say should remain an inviolate secret between them.

✣✣✣

Tarapada has become ancient. He is now seventy-three. His bushy hair has diminished in density, randomly grey and most often unruly. He looks like a has-been and harnessed to isolation. In his own family where his son Krishnapada and his daughter-in-law Balaka decide the course of life, Tarapada has cocooned himself with thicker silence and obscurantism. Shanti is no more by his side, taken by cancer about a year ago. The sanctuary that calmed his nerves once in his moments of turmoil is now vacant of its only inhabitant. His nights are sleepless, almost. Whenever he closes his eyes, he discovers himself in blank space, surrounded by fractured-neck apparitions with protruding tongues, mocking his very existence. He feels being consumed by ennui.

Son Krishnapada has chosen to avoid daylight. He works at a saw-mill owned by a timber merchant in the night and sleeps in the daytime, going out only when absolutely necessary. Being a hangman's son keeps him imprisoned in what he calls a hex. Krishnapada keeps reminding his father of the woes that have befallen his life, his wife's life. 'People speak in hushed tones about me. Whenever they see me, they point at me with wary eyes, as if I am not human. If only you were somebody else, father.' Alcoholic fumes escape his mouth whenever he speaks, unsettling Tarapada, who has never drunk or smoked. He keeps looking at his son in disbelief–his creation has outgrown him without remorse, without empathy.

✣✣✣

And Balaka, the small-bodied wife of Krishnapada. Her face was an advertisement for cosmetic brands, much in contrast to her middle-class background, and too out of place in the suburban setting of the house. She was loud, domineering and had little or no concern about how she was perceived. From the day she and Krishnapada got hitched against the will of her parents and of Tarapada, she threw her carefully crafted gentility to the wind. She seemed to be on a warpath to defy everyone who crossed her path, even her parents who were aware of the Das family's background. And there was not dearth of ire for Tarapada who, before the marriage, had found her to be too independent for tradition.

Balaka was determined to live her life on her own terms at her in-laws' place, even if it meant being rude. She played the role of the aggrieved to perfection, chastising her husband and father-in-law for her pretentious misfortune of being in the wrong house.

After Shanti's departure, Balaka started treating Tarapada like a misfit in the household, an appendix that hung like an imperfection.

Even though Tarapada did not approve of her, he tried to make peace with Balaka. '*Bou Ma*, why don't you and Krishna go out sometimes? We all can take turns to do the chores.'

'Go out and do what? Be asked if I am the daughter-in-law of a killer? I came into this house because of my love for your son, not to share the ignominy of your life in public,' Balaka would put her foot in her mouth. Squirming in embarrassment, Tarapada would withdraw himself into his own room. But then, in a small house, frictions were inevitable, particularly with Balaka's intolerance for the 'old hag'.

If that ill-will had remained only in her speech, Tarapada could still have afforded to not get himself affected by her barbed comments. But then, Balaka's exhibited dislike for him spilled into actions. The portions of food being served to Tarapada had begun to decrease in servings, and the general care a septuagenarian needed was far from being offered.

'*Ar kotodin ei buro ta ke khawate hobe* (For how long do we have to feed this old man),' Tarapada had heard her say to Krishnapada one day. He would stand in front of Shanti's picture on the wall and burble. *Do you hear what they say, Shanti? My hands might have taken lives but these are the hands that fed the family. Are you listening?* And then he would start to smile, shaking his head from one side to another, tired of dissecting his own life.

Balaka had even stopped lighting the evening candles in front of Shanti's picture. Whatever little light there was burned only inside Tarapada, illuminating his memories of her, but he had layered his life with so many bruises and so much of uninvited scorn that the walls he was encircled by seemed to be throttling him. Emboldened by her husband's condescension for his father, Balaka became increasingly impenitent towards Tarapada, treating him like a flaw.

Tarapada refused to add to the vitiated atmosphere. The more the neglect, the greater was his desire to live another day. He might have aged but the preliminary sketch of his once muscular body still remained firm. 'What if I find a job for myself,' he had murmured to himself during one of his nocturnal wakefulness. But who would want to give a seventy-three-year old former hangman a job, and that too a menial one? The only skills he had were now part of his ignoble past. He was angry with himself, so angry that he felt the brutal calm he was once feared for was returning to take control of his mind. He knew there was no battle to be won or lost, for he had always been the conclusion.

He went out to the marketplace he hadn't been to for months. Tarapada stopped by the fruit stall, surprising its owner Biswambhar with his visit in a long, long time.

'As far as I am aware, you don't eat fruits, Tarapada Da,' Biswambhar said inquisitively.

Tarapada smiled in appreciation of his memory. 'You are right. But you know, these fruits are for Shanti. Her first death anniversary is coming up tomorrow. Offerings have to be made during the *pujapath* (rituals), isn't it?'

✣✣✣

Tarapada used to be an early riser but after retirement, his disturbed nights made him go to sleep late. It was never in his nature to waste the small hours but mental fatigue left him at the mercy of sleeplessness. One morning, the noise from a commotion stirred him up from his bed, just when he was getting a rare dose of sleep. He peeped out of the window. Neighbours were standing outside, talking animatedly amongst themselves, and pointing at his house. There were old and young men, housewives and girls, all in their night-clothes, as if they had frantically responded to an alarm bell of an exigency. The entire neighbourhood had converged on his house. Tension was in the air.

And then, he heard Krishnapada wailing, his cries rising above the sounds of disturbance. Tarapada rushed out of his room. He found Krishnapada sitting in the courtyard, his cries interspersed with incoherent speech. The door to the room of his son and daughter-in-law was ajar. Balaka was swinging gently by a rope that plunged from a tilted ceiling fan, with a toppled wooden stool lying beneath her hanging feet.

One by one, neighbours started clotting into small groups around Tarapada's forecourt, none wanting to enter his house or ask him or his son any questions about the incident. Everybody knew Tarapada but nobody wanted to be a witness that the police might ask questions later. They spoke among themselves in hushed tones watching Tarapada sit alone in stunned silence. His tearless eyes seemed trained on nothing or nobody as if his entirety was being held hostage by a phantom mind, surreal in its enormity, far removed from morbid reality.

The crowd was becoming larger by the minute as people began speculating the turn of events. 'Poor Tarapada,' somebody said. 'How unfortunate this man can be! 'First went his wife and now a young life.' It was Sadhu Khan, an elderly man whom most people in Majhipatti deferred to for his underground past. Sadhu stepped out of the crowd and walked towards Tarapada. 'I am so sorry to hear about it, Tara,' Sadhu said as he placed a soft hand on his shoulder. Sadhu was aware that Tarapada and his family were beset with frictions but he couldn't imagine that things would come to such a pass.

'But why, Tara, why?' Sadhu asked almost inaudibly. Did Krishnapada's alcoholism cause irreparable damage to their marital life, or was it his constant absence in the night? Was Tara's son seeing someone else? But that's not possible. Krishnapada, Sadhu knew, could be anything but unfaithful. He had learnt his lessons in loyalty from his assiduous father. Whatever the reasons might be, they had obviously driven Balaka to a point of no return, or else why would a mother leave behind a child who was just over a year old? The baby, named Haripada in keeping with the naming tradition of the family, was found sleeping on the bed.

'Don't be unnerved, Tara. This is not the time. The police will come soon and you may have to deal with their questions,' Sadhu said with an element of finality.

Hours later, the police came to take Balaka away, to be dissected on an autopsy table, far away from two dispirited humans who stood like vandalised pillars among ruins.

It was an open-and-shut case. Curious neighbours returned to their everyday life, Krishnapada forced himself back into work to forget and Tarapada sat brooding like a dethroned king in a wasted empire.

✣✣✣

Krishnapada had started to grey. In the five years since Balaka's untimely departure, his body and mind had begun to show signs of degeneration. The loss was too deep to be repaired. At the same time, pangs of remorse at not being able to care for his father while he could, was tormenting him. He was caught between absence and conscience, unable to free himself from their punishing clutches, no matter how much involved he was in work. Even an increase in his alcohol intake failed to salve the orifice of his wounds that, even if inconspicuously, were still bleeding. At home, he spoke little and Tarapada littler.

A stream of silence ran between them. The only relief they derived from the bottom of their numbness was Shyamapada, or Puchkun, as he was nicknamed for his cute looks. He looked ahead of his age in appearance as he was growing fast, like his father and grand-father did in their childhoods. The kid loved transmitting Tarapada and Krishnapada's messages for each other, often layering them with his own child-like inventions. The silence had still remained impregnable.

Not that Tarapada hadn't tried to invite some order into the disarrayed household. 'Why don't you get married, again? You are only approaching middle-age. Think about the kid, he needs to be raised by a mother and not by two living fossils,' Tarapada had tried to reason with his son a couple of years ago. Instead, Krishnapada had hired a permanent housemaid, who though not adept at raising a child the way he wanted, proved good enough as a back-up.

'If that's what you want, so be it,' Tarapada had said with a sense of resignation.

❖❖❖

Niladri had one more year left at work. His legend had become cross-border. The number of felicitations celebrating his exploits came with irritating regularity for him. He wasn't a pompous man who would go to town with his every hit. He preferred to be the mastermind of detection, and with age he had become more of a thinker for his junior colleagues than an intrepid spearhead which he once used to be. Yet, once in a while, he had to leave backroom when the challenge would become too tough for young detectives.

It was raining that day, delaying his departure for home. Drinking his third cup of tea in an hour, he bent over his keyboard to open a word file into which he was hammering the critical nuggets of his experience as a detective. Niladri was writing an autobiography. 'Why don't you write a book on the art of detection. There's no one better equipped than you to do that,' a publisher friend had opined over a drink at the Police Club. But Niladri wasn't the kind who would talk about himself, as everybody knew him to be. And neither was he a writer who would be able to disambiguate his thoughts into prose. 'But you must, Niladri,' the publisher had insisted, 'for what you would write down would be gospel for your young colleagues who wish to emulate you.' The idea had struck Niladri as worthy of a cause.

Niladri had solved apparently-impossible cases and there were some he had delegated to his juniors for they appeared a piece of cake to him. He thrived in battle of wits that gave him a high he would not even get from his trademark 12-year single malt at the club. In his 35 years of service, Niladri never had to fire a shot – though he carried a service handgun–or be on a breakneck chase of criminals through winding city lanes. He was a man who connected invisible dots to discover patterns, and he preferred his thinking to be immaculately processed in undisturbed solitude.

He hollered for his junior colleague Saurya, who was sitting in a state-of-art cubicle just outside Niladri's office. Niladri usually didn't ask for assistance from his colleagues. He had his own methods and his own time, which ranged from minutes to months. Saurya wondered what it could be that his boss was summoning him.

'Yes Sir?' Saurya, an up and coming police detective, stood at the door, expecting to be waved in.

'Could you please get me the files of those cases that have been closed?'

'Of course, Sir, in a jiffy,' Saurya said, turned on his heels, and vanished from the door. He was his Man Friday. Soon, several plastic folders landed on his desk. He needed them to figure out the thought processes of his junior colleagues and based on what they had reached a particular conclusion, whatever that might be. Case comparisons, he thought, could be referred to by the next generation of policemen on probe.

His eyes sped through several files. Each was as everyday as the other. Nothing was amiss in the tediously worded contents. He wanted to leave for the day. Even if his mind was still as sharp as it could be, his ageing body was not being obedient lately. There was just one last file. He placed the file under the table lamp that craned its neck in an arc towards the surface of the table. A sticker on the file said: 'Balaka suicide case'. He remembered the case. A young housewife had hung herself to death about five years ago. Niladri opened the file and started reading. Each line seemed so mundane and predictable–a housewife taking her own life out of frustration, a common occurrence that deserved only a small paragraph in newspapers. *But hold on! What's this?* The forensic report said traces of banana were found in the rope that was used for the suicide.

What???? Banana??? But why???

His mind began racing, tapping into his vast reservoir of knowledge, experiences and instances. He saw dancing dots circulating in a maze, asking him to connect them, to give them a shape. And then it struck him like a thunderbolt!

Many years ago, he had interviewed a hangman who had shared a secret with him a few days before an execution took place. He was one of the very few hangmen in the whole world who used one particular method to ensure that the hanging rope never jammed. Since he was a Hindu, he refused to use cattle tallow to lubricate ropes. Instead, he used mashed ripe bananas, something which the hangman had claimed to be a ploy handed down to him by his father, who was also a hangman in his time. Niladri had avowed himself to keeping the secret, as desired by that executioner.

The flow of blood in his head was roaring like a locomotive. He could see the dots becoming linear into a facile line of common sense. His *magnum opus* was ready.

'Saurya, get the car ready and the force on board quickly,' Niladri screamed.

'Where are we going, Sir,' the bewildered junior asked, trying to connect his boss's calm composure to the unfamiliar excitement he was witnessing.

'We are going to Majhipatti.'

⁂

SCENT OF CLAY

The entire village has come to know that Togor stands naked in front of men.

Scandalised, the usually quiet and sparsely populated village now has a piquant topic to discuss other than its everyday unease over rising prices. Balaram's tea shop is where they meet, speak, crosstalk over rounds of tea and go home to their chores. They also listen to Sudhir, who is in his early fifties. He is the only one in the village who wrote a matriculation exam in English and can afford himself cigarettes. And so, he is revered, as if he is the village chief, a chap who knows 'Ingriji' (English).

The atmosphere was heavy inside Balaram's shop that morning, not because of merging *bidi* and cigarette smoke that were creating apparitions in the claustrophobic air. The men wanted to know if Togor should be declared an outcast.

'But we need to talk to her before we take a decision,' mulling, Sudhir blew out rings of smoke.

'Why should we talk to her? She has degraded the name of our village,' said a young man supported by a chorus.

Falling into silence, Sudhir looked out of the shop, at the clear sky and the row of trees that lined the bank of the river that flowed close-by. He could see migratory cormorants dive into the waters for fish and seagulls with their brilliant wing spans circle in the air over a porpoise that broke surface only to disappear quickly. A demure winter sun skimmed the waves to reach the bank, dulcetly bringing the brilliance of wildflowers back to life after a night of mist and dewdrops. Bleating, a herd of goats, big and small, munched on fallen leaves beneath a jackfruit tree and common mynahs hopped in pairs from one branch to another in a merry dance. Creation was unfolding its many gifts in an explosion of gaiety that reminded Sudhir of Togor. She used to be almost everything that was emerging from the morning in front of his eyes. Sudhir has seen Togor take birth. Her father was a close friend. He had carried Togor on his shoulder when she was small as he used to take her around the village to keep her from throwing tantrums at home. He had bought her clay dolls, taken her to the bank of the river and seen the awe in her eyes. He couldn't imagine that restless, innocent girl would grow up to do something that would have the entire village lined up against her. He wished what he was hearing had no substance.

Sudhir turned towards the men who were waiting for him to speak. 'We need to talk to Togor first before we can take a call.' Togor was in Kolkata, he knew.

'When will she be here?'

✣✣✣

Little Togor ran to the river to make dolls.

Towards the bank of the Ganges she dashed, unmindful that she was leaving her footprints on wet concrete. In the Belari village off the Uluberia town, the local boatmen were building a platform that would support a pier to the waters where a narrow Damodar coyly met the vast expanse of the Ganges. The concrete had just been poured and leveled. But Togor didn't care. She had to run, and run fast. A big boat with a high sail was about to leave. The local masons who were building the pier were playing cards in a nearby hutment, leaving the wet concrete to solidify in the hot summer sun of June. Loaded with soil dug out from the bank, the boat had already started to unfasten a thick rope that had it tethered to an ancient *gulmohor* tree.

Frantically waving at the weathered old man helming the boat, Togor let off a cry that glissaded over the waters gushing towards the delta. '*Majhi Kakaaaaaa, darao!* (Boatman uncle, wait!)'

Startled, the man looked at Togor who was already close to the boat, the ripples flattening at her feet. 'What is it?'

'Why are you taking the soil? What would you do with so much soil?'

'Well, we're taking the soil to Kumartuli. Now, you little girl, go home.'

'Give me some, please,' she pleaded.

'What would you do with the clay?'

'I will make dolls, a mother doll,' Togor stood there expectantly with her small palms cradled and raised like a prayer. The man scooped some clay out of a huge cane basket and dropped it on her palms.

The oarsmen began to row, the gap between them and Togor increasing with each of their rhythmic strokes as she stood wondering where Kumartuli was or whether Kumartuli was a place or a human being.

Gangetic soil from the Uluberia banks used to be ferried to Kumartuli in northern Kolkata, a potters' colony where mud sculptors would take months using it to build clay idols of the Goddess Durga. Togor wanted to make dolls with that clay, though she could never lend shape to any. The spongy unruly soil refused to obey the commands of her small hands. Yet, she would continue to play with the soil for hours together in the small courtyard of her house. Traces of dried-up soil would remain on her clothes, her body, even when she went to sleep. Her mother would often admonish her in fits of anger: 'Would that clay fetch us food?' That was seventy years ago when Togor was a seven-year-old girl.

❖❖❖

Ramtanu, a school dropout, worked as a petty salesman at a grocery store in Uluberia town 18 kilometers away. He would ride his old bicycle to the town every morning at eight to be in time for work and cycle wearily back home well after dusk, hungry and completely exhausted. The rigorous routine was killing him, almost. He wanted to open his own grocery store but his earnings were way too paltry to start any business.

He couldn't either take a chance with livelihood. The pittance he would bring home, though falling too short of needs, was feeding the family nevertheless, even if it meant meals as meager as coarse rice and lentils.

'I don't know how long I would be able to pull on like this!' A sense of despair covered his tired face as he spoke to no one in particular, though Lakshmi was in earshot. He had married her when she was 17 and he, 20. Belari, like many other villages in the region, had been repeating ancient conventions through the ages remorselessly, and early marriages were one of them.

With a daughter and a wife to look after, and his inability to do that with the ease he sought for his family, was weighing him down. The dreams he once had had been reduced to blank vision. There were even days when he would stand near the railway tracks that ran parallel to the village, contemplating to bring his life to an end. But he would always abandon the thought and return home knowing that one life gone meant the end of two more.

Back home, Lakshmi needed medical attention as she was frequently coming down with severe bouts of coughing. The breezy winter on the banks of the Ganges could test the endurance of even the strongest. The thatched hut they lived in did not have thick walls or fortified windows to keep the cold out. Two old blankets, their woolly surface thinning with time, covered Ramtanu, Lakshmi and little Togor. Ramtanu would toss and turn in the bed, Lakshmi would shrink like a foetus and Togor would sleep snug into the cold body of her mother, oblivious of another ruthless day preparing to befall her family.

One night, as Ramtanu and Togor were sleeping, Lakshmi woke up coughing violently. Soon, her mouth started spewing blood, and more blood, as the hours grew. Ramtanu rushed to fetch her water but she was in no shape to drink it as the crimson spurt that welled up in her esophagus made breathing difficult. Lakshmi was choking, collapsing. She could see darkness descending on her eyes. It was not the cold; the lungs of an overworked, mal-fed woman had been ravaged by tuberculosis. The disease had crept in unobtrusively. Ramtanu rushed out, freed the bicycle that was tied to a wooden post in the courtyard, and disappeared into the mist that had rolled in from the waterfront. But the local quack lived four kilometres away, which meant almost an hour of cycling and another hour back home. By the time he returned along with the self-proclaimed medical practitioner, the sky had turned a faint pink and the bed inside his hut red. Lakshmi was gone, her one arm stretched, touching Togor's head, who still slept without knowing that her dolly world had crashed all of a sudden.

If Sudhir hadn't restrained Ramtanu that morning, Togor probably would have been orphaned. '*Ami akta pashondo* (I am evil),' Ramtanu was berating himself as he picked up a kitchen knife, attempting to slash his wrist. 'What are you doing? Think about Togor. Control yourself, Ramtanu,' Sudhir firmly grabbed him from behind, calming his old friend down. Ramtanu slumped to the mud floor, his face concealed behind his palms. By then, the whole village had gathered in front of the house, with some placing tender hands on Ramtanu's shoulders and some others preparing to take Lakshmi to deliverance.

And Togor watched from a distance. Her mother doll will never be made.

But what will happen to Togor? Ramtanu knew that he had to resume work for Togor's upkeep. At the same time, he could not afford to leave her behind in an empty home. It had been a week with Lakshmi gone. Ramtanu had stayed home these seven days to regain his composure.

Still, the answers were elusive. He cried out,'Tell me, what should I do, Sudhir?'

Despair was setting in. At times he would cry when he would be alone, and at some other times, he would break out in uncontrollable laughter, bordering on insanity. Ramtanu's sister Lalita could no longer see him disintegrate day by day. She offered to take care of Togor. 'Togor goes with me,' Lalita made a no-nonsense announcement. She was in Belari to attend the funeral. Lalita was a childless widow who lived in Bhowanipore, in Kolkata, where she worked as a maid in the house of an artist of some acclaim, one Mr Amiya Bhattacharya. Lalita took care of the house in a manner as if it was her own. She also moonshined between breaks at two other homes.

Lalita kept a busy schedule, earning enough to rent a room for herself where she cooked frugal meals. If one mouth could be fed, so could be two. Her room was small but big enough for the one with maternal leanings keen to mold and the other waiting to be fashioned. In Togor, she saw the child she never had.

For those few days she stayed home in Belari, Togor slept alone, for her father who shared the bed just one feet away was far from being another existence for her. She hardly saw him in the house, even when her mother was alive. Missing Lakshmi in an empty bed, Togor would sleep clutching an old saree. Her mother was gone but the saree smelt of her.

The day she left, many in the village had gathered at the pier. Holding Lalita by the hand, Togor took one tiny step after another, walking barefoot on the bank to board a boat to Kolkata.

As the boat pulled away towards the middle of the river to gather pace, Togor looked at the bank. It was empty. Those who had come to see her off had already left, not waiting for the boat to go out of sight, like goodbyes were and like farewells still are, as if she was good riddance. But the soil she had loved so much would not leave her alone in a world unknown to her. She sat hunched over her knees, looking at her feet. They were laden with mud.

❖❖❖

Wherever Lalita went for work, she would take Togor along with her, as if they were travelling in a flitting passage of time in which a child was being made to learn lessons that it wasn't prepared for. Month after month, year after year, she kept circling in a strange orbit. Togor was just a passenger with no destination. The life that Lalita had given to her, she knew, would not take her anywhere although she felt indebted to her aunt. She would be gripped by such thoughts when she would be alone. The girl who once ran freely back and forth between a homestead and a river was now limping inside her, hurting, scared and without a hand to hold to grow out of her almost baby steps. Little Togor and her dreams had probably died the day the river took her to Kolkata. And that small girl Togor kept looking for as she kept asking herself questions to which there was only one answer: '*Parli na to, amar putul bagan ta shajate* (So you have failed to create my garden of dolls).'

✣✣✣

The crash course in life's trials has hardened Togor to the innocence with which she has been winning the world to her side so far. She is a grown-up girl now, has learnt to cry and hurt, surrender to sentiments and retrieve herself from anguish to re-live the life she hadn't chosen for herself. And Lalita is older and enfeebled by a debilitating back pain she contracted from long hours of hard, manual labour. She has given up work in many households. Neither is she working anymore for Mr Bhattacharya. The artist has moved to a bigger house, his own, in a different part of the city, too far from Lalita's home. Before the man left, he had paid Lalita an extra month's salary. 'And Lalita, if I can be of any use to you in the future, call me,' the man had said to Lalita reassuringly, handing her a piece of paper with a phone number on it.

✣✣✣

'You see, Togor, I am scared to think about your future. Who will look after you once I am gone! No matter how grown-up you are, this is a city. It will consume you quickly if you don't know your way here,' Lalita knew she had to acquaint Togor with the reality facing both of them.

Togor's eyes were moist. Flashbacks of blood and a red bed had surrendered to vagaries of time. She could hardly remember the face that slept peacefully on a bamboo stretcher four men had carried to mark the end of a troubled journey thirteen years ago. Her links with Belari had become tenuous. She could visit her father only when Lalita allowed and escorted her to the village, that too for a few hours. Lalita didn't want Togor to experience the dread of that terrible day again.

But the woman who sat in front of Togor was not any figment of memory; she was starkly real. The words she spoke were spearing into her heart. This was the woman she looked up to every day, this was an epitome of kindness that had shielded her from life's foibles. Togor hugged Lalita, whispering to her words of comfort.

'Nothing will happen to you, Kaki. So easy to say I'll go, right? I won't let you go. Why don't you find me a job, instead?' Togor buried her face into Lalita's lap to hide the tears she was shedding for the screams of nothingness she heard every day.

Lalita held Togor's face in her palms and looked at her with keen eyes. At 20, she wasn't unsightly but not fetching either, though she was curvaceous, frighteningly enough to invite lust. She could cook, clean, wash, shop, stitch clothes and sign her name in Bangla. Yet she couldn't be sent to households for work with that body. Desolate afternoons when men were at work, mothers slept and young boys read banned books were often together a recipe for disaster.

And then it struck her!

'Wait,' Lalita told her as she limped to a rusty trunk kept in a corner of the room. She flipped open a diary to fish out a piece of paper she had preserved inside the pages. 'Stay home, girl, I will be back in a jiffy,' Lalita said as she walked out of the room.

'Could you please call this number for me,' Lalita asked the young grocer who had his shop next to her house. The man looked at the six-digit number and started using the rotary-dial phone. 'Speak,' he said handing the receiver to her. With bated breath and trembling with anticipation, Lalita began speaking. She knew if there was salvation, it was on the other side of the line.

✣✣✣

One of the four cleaners had dropped out of sight without warning. The man was absent from work at the City Art College for over six days. The other three—all men—were grudgingly filling in for him. Cleaning the expansive classrooms and studios at the college demanded more work hours but without extra pay. Besides, they were not working as a team. Each had his or her own complaints and excuses. Sparks had begun to fly. The issue was reaching a flashpoint.

The bursar of the college walked briskly into the office of the principal. 'We have a problem, sir, which needs immediate attention.'

'What is it?' Principal Amiya Bhattacharya asked without lifting his eyes from a book he was reading. Bhattacharya was known for managing crisis with as much finesse as the strokes of his brush made evident. He was a renowned painter whose work had travelled abroad. Like most artists, he had a beginning beset with struggle but his genius couldn't be overlooked for long by art critics. He had risen through the ranks, starting as a member of the visiting faculty at the same college where he was the Principal today. His experiments with the impasto brush strokes had set him apart from his peers.

The bursar informed him why the situation concerning the cleaners was spinning out of control. 'Why don't you hire one more? You are the person who handles finances and human resources.'

That was not easy. The pay was low. 'Not that I haven't tried, but I haven't yet found one cleaner who is willing to accept the salary we offer.' The bursar was abandoning the problem to his boss.

'I see,' Bhattacharya said as he leaned back into the high chair, mulling.

It was exactly at that moment the phone on his desk rang, interrupting his thoughts.

It was Lalita. Bhattacharya struggled to recall who the caller was. Lalita? But once he did, a smile broke out on his face. He was being hurled back to a time when he and his carefree journey into art needed order at home. The food would be on the table on time, the hot water in the bucket in winter and the floor would be cleaned of the patches of colour it would be invariably covered with after each artwork. Lalita had tidied his everyday life with care, almost maternal. *By the way, she also used to bring a child along. What happened to her?* He began to listen. The words spoken at the other end of the call bordered on the lachrymal—an old woman was uneasily reminding her former employer of the word he had given to her a long time ago.

Bhattacharya was smiling as he spoke to the bursar. 'There you are! Your problem has been solved.'

In one sweep of turning fortunes, Togor was wrenched out of the comforting shade Lalita had cast on her all these years. Two days later, Togor joined the City Art College as a cleaner. With the shade gone, Togor wondered if this was the beginning of a time for her to find her own place in the sun. Overnight, a woman was born, like many before her, to live or die by hope.

Togor had broken the glass ceiling. The cleaners initially were uncomfortable in accepting Togor as one of them, for she had gatecrashed a male bastion. Togor too, was ill at ease to blend with them. But busy work schedules, crunching deadlines and her affability soon flattened whatever misgivings they had about Togor. It never left her mind though that the new life she was building would resonate with two other lives in their last vestiges—one at Bhowanipore and the other in Belari. During work breaks, she would idle her thoughts into the repose she found in Haran, with whom she was slowly bonding. To her surprise, she had discovered that Haran lived in Uluberia and had a relative in Belari.

Within a few weeks, Togor had picked up the ropes of her work. She didn't require to be shown her tasks anymore. As she went through her paces, she remained overawed by the humongous size of the college and its properties. But what had raised her curiosity were dolls made of clay, some were of life size, some smaller. She wanted to touch those dolls, caress them, and breathe in the scent of clay that still lingered in her mind, inconspicuously invading her senses. The *majhi kaka*

(Boatman Uncle), the boat, the rippling waters were rising from the deepest recess of her subconscious, suprising her with unbidden memories that for long had remained buried on the muddy banks of the Ganges.

Togor was still living with a fistful of moist soil in her heart.

❖❖❖

'Togor Di, please turn a bit more towards your left,'

'Why?'

'I can't get a clear profile of your left shoulder,' Tuhin said.

'Togor Di, I am not getting a view of the belly region,' It was Animesh.

'Togor Di, can you cross your legs?' Rajat's voice reached her from one corner of the studio.

Almost like a contortionist, Togor was twisting and turning her naked body to answer the creative urges of students. Every inch of her womanhood was being shaped by pencil strokes on paper, in maquettes, and in their minds as her body laid bare anatomical motifs to fire knowledge and imagination in curious minds.

At times, light would be focused on her in a pre-determined manner to highlight certain features of her body—from head to toes—to help students feel the underlying emotions of the human physique. She, of course, did not understand what impressionism or realism was, but she realised that she finally had a purpose in life. She felt no shame in doing what she did.

She had inhibitions, though, in the beginning to undress in front of students. *The way time has cannibalised my life, would these men too want to take a piece each of my body in the name of art one day?* She had little time to contemplate her situation. Togor had taken the plunge into swirling waters, and nobody else would swim for her to stop her dreams from drowning again. It was her and her alone.

Togor's transition from a cleaner to being a nude model was by chance. One day, as she was cleaning the Principal's office, she overheard a conversation between him and a professor of fine arts.

'Mr Roy, now that it is part of the curriculum, we need to address this issue,' Bhattacharya said warning, 'We're running out of time.'

The professor was trying to convince Bhattacharya that the task on hand wasn't a shoo-in. 'You know, we can't even take out an advertisement.' But the Principal wouldn't relent. 'Why can't we? The pay is good, five hundred rupees a month for two sessions a week.'

The professor steered clear of engaging Bhattacharya in a war of words in the effort to find a woman who would pose in the nude for students. No matter the fees, to find a woman with the right kind of anatomy for drawing and sculpting lessons and that, too, using the city's art network to get one, would be near-impossible. A female nude model was rare those days. Even if a candidate was found, her background needed to be scrutinised. Besides, it was an assignment that required complete secrecy to shield the identity of the model, who must give a written oath saying she was not being forced into nude study against her will.

Togor had stopped mopping the floor. Five hundred rupees! Her head was spinning. She closed her eyes to take a deep breath and in that very moment, a thousand flitting questions started daring her sense of reasoning. *What if I offer myself for the job? Who will know and who will not know about it? Will Mr Bhattacharya tell Kaki? Chhi chhi, what am I thinking?* She could visualise the disaster that would ruin her and Lalita's life. Neither could she accept the fact she would be shorn of her dignity if she undressed.

But then, it was big money for her. Ease of life for all whom she loved and her own desire to flower as a woman formed a fusillade of aspirations that kept pounding her mind, at that very instance, in that very room where her courage or the lack of it would determine the next course of her life. She looked at the Principal and the professor. They were still talking, not knowing that a storm was raging just 10 feet away from them, toying with a woman caught between modesty and allure.

Shedding all the diffidence she might have had, Togor walked up to the principal, each tentative step drawing her closer to a fate waiting to be designed by her.

Summoning courage, she said, 'Sir, can I get that job, please?'

'You?' Bhattacharya almost jumped out of his seat. 'Do you have any idea what it means?' Togor shook her head to assure the Principal that she understood what the job required her to do.

'But what would you tell your folks back home? To your aunt?' The professor was equally dumbfounded. Both he and the professor were men of repute, known as astute observers of human behavior. But to have a housekeeping girl volunteer for a role that even the doughtiest might not readily accept, man or woman, challenged their prudence.

Togor stood rooted to the floor, searching for words. A fire was building in her, thrusting her towards a point from where she didn't want to return. Slowly, pausing between sentences with deep breaths, she brought the Principal up to speed about her situation. She was advantaged in being obscured by anonymity.

Both Bhattacharya and Roy had kept surveying her, to understand if the Rubenesque anatomy that presented itself to them out of the blue was a boon or a risk. Then they looked at each other, finally nodding in agreement.

⁂

Her heart is pounding, as if it will explode. Step by step, Togor is approaching the studio where excited students are waiting to have their first real look at the live nuances of human anatomy. Her mouth is dry, eyelids trembling and her cheeks are turning pink. Her legs are refusing to carry her body. She can still refuse to undress and return to her cleaning job. But as she sees the door of the studio half open, a strange burst of power runs through her body. The drums of destiny are building to a crescendo, beckoning her, exploding inside her head. And then, there was silence. The lights dim as she takes up position on a slightly raised podium to illuminate knowledge with the brilliance of her being.

After two weeks, Togor started easing into her role, knowing that the emotions that flowed from the naked contours of her body formed reality's bridge with quest. In the eyes of the students, she could see respect for her and awe akin to a newborn's first look at the earthy world. They almost bowed when speaking to her, careful not to be brusque, reserved not to hurt the aura she was casting on them. Of them, Tuhin was the closest to her. The acquaintance he had made with her was deepening to a point where they had started to behave like siblings with each other. Even though Togor was much older at 35, it never occurred to her that the social distance, as decreed by the college management, needed to be maintained between a student and a model posing in the nude. Tuhin wanted to hear Togor's story but she had little to tell. *What would she, a face in the teeming millions, have to say about herself*, Togor wondered. To not disappoint Tuhin, she would prise vignettes out of her life, including the years of her childhood. She spoke about her house, her parents, the river, the cormorants, the journey to Kolkata and, of course, the figurines she couldn't make. 'You know, Tuhin, I could never create the eyes, the mouth, and the nose on the dolls. I was so small then.' Her dolly world had remained faceless forever.

Immersed in her work, she was getting by. What, however, bothered her was that she was living a life of lies. At home, Lalita would want to know sometimes how she could help ease their lives with such small pay. She was under the impression that Togor was still working as a cleaner. She had made it clear to Togor that she disapproved anything that was not honest or moral.

'Don't worry, Kaki. Everybody at the college loves me and so, they reward me with cash sometimes, like *bakshish*, you know. And then, there is overtime pay,' Togor said to disarm her of her concerns. Togor cringed as she struggled to hide reality with a fake smile. Even the grocer next door or the shopkeeper who sold cheap lipstick and artificial earnings to her wanted to find out how the sudden elevation in their standard of living, even if by a small measure, had happened. She had to invent stories almost every day. She knew she was stretching her inventory of lies too thin for it to snap someday.

Another problem that had begun to plague her life was the nosey cleaning staff. They were grudging her the pay she was receiving and resented the idea of talking to a woman who was baring herself to men. 'It would be a shame for me to be seen in your company,' Haran took her by surprise.

'Even you, Haran *da*? I thought we belonged to the same place.' The bridge to Belari she had been building with him had collapsed.

✣✣✣

Togor still comes to Belari sometimes to look up her father. With age, Ramtanu has become diseased. A small government-run medical clinic has come up in Belari. Togor takes her father there for check-up whenever she visits the village. Some buses have begun to ply between Howrah and Belari, signaling the arrival of change, even if it is only a semblance. Today, Togor is back in Belari, and Ramtanu, whose eyes usually light up every time she sees her, is refusing to even look at her. His eyes are trained on the floor, his head hanging on his chest, as if he is in mourning.

'Baba, what has happened, Baba?'

'He has no face to answer your questions?'

Togor turned swiftly to find her Sudhir uncle standing in the middle of the courtyard. He had grown old too like

Ramtanu, his frail body being supported by a crooked stick he held in his right hand.

'Sudhir uncle, so nice to see you again. But what about Baba? Is something gravely wrong with him?'

'No, he is all right. In fact, everything is wrong with you.'

'I don't understand, uncle.'

'Don't speak a word. Just listen, Togor.'

Sudhir was at pains to let Togor know what he had learnt about her, but he had to, otherwise she would face a witch-hunt in Belari. 'We have heard what you do for a living and the village disapproves of it. People are scandalised. You must never return to the village again.' What he had said conveyed a sense of finality to her.

She knew her most intimate secret was now being bared to a kangaroo court, waiting to be torched. A wound had opened in her life fortified with lies. She could immediately sense how the word had spread. Who else, but Haran Da! For once, she wanted to fight back, to remind Sudhir how heartless the entire village was in sending her off at the first opportunity when one of them could have come forward to help her father in raising her. Nobody even cared to know whether she was dead, dying or alive. There was no point speaking to stones, for stones did not understand the language of the living. The die had been cast.

'But who will take care of my father?' Reverberating in the air, the question followed Sudhir as he disappeared down the road, with Togor holding the frail hand of an old man for whom she felt deep affection she hadn't experienced before. She kept holding the hand that fed her once until Ramtanu twisted himself free from her grip. She was truly an outcast now.

✣✣✣

Many years have passed since Togor went to Belari the last time. Ramtanu is gone. She only heard the news. Lalita was gone too. 'Can the human body ravage a life?' she often wonders these days. The wounds that she had returned with from Belari many years ago have stopped bleeding but not healed. Togor is now sixty-eight. Her vision is getting weak with age. The body that was once at the core of creation is now covered with thin rivulets of creases. The knees are packing up. Yet, she stands in front of the mirror every now and then, posing like she did at the art college, giggling, as if a child is lending destiny to form. Sometimes she hitches her saree up from one side of the mirror, baring her legs to have a sneak peak at them. Some other times, she would lie down, lift one leg laboriously up to the belly button and hide her face in the space between her cradled arms. Embarrassed, she will withdraw quickly but not dismiss the reflections that so lovingly remind her of artistic compositions she had once mastered. If only they could draw my eyes! There was treasure in them, so many images that kept transforming, so many moments that turned at will to create a mosaic that no easel wanted to capture.

Sighing, Togor returns to a sewing machine she had bought with her savings, stitching blouses and petticoats for neighbourhood women. Except Tuhin, no other student keeps in touch with her though she remembers every face. Tuhin has become a renowned sculptor. He had offered Togor a monthly help from his earnings but she had refused flatly. Whenever Tuhin visits her, he monopolises the conversation, talking about his profession. Togor understands nothing of what he says but keeps smiling with a sense of contentment—the forms that this student creates today were once nurtured in a cradle of an art form that she had prepared so lovingly. Tuhin is with her today, after a fortnight's gap, telling her that he has been commissioned by a Durga Puja club to decorate a pandal with his work. Clay work! She wants to burst out in delight.

Togor woke up to the sound of drumbeats that was wafting into her tiny room. Durga Puja had arrived. From her window, she could see hundreds of people in new clothes walking the festive streets of the city. She wondered if Tuhin was still busy with his *pandal* work. It was then that her phone rang. Togor had an ordinary mobile phone she used to keep in touch with her customers. It was Tuhin. 'Get ready, Togor di, I will be picking you up in an hour.'

'But why?'

'Don't you want to see the Pujo?'

Togor and Tuhin walked along a narrow lane that led to a big opening that served as a meeting point for the neighbourhood. The *pandal* that stood there looked like a temple glistening in the morning sun, its intricate façade towering over the crowds that had gathered. As they walked in, Togor froze.

The terracotta walls of the *pandal* were lined with sculptured motifs—each resembling Togor of another era, each jumping out of history. The refrains of the nude compositions that Tuhin had drawn at the art college were donning the walls, touching off myriad emotions in her. Keeping her eyes fixed on them, she moved towards the centre of the *pandal*, as if she was playing hide-and-seek with the mirror back home, only to come back to look at herself from close. Togor suddenly felt embarrassed for the first time in her life, a feeling that was taken away from her by the clothes she had shed a long time ago. The motifs were beckoning her to join them, in flesh and blood once again. All her life, she felt she had worked for a cause but never imagined that the very cause would one day make her feel like a mother who had given birth. She felt complete as a woman. Her aging body began to tremble. Deep inside, she suppressed the glee of seeing so many dolls that were standing like her, sitting like her, laying down like her, and looking like her, to wipe out the circle of anonymity that surrounded her all her life. Nobody else knew they were her, nobody looked at an old woman standing at the base of the wall in awe of the motifs. She wanted to scream—'It's me, it's me' to the world to announce her moment of truth but the tug of the secret she had kept all her life despite the Belari debacle was too strong to ignore. Coyly, Togor looked at Tuhin and he at her, between them flowing silently the combined symphony of a creator and a disciple.

Suddenly, Togor began to walk towards the exit, oblivious of Tuhin or the crowds that were building up inside the *pandal*. Shouting out her name, Tuhin scrambled to look for the woman who made his life, but she had melted without a trace into a sea of humanity.

✣✣✣

AMPHITHEATRE

These days, Moinak has just one aim in life—to save the earth from apocalypse. He thinks all the stars in the sky are conspiring to erase life on his planet. And so, every evening, he sits on a chair on the open terrace of his house and re-constellates the distant planets. He moves his arms in the free air, removing Mars to where Jupiter is and Jupiter to where Venus has been sitting since birth of time. Almost like a game of Chinese checkers. He finds the planetary positions too flawed, in an astrological sense, to be able to make life on Earth flourish. Today, he is focusing on Great Bear. He wants it to be reindeers, bringing gifts to human beings.

'Come Moinak, it's time for dinner,' Trishna called out from the door of the terrace, where she stood silently, like every day, watching her husband trying to orchestrate the great sweep of the universal mechanism like a master conductor.

Moinak still didn't get up. Mouth agape and his impassive eyes reflecting nothing but the light from the moon, Moinak kept looking into the sky, hoping to build his own astral world that he can control at will.

Trishna walked up to her husband and leaned towards him. 'Come, it's late. The food will get cold. They are not running away. Can't you see, the Venus has moved a little bit to the direction you want it to be?' she whispered the words into his ears like a lullaby.

Moinak needed to sleep. The drugs were kept on a plate next to his meal on the table. That's the only way she knew she could keep him alive in their disrupted world.

❖❖❖

The decrepit steps of a very old building, a remnant of the British era in the bustling sprawl of Chandi Chowk in Kolkata, went up to the second floor before being halted by a terrace. Moinak's destination was the first floor, where among many small offices was a glass cubicle with a wooden table, two chairs and several shelves filled with new and worn-out files. On the table was a square pad made of blotting-paper, a vial of writing ink, a fountain pen, and a writing pad. The cubicle was not air-conditioned. A World War II fan hung from the ceiling, its pock-marked blades labouring to complete the circles they were meant to. On the back wall, a sooty exhaust fan was whirring to throw out the combustible air inside. It all looked so primitive. Behind the table sat a man, about sixty, with a nose like Sherlock Holmes, thick brows and thin lips. His eyes had a discenring look about them and the colour of his skin was so pale that it appeared embalmed. Moinak wondered whether he had unearthed a sarcophagus. He and the man had only spoken on the phone. This was the first time they were meeting and Moinak had a feeling that it would not be the last.

'Come in, please. Mister Moinak Chatterjee, I reckon?' said Nibaran Banik as he gestured to his visitor to take a seat.

Moinak nodded as he seated himself. 'I am in a bit of a hurry, Nibaran Babu. Do you have the *kushti* (personal horoscope) ready? I have to take my daughter for her vaccination.'

'I have prepared the *kushti* for your daughter on the basis of what you told me on the phone,' Banik said as he handed over a yellow-coloured scroll to Moinak.

The brand of astrology Banik practised had a variant. To the rich, he was bad news. He was anything but a quack. Quite often, he would use half-truths and lies to find a way into the wallets of his wealthy clients. He had mastered the science of astrology which was being practised with honest intentions by thousands of his ilk and believed in by millions across the world. He knew he was a blemish on a noble practice. But he didn't give a damn about how people would remember him as—probably a genius gone rogue? He needed more money, plain and simple. He was just being untrue to his profession. Banik's needs were dominated by tall medical bills which he was barely able to pay with whatever his predictions fetched. Arthritis and a rheumatic heart were slowly getting the better of him, causing his mind and body almost unbearable discomfort. He soon realised that his mastery of astrology and gullible clients were a rewarding combination. Keeping rich clients thrashing like a fish hooked on the line became his main practise. And Moinak was a rapidly growing entrepreneur who appeared wealthy.

Moinak could guess that he was being overcharged for just a *kushti*. But what he didn't know, as he sat on the chair in the small cubicle, was that he was facing a merchant of fate.

Yet, the *kushti* was important to have. He wanted to know which course his daughter's life would take in the years to come. As he went through the scroll, he couldn't make out what it contained. There were only diagrams and words written in chaste Bangla and Sanskrit, neither of which he was familiar with. What made it more difficult for him to decipher the content was the extremely cursive handwriting of Banik. Astrologers were infamous for their cursive handwriting, but these looked like small whirlwinds one after another, rising into the diagrams, as if a terrible storm was gathering.

'I am sorry. I can't make head or tail of this. Could you please let me have the gist quickly?' Impatience was showing on his countenance. Like any new father, Moinak too was more than keen to find out what fate had in store for his little girl, whom he saw as a divine gift that had arrived in his family after several years of conjugal incompatibility. Antsy, he looked at Banik.

'Let me explain her planetary positions to you in short.'

He went through the *kushti*, dissecting each line for Moinak, who was swallowing every word he was uttering. Banik suddenly paused, leaving a few concluding lines hanging unread in the foul air of the small cubicle.

The pause was almost dramatic. Banik wanted Moinak to be irreversibly impacted by the unread lines at the bottom of the scroll. Even Moinak could sense that those lines concealed the summary of the entire scroll.

Banik coughed, cleared his throat and prepared to deliver the final line like a thespian in the last act.

'You see, Mr Chatterjee, nothing is a given.'

'I know, Nibaran Babu. I have been through my own ups and downs.'

'Well then, here it is. On the fifth of March, twenty-two years from now…' His hands trembling, Moinak wrote it down on the back of the scroll.

Concealing a smile, Banik kept looking at Moinak. He knew his fast deteriorating health wouldn't allow him to last that long for anyone to call his prediction right or wrong. After all, he was an astrologer, who told the future. This time, he realised that he was telling his own.

❖❖❖

Exactly ten years later, Banik passed away following a cardiac arrest he suffered in his chamber. His rheumatic heart had called it a day. His body was discovered by the caretaker of the building. Since Banik had no family, his last journey started from that dilapidated building in Chandni Chowk and ended at the Nimtala crematorium. Nobody cried in his wake. Nobody remembered him thereafter. He left no money or property behind, at least that's what strangers who performed the last rites understood. Nobody came forward with claims either. Only a few clients and one particular shaken man who had often visited him, seeking remedies for predictions, remained as the residue of his life. Once in a while, he would give that man a gemstone for his daughter to wear, or a hymn to be chanted at dawn. But that was all he could do for this client—some little hopes he knew weren't remedies but his client grabbed them as lifelines. But now that Banik was gone, the client had no other option but to take his fears to other astrologers. Even they said Banik's calculations were flawless. Nobody could peel back the spurious layers of astronomy he had so cunningly crafted with his genius to construct the *kushti*. That client became a mental wreck.

✣✣✣

Years turned and so did Madhulika, from a sprightly young thing to a girl in advanced teens. Her growing-up was unusual in more ways than one. Madhulika found her parents to be increasingly keeping her movements under strict vigil. She wondered why, especially her father, wouldn't let her out of his sight for as long as he could. There was hardly a moment she had to herself whenever she was at home. She realised that she was being treated like a rare gemstone kept in a chamois-leather pouch inside a bank vault. It's just like that, the gemstone was meant for private viewing, within the walls of a wary home.

If she woke up with a plethora of wishes, some would be fulfilled and the rest would be dismissed as teenage tantrums. Not that they weren't doting parents. Yet, there were no takeaways for her, no birthday parties to attend, unless accompanied by either Moinak or Trishna. Neither was she allowed to go to school, and later to college, unescorted. She found the web of protection that her parents had woven around her impossible to breach. A deep sense of being stifled was consuming Madhulika from inside. She felt outraged as she fought the futility of trying to live her girlhood. She resented being a girl shackled for no fault of hers.

She would open the window of her room to see the mornings and the nights that unfolded outside the boundaries of her house. She would find fritters shops raising their rusty, corrugated shutters in the morning to serve hot breakfast. She never missed out on the old men and women, and fitness freaks walking back home from their morning workouts. And then the bus that would speed away from under her window, carrying people to work, made her wonder what all the rush was about. Young boys and girls like her, in their colourful uniforms and chattering among themselves, would enthusiastically walk towards local schools. They were on their own, but she wasn't.

She was unable to be a part of the world that changed like a kaleidoscope every moment. Madhulika would stand behind the window in sharp contrast to the dynamism of that world. Even though both her feet were grounded inside her room, the fantasies she nursed would fly unchained into the free universe that she so dearly wanted to be hers. She would keep looking through the window for hours, her mind rebelling. The call of the firmament was becoming unbearable for her. She wanted to tear apart the iron bars of the window to let her body merge with the streets, the people, the murmuration of the warblers in the sky, and the brilliance of days and the calming mystique of nights. Yet, she feared that these wonderful sights of life might soon be rationed for her by her parents. Who knows!

Much as she tried, she couldn't make out why her parents were behaving the way they did. She found her father losing weight by the day. Almost emaciated, he had become easily irritable while the frequency of her mother's visits to the *pujor ghor* (Puja room) increased. They took turns to keep an eye on her and that meant even pressing an ear to the door of her room when she was fast asleep.

Madhulika felt like running away for good. But then, she was only 18, and not prepared to take on the world at large, no matter how appealing it was to her. The freedom she so wished for was trapped in the clenched fists of her parents.

To deflect her mind from the agony of captivity, she took to reading books. 'Yes, you can have books as many as you want. Just name them,' Moinak had said to her daughter one day.

Madhulika began reading anything she could lay her hands upon. Whether it was an autobiography of Malala Yousafzai, or fiction based on call centre stories or a compilation of articles on the global movement for equality—she gobbled up everything like a hungry traveller who had just walked into a roadside inn after a long journey.

'Baba, you know the fall of Bastille marked the beginning of renaissance?" she had asked Moinak one day. What the hell is Bastille? Moinak had no idea. He could sense that Madhulika's mind was maturing fast. Probably, my daughter is intellectually precocious, he wondered. But what he didn't know that she was forming her own opinions, like an 18-year-old does, with or without being in protective custody.

✣✣✣

Four years had passed since Madhulika had wrongfooted her father with that Bastille question. Not that she would let go of him or her mother. The questions that once used to be sparse had turned into a fusillade. Some they would answer but most of the time, they would look at their daughter blankly, failing to notice she now had a mind of her own that would weigh orders before accepting any. It was a matter of time for her to confront her parents, and as she did, her parents switched to their trademark parrying.

'Why do you keep guarding me all the time? I am an adult now. My friends make fun of me on the sly. They think I am like a doll. What is it about me that has been bugging you for so long?'

'Come on, dear. We love you so much. You are our only child. Have we never fulfilled your wishes? All you have to do is to ask,' Trishna circumvented the question in an effort to ease the tension that was building up.

Madhulika recoiled without a fuss. There was no point seeking answers from her parents. If not loudly, she has been asking all her life. What surprised her was the fact that her parents hadn't spent their childhood or their formative years like she had. Almost like bedside stories, Trishna had told her how free she and Moinak were to make choices for themselves when they were growing up in lenient families. This piqued Madhulika. She knew there had to be a reason why her parents were acutely protective of her. It did not make sense.

Her mind remained in turmoil, but the clues to solving the puzzle weren't forthcoming. That was until the day Madhulika went hunting in her mother's closet for a gaudy saree to wear to the freshers' welcome function at her college, obviously accompanied by one of her parents.

It was then that she discovered something hidden behind a stack of sarees her mother no longer wore. It looked like a rolled-up calendar, yellow in colour and broken at the edges. Slowly, she unrolled it. There were diagrams, which made no sense to her. What is this? Then her eyes fell to a line at the bottom of the scroll. It was the gist of the diagrams, written in simple Bangla and the handwriting was her father's. Dumbfounded, she sat on the floor, legs crossed. Rather than shock, a burst of rage ran through her body uncontrollably. This is preposterous!

Moinak and Trishna heard their daughter scream. They rushed to where Madhulika was. They found her sitting on the floor in front of the open closet, with the remnants of the *kushti*, torn into bits, surrounding her like dry yellow petals. 'What the hell is this?' She was screaming at the top of her voice. Recovering from his initial shock, Moinak tried to pacify his daughter. 'Relax, Madhu, relax. We were about to tell you but then you found it yourself. Stay calm, please.' He was pleading.

Finally, it dawned upon Madhulika. In one stroke of discovery, the pieces had begun to fall into the places where they were meant to.

✣✣✣

'Wake up, dear, wake up. Have your bath quickly. You have to say the prayers.' Madhulika was reading an old book titled *The Alchemist* late into the night. She had planned to go through some parts of the book once again after breakfast, to understand the shepherd Santiago, who had learnt to listen to his heart. She had been so enamoured by Santiago that the shepherd boy had become her alter ego. She wanted to liken her life to Santiago's rise from ruins in pursuit of dreams, for she felt her own ruins within the four walls of her room would one day be the reason for an unbridled journey into a treasure hunt. For her, Santiago was emerging as reality from the pages of fiction, urging her to return to where her dreams had begun. That was the treasure she hoped to find some day. But then, Santiago discovered an alchemist who shone a light on his path; Madhulika only had impregnable walls that had obscured that light from her.

She struggled to open her eyes. When she did, she could see her mother standing near her bed, repeating the wake-up call. Santiago can wait, all that listening can wait, too. It was her mother she had to listen to now.

'Prayers? But why me?'

'Don't you remember? This is the day...'

Silence was all-pervading.

Trishna hurried out of the room without speaking. Madhulika started laughing as she concluded that what her mother had said a few moments ago only illustrated her parents' misplaced beliefs. She left her bed, went straight into the shower and a few minutes later, walked into the *pujor ghor*, struggling to suppress beneath her countenance the scorn she had for all this.

After Madhulika said her prayers, she was made to sit in the middle of the living room flanked by her parents and in front of a pantheon of gods. She noticed that some relatives had come in early to take part in the puja. As the morning grew, some more relatives and neighbours walked in, forming a ring around her, as if they were in an amphitheatre to watch a gladiator perform. Nobody talked. Even if they did, they spoke in whispers into each other's ears, their curious eyes never leaving Madhulika.

She was getting torn apart by contrasts. The girl in her wanted to relent and the woman that she already was would not listen. The long pent-up fire in her was now impatient; its flames rising fast through her body, exiting her soul, and re-igniting her aching. 'Is there any way out of this, Santiago?' she asked in her mind. The ignominy of her being at the centre of a farcical show was getting to her. And then, a sudden calm descended on her. Her sight began to fly beyond the gods in the room, the people and the four walls, towards a void where matter was transmutating like alchemy, forming into a mass emitting light to illuminate her thirsty eyes. *Ah! Santiago! Now I know.*

She stood up. This circus of the absurd, or the ruins, has to stop.

'Where are you going?'

'Ma, I am uncomfortable in this saree. Let me change into a salwar kameez since I guess I have to sit out this farce no matter what time of the day it ends.'

'Okay, don't take too long.'

Madhulika stepped into her room, took out a dupatta that she thought looked almost like the tunic of Santiago, and flung it around the ceiling fan. No point keeping a room full of people waiting.

It was the day twenty-two years ago Moinak had met Nibaran the astrologer.

UNSOLD

Rukmini was feeling exhausted. She deserved to be tired at sixty, at least that's what she placated herself with, especially after over three decades of private practice as a physician specialising in medicine. Rukmini had already dealt with twenty patients since she commenced her office hours at her consulting chamber that day. She wanted to leave for home a little earlier than usual. The shadows outside her chamber were lengthening, and so was her tiredness. She pressed the intercom button to tell her front office assistant Hari, that she would be packing up for the day.

'Just one more patient, ma'am. He has been waiting for long.'

'Okay, Hari. Send him in. But no more for the day, please.'

Accompanied by a woman, probably his wife, a middle-aged man with his torso thickly bandaged, walked in with strenuous steps. Rukmini gestured to the chair opposite hers. She could sense that the man was in great discomfort. 'Tell me,' she said to open the conversation. The man was a fisherman in the Sunderbans. He was a victim of a tiger attack. His wounds were not healing the way they should have and so, he decided to consult Rukmini, whose undisputed fame as a doctor had reached him through references.

'A tiger attack?' Rukmini almost jumped from her seat. Within seconds, her clinical focus crystallised before this uncharted territory—a case unlike any in her medical practice.

'Where in the Sunderbans are you from?'

'Would you know, Doctor? It's a village called Boro Mollakhali,' the man winced in pain as he answered.

Rukmini stifled a sigh. She was aware of how the Sunderbans pulled deadly surprises on men and women who chose to dare the wild, but to have a tiger-attack victim sitting right in front of her was a stark reality she never imagined she would have to face one day.

'Is the stranded launch still there on the bank of Boro Mollkakhali?' Rukmini asked randomly without lifting her face as she began writing the prescription.

'Yes, ma'am, yes. It is still there. The children of our village still play hide-and-seek inside it. The launch is the landmark of our village, though it is just a skeleton of what it used to be.' The man stopped speaking just when he appeared set to reel off more about the launch and his village. Bewilderment was writ large on his face. 'But how...how do you know about the launch?' between laboured breaths he asked.

Rukmini did not say another word as she handed over the prescription to the man who, still baffled, walked out of the door, not knowing that he had unwittingly opened another wound to bleed silently behind the doctor's table.

An hour later, Rukmini walked into her apartment and slumped into a sofa. Next to the sofa was a chest of drawers on which stood a photograph she had downloaded from her first android phone many, many years ago. Carefully arranged dots of sandalwood sap adorned the frame. She kept looking at the picture with a vacant gaze, oblivious to the turbulence that was building in her mind.

✣✣✣

Khuki was six year's old when she lost her father. A fisherman, Nibaran would set out on a small boat along with his team when the eastern sky would still be unlit. The catch used to be evenly distributed among the fishermen. Nibaran would bring a few fish home and sell the rest to the local market. His earnings were not as much as he wanted them to be but were enough to keep the family frugal. On one such hour between a collapsing night and a rising daybreak, he had left for fishing after his wife Mala loaded the boat with a sack full of puffed rice, jaggery and a jerry can of water. While bigger boats had makeshift kitchens, and even bathrooms, the smaller ones required to carry food from homes as fishing would usually continue through the day until late afternoon.

The skies had begun to lose daylight that day but Nibaran and his men still didn't return. Mala was worried. She had noticed strong winds disturbing the steady flow of the Matla river that flowed by the village. *Strange! This has never happened before.* Dusk merged into the approaching night and the night into a deeper darkness, but still no sign of them.

Then she heard her name being called out from the courtyard. They were the other fishermen, appearing shaken, distraught, and without Nibaran. They were struggling to tell her something. Mala, a woman born and raised in the Sunderbans, could sense the ominous portent of that night-time visit. She fainted without warning. Nibaran had been taken by a tiger when he went to relieve himself near the treeline along a fishing creek.

Overnight, Mala was pitchforked into playing a role she wasn't prepared for. But what bothered her was her inability to find out the impact Nibaran's death was having on her children. Well, her son was too young. He could be kept out of the circle of her concern. But Khuki? Was she affected by the absence of her father? Although Khuki continued frolicking with her friends, picking *jamun*s and playing *keet-keet* (hopscotch), she would go missing from time to time. On one such occasion, Mala had discovered Khuki sitting inside a big abandoned boat, stranded on the bank near the pier, and gazing at the river, as if she was expecting something to emerge from the horizon.

'What are you doing here?' Mala couldn't conceal her angst.

'Nothing, Ma, I am just sitting here watching the boats.'

'Come on, let's go. You and I are going to Godkhali.'

'Nooooo, I am not coming with you.'

A sea of humanity was rising from a river—in tens, scores and sometimes in hundreds, one by one, or one into another and one beside another, or even all of them together. Each oblivious of the other, buried in their own thoughts, was being disgorged by big, medium and small motorised boats that jockeyed for space at the Godkhali pier. It was the busiest of the many piers that connected the mainland with the riverine web of the Sunderbans.

The boats were doing good business as it was tourist season, though regular customers were as many as the visitors. Scores of vacationers from Kolkata and adjoining areas were either disembarking or boarding, cautiously climbing up and down the steps between the pier and the road up. Cars and buses were honking in and out of the crowded parking lot as touts merged with the milieu to look for gullible tourists.

Amidst all this, nobody noticed a little girl, barely eight, acting obstinate. She wanted to go back to the boat that brought her and her mother to Godkhali. But the mother would not loosen her grip on her daughter's arm. Mala was afraid that Khuki's tantrums might draw attention, something she wanted to avoid at any cost. As it is, she had journeyed for three hours on a boat with a sense of trepidation. Each passing minute on the boat had caused her palpitations to increase as she wasn't sure if her journey from her village in Boro Mollakhali would end in trouble or the way it had been planned. 'Behave!' Mala had hissed to her daughter. And Khuki, realising that she would not be able to break free from her mother's grasp, calmed down. Soon, they vanished into the chaotic rush unobtrusively. They walked towards the parking lot where a man waived at them from the driver's window of a car. A woman in the back-seat made space for Khuki and Mala.

'We will drop you off at the next crossing,' the driver, a thick-set man, whispered to Mala as he gunned the engine to life. Mala gave herself one last-minute gasp to becalm the feud her mind was having with her reality. One half of her heart was being disobedient. The other half was overwhelmingly intransigent. It was too late to be a peacemaker.

Khuki, drowsy, half-asleep, was tired, very tired from the long journey she had to endure in an overcrowded boat.

She had been woken up very early that day so that they could catch the first boat out of Boro Mollakhali.

Just a few hours ago, Khuki's plaintive cries had rent the afternoon air as her mother was dragging her away from the mud hut she knew as home. Since the death of Nibaran, the household had little means to feed four mouths—Khuki, her tiny brother Buro, her widowed grandmother and Mala herself.

Destitution was tightening its chokehold on the family, bit by bit, reaching a stage where even living for the day had become difficult. Day after day, Mala would pluck wild *kolmi shaak* (water spinach) that grew in abundance around the local ponds, or dig up *kochu* (taro roots) to boil and offer them as semblance of food to her family. Her health was deteriorating, and so were Grandmother's, Khuki's and Buro's. The children were so emaciated that they looked like walking skeletons. Wasn't there a way to live a better life, Mala would often ask herself. There was, waiting to be explored. But that road was laden with risks, and blatant avarice. Mala knew she had to take the call, even if it meant degrading her own motherhood with a sacrifice she was willing to make.

With one hand, Khuki was holding on to a dry tube-well in the courtyard of her house, refusing to let go. In her other hand was a doll made from rags. She could see her Grandmother and her tiny, younger brother stand in the doorway, looking at her unmoved. Using force, Mala pulled her away from the tube-well. Some neighbours had gathered to watch the unfolding scenario, but nobody said a word. Khuki's cries didn't mean a thing to them, for many homes in the village still reverberated with such cries. They were used to loss and desperation. Losing was so routine in the Sunderbans that it had become a way of life, without questions.

While being wrestled back by Mala, Khuki extended her right arm in the air in one last attempt to reach out for her grandmother. 'I won't go with you. I won't,' she was sobbing. She didn't know that between her and her mother stood fifty-thousand rupees—the price of her life, the pull of which was much stronger than her feeble, young hands. From the hands of her mother, Khuki was in the clutches of a stranger in a car, unwilling to begin another journey.

Khuki woke up from her slumber in the arms of the woman in the back seat. She tried to wriggle herself free. In despair, she began to bang her two small fists on the rolled up windows of the vehicle. But the woman pinned her down into the seat in a vice-like grip. In the trail of rising dust that followed the car, her mother had begun to look like a granulous photograph. The car began to pick up speed; it had to hit the highway quickly before passers-by became curious. The woman and the driver didn't want to be spotted with a small, rustic girl in a car that looked completely out of place on the dirt-roads that ambled towards the highway. As the car tore away from

Gadkhali towards Kolkata, Mala stood there watching a part of her life disappearing. She was choking on her breath. She could feel the tumult building deep inside her chest. But then, the die had been cast.

✣✣✣

Khuki was a child, just eight years old when she was taken to Kolkata. Initially, she would throw a fit. The first few days saw her raise a ruckus. She refused to eat, kicked the closed door and screamed at odd hours. But not for long. Khuki was soon getting used to her new home in a city she saw for the first time in her life. She couldn't imagine that lights could be so colourful and burn so bright in the night, as if a thousand stars had descended from the sky to caress the surface of the earth. Up until then, evening lights, for her, meant the kerosene lamp her mother would light up in the night inside the hut, and the Milky Way that stretched across the unpolluted skies of her village, with blinking stars weaving an illuminated tapestry in the vast expanse above her. She looked in amazement at the beautiful neon lights that relentlessly burned through the evening, lighting up sidewalks, cars and human faces in varying hues.

But she could see them only through a small opening in the curtains of the small room where she had been kept along with two other children of her age, twin sisters Minu and Sonu. They were made to share a large bed under an old ceiling fan that would break into a racket the moment it would be switched on. Two thick curtains remained constantly drawn on the two windows of the room and a wooden closet with a life-size mirror stood in one corner. It was in the front of this mirror, Khuki, Minu and Sonu had to often stand naked for a quick inspection of their developing physical attributes by a middle-aged woman called Rani, the one who had kept Khuki out of sight in the car. Khuki was eleven and showed the promise of growing into a pretty young woman.

The girls were being regularly groomed by Rani, who screamed at those who would dare to be in the vicinity of the room. Slowly, their rusticity was peeling off. Khuki's matted hair had been cut short and bobbed and, instead of skirts, she was made to wear salwar kameez. The food she was served was heavenly compared with what she had been eating at home. Two toasts, a boiled egg and a glass of milk for breakfast and rice or rotis with dal and sabzi for both lunch and dinner. In these three years, good food and constant mollycoddling by Rani had worked a great deal towards weakening her memories of Boro Mollakhali. Her young, unassuming mind drew her close to Rani, to whom she clung on, as if she was her guiding light.

❖❖❖

The man who had driven Khuki from Gadkhali to Kolkata was the Uriah Heep of the area. He answered to the name Jugadu, though it was not his real name. That's because he could 'arrange for' almost anything. Jugadu couldn't remember where his home was. All he could recall was a train ride many years ago. He had landed in Kolkata as a lost child, growing up begging on the streets. It was only a matter of time for the underground to welcome him. He walked the lanes and by-lanes of the city under the tutelage of successive street gangs. He was quick to learn the tricks of the trade. Pick-pocketing came easily to his nimble hands. With time, he became an expert in selling stolen jewellery and the making of country bombs. Pimping came later.

'Jugadu, here's your share from the sale of that necklace,' or 'Bhangar needs disturbance' and even 'the businessman wants an escort' became the refrain of his kingdom he had slowly created. His cunning was unparalleled; his trail, undiscovered.

The money he made could have made him live in luxury, but never for once was he ostentatious with his lifestyle, or loquacious. His services were often required, for he had developed such wide contact in different strata of society. Jugadu knew what exactly he had to do—which was a job he actually did not like as he never forgot that he was a victim of circumstances himself. Yet, the adrenaline rush he experienced in his cat-and-mouse game with the law and the money that changed hands to reach him through *hawala* kept him going. Over time, he became a legend of sorts who was spoken of in hushed tones at midnight card games in *dhaba*s and cheap bars, and deployed into service for a fee whenever any situation spiralled out of control.

Jugadu knew Khuki, Minu and Sonu were still a few years away from playing the role for which they had been brought. Until then, their upkeep had to be maintained, come what may because there were no ways yet the girls, bought for a price from their poverty-ridden parents, could be released into the urban wild. Whenever Jugadu saw the three girls, he would plunge himself in a throwback to his own past. He wondered, what if he were subjected to such captivity after being torn away from his home? How would he have felt or reacted? He knew what he did with the three girls was unpardonable. But so deeply was he buried in the catacombs of his underground life that all exit doors had already been permanently shut. And that's the reason why he felt so much for Khuki, Minu and Sonu.

Unlike him, Rani was heartless. She saw in the three girls a gold mine that waited to be harvested. But she was getting tired of waiting. Rani picked up her mobile phone and called a number she had memorised.

'Jugadu?'

'Yes?'

'I have to get the girls ready and fast. How long can I wait?'

'Not my fault. You wanted them young and I got them young. But I didn't like it.'

'What do you mean?'

'Rani, they are too young, even for business. I should have declined.'

'Anyway, I have a plan.'

'I am listening.'

'Remember the doctor who was fired from work by a private hospital for conducting an illegal abortion?'

'Yes, what about him?'

'Well, I have spoken to him and he said there are some medicines, something that he called steroids or something that can be given to the girls to make their bodies grow before time.'

'How is that possible?'

'I don't know. But that doctor said it is possible. He said it happens everywhere in the world. He also said a lot of sportsmen use such drugs to build muscles and improve their performances.'

'I don't know. Let me think.'

Jugadu fell silent. His mind began to claw into the depths of his knowledge in an attempt to figure out what exactly steroids were and what they meant for a human body. He suddenly remembered having heard years ago that a Canadian athlete, who had used such drugs to cheat in an international race, had suffered terrible after-effects, including the ignominy of developing breasts like a female's. 'Okay, so it can happen,' he said to no one.

Jugadu called a contact who sold hallucination-causing drugs to a street peddler.

'Well, Jugadu, they can create muscles and enhance physical attributes but they can also kill.'

'Kill?'

'Yes, if abused, these drugs can cause death.'

Jugadu lighted a cigarette and blew smoke rings into the air as he struggled to make up his mind. Unlike birth, he knew death didn't send its calling card. Maybe, one day, he would lie bleeding and unattended in the very world he plied his trade every day, knifed to death by a rival or shot by the police in an encounter. His body would lie unclaimed, like a dud coin. A child who had once arrived lost in life would, in death, stay lost to humanity.

Jugadu sighed. The lure of money suddenly lost importance for him. Three young girls were being primed to make a beginning towards an unfortunate end. He made up his mind.

That day, around seven in the evening, Jugadu went out for a walk. He needed to clear his mind. He walked almost a mile. Feeling grubby, Jugadu went to a man who was selling momo on the sidewalk usurped by street-food vendors.

'Give me half-a-plate.'

'Ok.'

The man returned to packing spicy sauces into polythene sachets.

'New arrivals,' Jugadu whispered.

'How many?'

'Three'

'What's so new about it?'

'All minors.'

Surprised, the man raised his eyebrows slowly.

'Where?'

'At Rani's.'

The momo-seller returned small change to Jugadu. The transaction was over. Not another word was spoken. Jugadu vanished into the crowded streets. That was the last anybody had seen of him.

✣✣✣

Special Officer Aritra Mitra had just returned to his office after making two arrests at a pub where a brawl had broken out over seating space. Terribly tired, he asked for a glass of water. Leaning back on his chair, he lifted his feet on the desk, picked up his mobile phone and began looking into the texts that had arrived an hour ago, when he was grappling with a drunk man inside that pub. It was then his phone rang. The number was unnamed but he knew it by heart. It was Praveen Rai, the dimsum-seller who, on the side, also earned some money as a police informer. Rai had remained a trusted source. Never for once had he failed Aritra.

Two hours later, when it was about 10 pm, Aritra knocked on Rani's door.

'Who's it?'

'Open up. It's the police.'

Aritra, his service pistol drawn, burst into the room, followed by several other cops who had joined the raid. In one corner of the room, they found three small girls huddling, overcome with fear. The rescue of the girls took long as some neighbours tried to block the path of the police in an attempt to prevent them from arresting Rani. But Aritra made it abundantly clear to the crowd that he would brook no answer if the police were stopped from doing their duty.

That night, the three girls stayed at the police station. Aritra took personal care of them, feeding them and arranging for them a place to sleep. Later, he called the state-run hospice called 'Alo' with which the police had a steady agreement for housing those rescued.

While Monu and Sonu's parents were tracked down and the twins returned to their home by the police two days later —Rani had begun to sing like a canary in the interrogation chamber—Khuki refused to be taken home. She even threatened to run away if she was forced to do so.

'What do you want to do?' Aritra had asked her.

'Please, please, Uncle, let me stay here. I want to go to school.'

✣✣✣

Khuki soon became the cynosure of all eyes at Alo because of her good nature and her remarkable determination for learning. Sutapa Dhar, the imperious warden at Alo, who ruled with an iron fist, was used to being pampered by a retinue that was made up of people from the hospice. Anybody new was required to be part of it as an apprentice. But, when she saw Khuki, she remembered the police officer telling her that this girl needed special attention. Sutapa, being an astute practitioner of social welfare, could notice a certain spark in the child's eyes. Within days, it was clear that Khuki's intelligence quotient was way higher than those who walked in and out of Alo like flotsam. The next thing Sutapa did was to get Khuki an identity card.

'Khuki, we need to have a proper name for you. How does Rukmini sound?

Rukmini? Khuki couldn't understand whether she was being expected to like or dislike the name.

'But Sutapa Aunty, what does it mean?'

'It means radiant or bright. In Bangla, *ujjol*.'

Rukmini was sent to a school that had been set up by the state government especially for girls like her. Even though she was behind other students in terms of years, it didn't take her long to catch up with her class and, eventually, with progress.

Nineteen to a dozen, stories like these appear only to be dismissed from memory like just another headline in the inside pages. The question of empowering women remains drowned in incomprehensible data. Yet, far from research and vows, somebody or the other is always authoring a turnaround story that drives strivings. Khuki, in a new avatar, was one such.

The bed on which Khuki used to sleep hadn't been used by any other inmate. Sutapa had not allowed anyone else near it; not because, in her subconscious, she was expecting her back. It was because the empty bed drove home the point that destiny is too ephemeral to be waited for. The bed was a trophy that belonged to her and the girl she had so carefully mothered. Sutapa looked at the photograph of Rukmini, captured in a frame and kept on her table. She was wearing a stethoscope around her neck.

Khuki, who had come to Alo as a child scared out of her wits, was hand-held by Sutapa as she grew up under her tutelage. She had guided Khuki like a lighthouse during her passage from puberty to adulthood, from school to college and thereafter. But Sutapa knew that Khuki wasn't as anchored as she herself was for Alo. A time would come when she had to leave. After school, Khuki took to pursuing medicine, which required her to be at the medical college which she was going to.

Sutapa and the rest of the staff at Alo had stood at the gate, giving Khuki an emotional send-off. 'The day you come back here, I want to see a stethoscope around your neck,' Sutapa wiped a tear or two as she waved her goodbye. And Khuki, indeed, had come back with a stethoscope around her neck, to be held for posterity by a simple picture-frame.

But Khuki, or Rukmini's story did not end there.

Rukmini, even though she was employed with a renowned private hospital in Kolkata, was required to travel across the country because she was empanelled as a medical consultant with a non-profit organisation. Its mandate was clear-cut—go to remote villages and far-flung areas where medical facilities were few and far between. The medical camps that were regularly held by the organisation in the impoverished areas acted as a quick-fix for the ailing but Rukmini knew the services her team provided were only as good as their last visit. More leg-work, more surveys and more medical facilities were needed to bring some hope to the people who were too poor to be advised treatment in city hospitals. There were even villages that didn't have electricity. Stories like these struck a chord with Rukmini.

'Are there really villages that still don't have electricity?'

'Yes, Rukmini. There are many. Would you like to visit some?' The medical supervisor of one of the camps was sure that Rukmini could be convinced to visit these villages that had remained as a footnote for long on the list of priorities of doctors.

'Please draw up a plan for me, sir? Not only I will visit, but I will also hold a medical camp in some such villages.'

'All right, Rukmini. Let's look at next week.'

***

Seven days later, Rukmini and her team walked into a village that was beautifully idyllic. It was a long haul to the village from the Godkhali pier. Small waterbodies, banana plants, big and small trees, huts, cows and water buffaloes grazing and the light-green sweep of paddy fields combined to create a picturesque canvas Rukmini had never seen before. The village seemed to be frozen in time. Everything that was supposed to be in a village like this was in place in perfect harmony with nature. The only thing missing was electricity. The village seemed to have no name.

The village chief walked up to greet them. 'Doctor madam, the site of the camp is that side,' He pointed to his left.

'All right, but I would like to go around on foot for a while. Is there someone from the village who could show us the way around this place?'

A young man, about 20, wearing only a rolled-up *dhoti*, joined them. 'This way, doctor madam.'

Rukmini began to walk, through slush, negotiating the natural upheavals beneath her feet. At a short distance, the team could see a cluster of mud huts peeping from behind a row of trees. She increased her pace.

'This way, Doctor madam.'

'No, it's this way.'

'But there is no path there.'

'There is.'

Rukmini parted a thick bush to expose an old path, almost reclaimed by nature. Only a keen eye would be able to make out that a pathway once existed there.

'How did you know that there was a path here? Even I didn't know,' the young man said, visibly surprised.

She paused where the path began. It looked so familiar to her. 'That's right. How did I know about the existence of a path here?' Rukmini smiled as she began to walk again. A few seconds later, she was almost running. Suddenly, she broke into a run and jumped, as if trying to pluck something out of the air. 'Wasn't there a low-hanging tamarind tree here?'

'Yes, there used to be one, but a cyclone two years ago had uprooted it.'

She continued to run through the foliage, parting each bush to make way, and came to the edge of the treeline that surrounded the cluster of huts. Breathing heavily, Rukmini walked towards the thatched-roof houses. As she approached one, the tail of her saree got stuck in something. She looked back to find an old tube-well, rusty and useless, in the middle of a courtyard. She freed her saree, took a few steps and found herself in front of a house whose roof had almost been blown away, apparently by the storm. It looked like a deserted home of a very poor family. Transfixed to the ground, she kept looking at the house. She found the image that was in front of her changing, as if from the depths of the past, another picture was emerging slowly. A small hut with an old woman and a small boy were standing in the doorway. They looked like signatures of an artist emerging from beneath an old painting that was being restored. She could see the colour of the broken door changing into green and a red *gamcha* (traditionally patterned towel) hanging from a window. A doll made from rags was leaning on the mud-wall of the house, smiling at her.

'Does anybody live here?'

'Yes, an old woman suffering from tuberculosis and her son who works in the field.'

'What about the woman's husband?'

'He died long ago.'

'Anybody else? No relatives?'

'Yes, she had a daughter but we heard the child was taken by lifters at a fair in another village many years ago.'

Rukmini smiled.

Rukmini pulled a cotton mask across her mouth, summoned her assistant and walked into the hut. On a bed was an old woman, or a skeleton which barely resembled a human being. She sat next to her, uncoiled her stethoscope and pressed it against the woman's chest. Her hands were shaking. A storm that had risen in her life a long time ago was once again building, threatening to overpower her. The pique of the moment was drilling itself ruthlessly into her heart. She looked at the woman again. She was dying; her days were numbered. Rukmini uncoiled the *orna* (veil) from around her neck and used it to wipe the sweat from the forehead of the sick woman. Then she ran her fingers through the woman's hair in an attempt to comfort her.

'Where's your son?'

The woman couldn't speak. Instead, she turned her head towards the door, indicating that her son was not at home.

'Is it hurting too much?'

The woman nodded. *Was it comeuppance?* Rukmini wondered. She took out a syringe, gave her a shot and turned towards her assistant and the village lad. 'This would reduce her pain, but for only a few hours. I am leaving some medicines for her. When her son returns, explain the dosage to him.' She also left some money for the medicines.

Rukmini knew the woman would not survive a journey to a city hospital. She was beyond cure. 'Keep me informed about her, please. I will leave my number with the village chief.' She fished out a cell phone from her purse and took a picture of the woman.

'Why are you taking her picture?' the man in the *dhoti* asked.

Rukmini didn't reply. Instead, a tender smile emerged on her face. She kept a hand on her chest and bowed out of the hut, as if in respect for the dying.

'Does she have a heart disease?' The young man, seemingly nonplussed, asked.

'No, she never had a heart.'

The man in the *dhoti* wondered if he would ever be able to understand the language these city people spoke or what they usually meant while speaking.

Rukmini stepped out of the house slowly and paused near the derelict tube-well. She took a deep breath, looked at the house one last time, and walked out of the courtyard. She had lives to save, like that of her own had been, so many years ago. This was not the time to romance memory.

✣✣✣

A ROOM TO FORGIVE

Drop by drop, milk slid down the cotton-wool wick into the dry mouth of the infant, like raindrops on withered green. That was the only way the starving baby could feed. It was too weak and the mother, far from being healthy enough to be able to suckle her baby. A mother's joy of feeding her child with her own nectar now hung loosely from the tip of a wick.

She rocked the baby boy gently while softly singing lullabies she had herself heard as a child. Holding the baby close to her chest, she breathed in the milky smell of his translucent skin. That incredible feeling of having a part of her own heart beat on her bosom chased her agonies away, even if for a few moments. And as two lives spoke in God's own language, she found one day it was only her heart that was beating. The other had stopped forever, lost to heartlessness.

✣✣✣

Many birds crisscrossed the air of the Belonia village in south Tripura but the cuckoos and magpies fascinated Amala more than any other types. After every squall, they would sit side by side, trapezing on the swinging telegraph wires and tweet mellifluously. Their singing caparisoned the damp monsoon air. From the slush and pools of water down below, toads croaked themselves hoarse, in a very off-key contrast. To Amala, it seemed like an orchestra of the mismatched. Yet, she found an odd duet between land and air that only she could sense—the toads complaining like grumpy old men and the birds tweeting 'nothing doing, nothing doing, nothing doing' in a steady rhythm. She would break into peals of laughter, imagining that the birds were completely disregarding the whimpering toads.

'What is it? What's making you laugh like that?' her mother had asked.

'Ma, just see how these birds are singing.'

'What's there to see? They do it every day.'

Amala did not say she was laughing because of the invisible toads. Her mother would not understand that a small girl in a frock with hair knotted in red ribbons was plucking simple joys out of the air to feed her fantasies. One such was the Champui Hills she could see at a distance from her house. A scarlet stretch of blossoming Sinimungs ran along the face of the hills, which appeared to her like a thick red border on a white saree. And then, there were days when sudden flights of yellow-winged butterflies burst from wildflower bushes, looking like glistening dandelion seeds scattered into the sunlight. Even the clouds that piled on each other or flitted were either castles of fairies or elves playing hide and seek. '*Ki je bolish bapu, bujhi na* (I don't understand all this),' her mother Kumudini would say to her.

'Today I saw a ladybird on a taro plant. It looked like one of the red buttons on my white penny frock,' she wrote down in her beautiful handwriting in a small notebook as her fantasies spoke to her nineteen to the dozen. Be it a clutch of words, short poems or her random thoughts, her writings mirrored a brilliant mind. And it was that mind her teachers at the village school found to be extraordinary. 'She is prodigious,' Headmaster Binayak Deb would often tell other teachers. As impressed were her neighbours, 'What all she knows, how well she writes!' Everybody was hoping that one day this little girl would bring glory to the obscure village.

'We would give her a *britti* (scholarship),' Mr Deb announced one day. Though other teachers knew she was talented, they felt a *britti* was out of the question. 'That's going too far, I'd say. She is only nine and in class four,' the mathematics teacher had said. 'Why not? Girls in this school get to study only up to class four. We don't know what would happen to her hereafter, but a *britti* would surely support her further studies,'

Mr Deb had said. Amala had little thoughts about her *britti*. Her red ladybirds would be blue buttons sometimes, the elves in the sky would exchange roles with fairies, and the cuckoos would continue to tease the croaking toads.

The *britti* sat idle on her life until Mr Deb came to her house one day to stir up the question. 'I am telling you Mr Saha, your daughter is very talented. Please do not waste the *britti*. Let her continue her studies in some other school,' he had pleaded with Amala's father Biplabkanti.

But Biplabkanti had other ideas.

❖❖❖

And Amala kept running through the magpie woods towards more imaginings—writing down what she saw and reading what she didn't know. The universe was unveiling newer wonders to her every day. Her fanciful curiosities were heightened to a point from where her young, raw mind refused to accept the fact that she was too small to always have her way. In a family of doers, she was the only dreamer. 'I don't know which way this girl's life is heading,' Biplabkanti said one day despairingly to Kumudini, expecting her to share his concerns. 'You could have at least let her continue with studies. You didn't do that. Why complain now?' she shot back. Biplabkani recoiled into silence. He knew the small purse that the *britti* carried wasn't going to be redeemed. He had spent it on running the family. After all, he was just a dispatch clerk at a British-owned sawmill in undivided India. 'Unrest has erupted everywhere. The country is on fire. Many freedom fighters are hiding in Tripura. Just a few days ago, our barber Jibon was saying that more and more of unknown faces are being seen in Belonia. What use studying now, that too, for a girl?'

Amala never got to study again. The brilliance of her mind, her imagination, and her bountiful discoveries were being constricted into a chalk-marked circle her father had drawn around her.

And amidst all this, Amala was married off. She was only eleven.

'She is so young, why are you rushing her into marriage,' the local wise had pointed out to Biplabkanti. But there was no going back.

Her toads stopped croaking for her. The cuckoos flew to a new telegraph wire and the sky above Belonia turned so slate-grey and unvaried that the fairies and elves went back to their homes in fairy-tales. And the odes to the Champui Hills remained pinned down between the covers of a small notebook. Amala became a misfit in a world of designs.

✣✣✣

Weddings in the thinly populated Belonia were so few and far between that the news of a marital alliance being set up in any home would run faster than the wind through the talkative village. The antecedents of a groom or how good a daughter would be as a bride would monopolise conversations at saloons, grocery shops, the vegetable market and the post-office. The inescapable village grandfather, Suhrid Burman, who had a propensity for throwbacks, would hold court at the only tea shop to talk about the grandeur of weddings back in the day. And nosey wives would peek into neighbours' wardrobes in an attempt to best each other at the sartorial contest a wedding was for them. Nobody stayed uninvited. The whole of Belonia would come together as one large family to bid farewell to a daughter whom they would miss until the next wedding happened.

So, whenever Kumudini would clip her only silk saree to the laundry line on the forecourt on sunny days to rid it of mildew, Amala would know a wedding was just round the bend.

'Ma, am I not going to this wedding?' she would ask, eager to be part of a fanfare that would unfailingly re-equip her mind with more imaginings.

The clinking of the bangles, the laughter, the teasing lilt of the *shehnai*, the smell of food and the all-pervading bonhomie in a colourful crowd of people had their exclusive appeal for

Amala. She would look at the whole show from an unpeopled part of the house, as if she was at the edge of the world spectating a distant galaxy being shaped by myriad brilliant forms. And when a man and a woman wearing garlands would begin circling a small fire under the *chhadnatola* (a makeshift place where vows are exchanged in a Hindu wedding), it looked like a game to her.

Amala would return home thinking about the colours she saw. But their dazzle would float in her vision only for a while, unlike the lingering scarlet of the Champui Hills.

✣✣✣

When her own moment at the *chhadnatola* arrived ironically ahead of her time, the bejewelled galaxy that once fascinated Amala had shrunk into a small pit of fire burning between her and the man who would be her husband. The *shehnai* was playing as usual but its lilt was drowning in noise—the sounds of laughter and the clinking of bangles seemed like a machined tedium. And Amala, who sat like a harlequin in a pantomime, waited to be told what's next.

As the wedding party became increasingly boisterous, Kumudini pulled Biplabkanti aside, away from the earshot of any. 'We have been deceived,' she whispered to her husband. 'I know,' Biplabkanti wore a confounded look as he seemed to be at a loss for words. He ran his fingers vigorously through his hair, clasping them in his fist to vent his angst at being travestied. But all he could do was to slump into a chair silently to express how hopelessly disquieted he was. By then, the situation had become irreversible as the rituals had already advanced into marriage vows.

Just a month ago, Biplabkanti had found a match, a young man of 26 named Chandranath Deb. Handsome and well-built, he taught Bengali literature at the Dhaka University and belonged to a well-off family of the Deotala village near Dhaka.

But when the groom took off his *topor* (a headdress for a Bengali groom) at the *chhadnatola* to exchange garlands with Amala, it was discovered that he wasn't Chandranath but his elder brother Surjokanto. Dhaka had sent to Belonia a wrong groom, and that was not by any mistake. Nobody said a word.

✣✣✣

Like a ruined artefact being retrieved from ship-wreck depths, she rose arduously from the cavity of her bed. Her dishevelled white hair that ended just near her ears looked like a porcupine's back, and the creases covering her face resembled rivulets spreading carefree into illogical patterns.

A dim light from a yellow bulb softly illuminated her forehead before sliding onto her nose and pronounced facial bones on her hollow cheeks. She looked so immutable having lived the years she weren't meant to. The old woman took a glass of thin milk from the female attendant and drank from it slowly, sip by sip, waiting for the fluid to diffuse somnolence. It was bedtime. The sedative-laced milk would bring her sleep but until it did, she and her loneliness would talk to each other softly, as always they did all her splintered life.

The hospice she lived in had been condemned to the crypt, where no flowers were sent on birthdays and no letters came except cheques from unseen sons and daughters.

The old lady wasn't bothered about empty letter boxes. She didn't want anybody to come in search of her. She had been a recluse all her life.

❖❖❖

Amala could not do away with Belonia tugging at her heart. But she became quickly aware that she couldn't afford to keep living in fantasies anymore that were once her own reality back home. The rules of the household were harshly set for her from the time she had stepped in as a new bride.

'The two of you have to live in the outhouse in the courtyard,' her mother-in-law Amravati made no bones about it as she pointed to a small tiled house with tin walls. That was not all though. Amala had to deposit her gold ornaments with her because 'they would be safe in my almirah'.

And then, her sarees followed the ornaments. 'What need is there for such a small girl to have so many sarees? I'll keep them arranged separately or else they will be spoiled. For now, let her use two.' Amala never saw the others again, including her wedding *Benarasi* (Banarasi saree).

Squirming with embarrassment, Surjokanta told her new bride not to mind his mother's behaviour. 'She is like that but you'll find out in the end that she has a soft heart,' he tried to console her.

'But, why do we have to live in the outhouse?'

He couldn't tell her why. He didn't want to lose face. Surjokanta wasn't an unpleasant man. He was a born layabout and appeared befuddled all the time in the after-effects of his alcoholism. He went fishing too in a nearby stream, where he would spend hours looking at the sinker, as if his whole world depended on its movement. Surjokanta was so carefree that working to earn a living was not in his lexicon. He was way too extravagant with time. In their household, respect and care were reserved for those who earned.

'Can you cook?' Surjakanto had asked. Moving her head from left to right and back, she had answered. So, food came from the main house but that was only in the night. All through the day, she would be famished. Her stomach would ache and her head would spin because of weakness. If hungry, she would drink bellyful of water. Amala was losing weight rapidly. With Surjokanto perpetually missing from home or returning drunk, there was nobody to take care of her woes.

One night, Amala was writing a letter to her parents, the first time since she arrived here.

'Respected Baba and Ma,
A billion *pranam*.'

Then she scratched the line out, sealed her lips with the forefinger of her left hand and stared into the wall. Was this the way they taught us to write letter to parents at school? Yes. So, she started again, on a fresh sheet of paper.

'Respected Baba and Ma,

A billion *pranam*. I hope both of you are all right. I am doing fine. My husband is a good man. So is my mother-in-law. They are taking care of me. There is no shortage of anything here. But both of you take care of yourself. Don't worry about me. Your obedient daughter, Amala.
P.S. Please do not throw away my frocks. I will wear them when I go home.'

The words were blurring. Curling up like a foetus, she began to weep, her body rising and falling like disturbed earth.

❖❖❖

It was raining so hard that afternoon that the window sill was wet, leading to legs of water cascade down the wall to create a small pool on the floor. The old lady's bed was near the window.

Droplets of water had gathered on her hair at random like pearl beads, making her head look like a shining crown. Somebody should shut the window, or else the room would be flooded and her bed would be completely wet.

'Where is this attendant!' she murmured to herself. The attendant was always missing whenever she wanted her to be around. She raised herself on her frail hands, and got out of the bed. She had to be very careful. The underfoot condition was treacherous, too slippery. Holding her breath, she began tip-toeing towards the window, which was swinging in and out like the pages of an open book in the air. She stood in the pool of water where the floor met the wall, and began pulling the window shut, inch by inch. One wrong step, and she would slip.

How many times has she fallen and risen!

❖❖❖

The chimneys of nearby factories spewed black smoke into the sky above Deotala. This made Amala sad, very sad. The sky was her playfield. She could lock her mind onto the vast expanse and spend a whole day without bothering about how her life down below would unfold. 'The cities are crawling towards me, to snatch away my little joys, my wondrous moments, my girlhood,' she wrote down in her notebook. As always, she was wise beyond her years. She often wondered if she could only wrap the sky above Belonia around her body and feel its cloudy softness on her skin, there would have been some solace. At least, her modesty would have been spared.

Two years had passed since her arrival in this house as an eleven-year-old bride. Time had taken its toll on her clothes. She was left with just one saree. The other one, tattered, had been turned into a mop. That was a problem nobody else could manage for her. To an extent, of course Surjokanta, but he was useless as ever. She would wash her only saree, wear it wet, and let her body-heat dry it up, causing her to often sniffle and cough.

'Can't you see I am falling ill?' she had asked Surjokanto. As usual, he had shrugged before going out for fishing. 'Worthless!' Amala had screamed, but nobody was listening. Or were they?

From his room in the main house, Chandranath heard her scream. He had watched his elder brother walk into the house on their return from Belonia, with a visibly nervous Amala behind him. The little girl in an unmanageable *Benarasi* saree looked like a gift hurriedly packed. He wondered if the decision of his parents to drop him from the wedding plans was right or wrong, but one thing was sure. Even though the girl was very young, she was too cute and would probably be a head-turner when she would grow up. But as of that moment two years down the line, she looked like a skeleton that passed for a living being.

Chandranath was impressed by the grit with which Amala was defeating her troubles and equally embarrassed for the way the household had caused them in the first place. How could someone live like this? No, something needed to be done for her, but how or what?

The opportunity came with an unwholesome beginning. When Amala was almost fifteen, she gave birth to a baby boy. The infant was so weak and Amala so dry that feeding it was like feeding a new-born sparrow. Just a *jhinuk* (a conch shell-shaped spoon) of milk came from the main house for the baby, which was too sharp and hard near its narrow end to be used for feeding. So, she made wicks out of cotton-wool to feed the baby that was too weakened by starvation. Hoping against hope, she had tried to nurse her son back to health. But then, all of a sudden the baby was recalled by the Creator, as if a father was taking his son out of a game in which nobody was willing to share the joy of being merry.

If Amala was heartbroken, she didn't show it. But that she was brimming with fury was all too evident. 'How many more lives do we have to lose before you people understand!' she had jabbed the forefinger of her right hand angrily into the air like a spear, pointing it at the main house while chiding her husband. She had become so exasperated with her living conditions that her loud protestations had become the only conversation between her and her husband. 'Do something, or else I am going back to Belonia,' she had said in a fit of rage, her no-nonsense tone catching Surjokanto completely off-guard.

Two days later, Amala was summoned to the main house by her mother-in-law. 'Listen girl, you can always make another baby, but don't do our heads in with your shouting. From tomorrow, you will make the room of Chandranath every day,' Amravati said to her.

✣✣✣

Gradually, Amala took control of Chandranath's room which always looked like the aftermath of a war. From dusting and mopping the floor to neatly folding his clothes that he would fling every which way, she began tidying up the room. She would arrange his books properly on the shelf. And in doing so, her old habit of reading returned.

'You read books?' The voice came from the door. Amala was quickly leafing through a book as nobody was around. But she didn't realise that Chandranath that day had returned from the university earlier than usual.

She was afraid she might be scolded for overstepping her limit. 'I mean…I was just attracted by the beautiful cover of the book,' Amala tried to explain.

'That's all right. But can you read?'

'Yes, I can read and write too,' she said. To try her, Chandranath gave Amala a writing pad and a pencil. 'Write something.' She began hesitatingly, but soon she started writing with flourish, about Champui Hills, about the untamed burst of the scarlet. Amala herself was surprised that she still hadn't lost her flair for writing even after so much of hardship. Now that someone was around to read, her gifted mind began taking baby-steps out of evanescence.

'Bird, you go
This is not your nest
Hold the hues of the skies
In your quivering breast.'

Nobody remembers the stars that burn out in daylight, Chandranath thought as he sat numbed after reading the short poem written by Amala. The simplicity of her writings, her expressions aflame with yearnings and the nomadic quintessence of her soul were slowly wrecking his scholastic calm. He began feeling an inexplicable attraction towards Amala as a sapiosexual sense would overcome him every time he would read her writings. Chandranath was hopelessly immured by her bewitching aura.

Neither could they realise that the layers of all that were forbidden between them were getting peeled off inconspicuously. A touch here and a smile there, moments shared watching rains or reading from a book of love stories together were slowly making their composure collapse like an embankment unable to withstand a surging deluge.

And then one Sunday afternoon, when everybody in the house was having a siesta and she was making his bed, they crossed the last mile of correctness. In a flash, he had dragged her into his chest. 'Chandranath, what are you doing!' she had said breathlessly but both knew it was just a coy pretence meant to delay her surrender. Soon, Amala was coo-cooing, whispering sweet nothings into his ears.

That one afternoon dramatically changed the way Amala looked at life. She realised she had a magical wand that no man could resist—her womanhood. So, in intimate moments flush with emotions, she would subtly ask for favours. Sometimes it would be a pen or a book, sometimes earrings or a saree and some other times even money. And Chandranath, who by then had become enamoured by her, was ever-willing to lend her life a semblance of dignity. The help that he was offering was no more out of pity; the stirrings he was experiencing in Amala's company were opening his heart to over-indulgence. And the constant petting gave her a high she had never experienced before. But then, much as they appeared as a pair made in heaven, both knew the relationship had an expiry date.

'What happens when you get married?' Amala had asked Chandranath one day as she stitched a loose button on his *kurta* while he was wearing it, her warm breath clouding on his chest. The question had brusquely pulled him out of rapture. He was aware the time was not too far when they would have to part—his mother was already sending his pictures out to match-makers. But he didn't want Amala to be foundering again when he would eventually move away from her.

'Please do not worry, Amala. You will be in my heart, always,' he had said.

The Champui Hills were calling her again. Every time she closed her eyes, she could see the scarlet wave. All that remained was to part the magpie woods and scale the hills. Come what may, she wouldn't stop running.

✣✣✣

People seemed to be spoiled for choice. A red blouse today, a white petticoat tomorrow and a blue bush-shirt the day after—Amala was stitching away diligently. She was an instant hit in the Deotala village where tailoring was never a cottage business. She was earning more money than she actually needed to live a simple life in relative comfort. The sewing machine Chandranath had gifted her was working wonders to turn her life around.

'*Eibar ektu shobhyo bhabe bash korle hoi na* (Isn't it time we lived in a civilised manner)?' The question was directed at Surjokanta. 'But Amala, don't we already have enough?' He was counting money and she, her dreams. A marked improvement in her lifestyle made her the envy of Deotala and a thorn in the side of her mother-in-law who couldn't stomach the fact that Amala was no longer at her mercy.

Yet, she felt incomplete as a woman. Sometimes, in the overreaching solitudes of her mind, the image of her dead son would rise like an indelible watermark. She knew the only way that wound could be healed was by having another child. So, when a baby girl arrived months later, she became a magpie-whisperer again. Amala named her Champui after the hills. No more wicks to be dipped in *jhinuk*s, no more feeding the baby drop by drop as Amala was gushing like a generous river.

But motherhood failed to lift her from the rut she had got herself in—her addiction for favours. Chandranath had long stopped being a yielding conquest for her. He was building his own family as a young husband. But many others were, on whom she began to switch her magic on. The innocent, dreamy girl from Belonia had been truly overpowered by avarice.

'Stay away from her,' would be the advice for men without endurance from those who weren't willing to be caught in her web of intrigues.

The air was rife with rumours. The fast money she was making, the men she was seen with in Dhaka where she shopped for textiles, and her garish clothes—they all combined to offer grist to naysayers.

Some of it had reached Surjokanta, who behaved normally in front of Amala. He feared that trickle-downs from the comforts the family was endowed with might vanish if he created a fuss. But in private, he believed his wife was being immoral.

❖❖❖

'We need to shift to another place, a bigger one,' Amala said, taking Surjokanta by surprise.

'But where? To Dhaka?'

'No, I'm thinking about Calcutta. And Dhaka, as you know, is in another country now. Look, Champui is growing up fast. We need to give her decent education. I don't want to give her a life like yours and mine. She would rot in Deotala.'

'True. I don't want her to grow up like you, Amala.'

'What do you mean?'

'Noting, really nothing. I was only thinking about her future.'

Surjakanta might have been a useless, rudderless man who revolved on his own axis. Money for liquor, bait for fish and hours to loaf away were what his life was all about. He had chosen to lounge in the glory of his wife unabashedly and Amala had long stopped minding his waywardness as long as he didn't interfere in her business. But to imagine a life away from Deotala was troubling him. This is where he was born, and every breath he took was from the free air of his village. To be prised away from Deotala would be like living in a body emptied of soul.

So, when the time came to leave, Amala walked out of Deotala with arrogance, Surjakanta with heartache and little Champui with boundless wonder.

✣✣✣

Champui was going to college which was not too far from her house in Bhowanipore. This was an old neighbourhood but nice and tidy. Bengali aristocrats had built their houses here. Yellow buildings with pillars, green French windows, arched gates and red balustrades set them apart from the modern match-box like houses of the nouveau-riche. But what Champui couldn't tolerate were the young rowdies who gathered at the tea stalls on pavements, building their rabid worlds over a cup of the brew as and when they pleased. Their catcalls and passes had become a constant nuisance. They did not spare even her mother whenever she went out. 'There goes the queen bee!' or 'What have we done to be so ignored!', many such deplorable remarks would come racing through the air at her.

'Ma, why do you let them go scot-free?'

'My dear, silence is contagious,' Amala had said to her daughter, expecting her to understand the import of her words.

And Surjokanta? The least said the better. He had added gambling to his repertoire of bad habits. He was every which way but loose. Little conversation would pass between him and Amala. There was never any affection between them.

Despite his own foibles, Surjakanta had never taken kindly to the means Amala had used to rise from the ruins of her life. His pent-up frustration at not being able to look Amala in the eye was decaying him from inside. Like a caged animal that violently claws the floor of its prison, Surjakanta had begun to bare his fangs and claws. He couldn't take it anymore.

Sparks started flying around the house as he and Amala engaged in a battle of attrition.

Hearing rubbish from Surjokanta had become a regular affair for Amala. Initially, she avoided answering him. But she knew her patience was running thin.

One night, in drunken stupor, he went to the extent of reminding Amala about Chandranath. 'What do you think? I don't know where you used to get the money from back in Deotala or what you do now?' Surjakanta had yelled at her.

'You know nothing. Tell me what you know,' she yelled back.

From time to time, Champui would join the heated exchange without taking sides. 'Baba, if you really have something to say, let's hear it, and Ma, why don't you clear things up so that he stops?'

But there was no stopping to the row that erupted every night with renewed accusations and counters. Once it came to such a pass that Surjokanta couldn't resist himself. 'You are a bloody whore and I don't want my daughter to live in the same house as you.'

A thunderbolt seemed to have vertically split the house. Champui stood stunned in the middle of the floor, amazed at the way her parents were out to degrade their own family. Amala slumped into a sofa, closed her eyes and took a deep breath, as if she had walked into an inn after a long and tedious journey. And Surjokanta, who stood at the other end of the room like an impassive mannequin, wondered if the arrow he had shot hastily could ever be retrieved.

'Champui, go to your room,' he ordered.

'No, she must also listen to what I have to say so that she can take a call about me being a whore.' Amala sat crouching in the sofa, her fingers digging deep into its velvet arm-rests, her body half raised, as if a maimed tigress was preparing to take a decisive leap.

'Where shall I start? From the beginning?' Her eyes were spewing fire and her voice as cold as revenge.

Surjakanta tried to cringe away from her fury. He could feel the rising flames in her eyes were about to incinerate his entire lifetime.

'Now listen. First of all, I was cheated in marriage. Your family sent you and not Chandranath with whom my alliance was set up. And then, your mother treated me like rubbish. You and your mother were responsible for the death of our first child. Champui, you had a brother who died soon after birth because of the heartlessness of your father and your grandmother.'

Shocked, Champui looked at her parents with disbelief. 'Is this true, Baba?'

Amala continued, as if she was a possessed woman. 'And finally, if I hadn't done what I did, the soil beneath your feet would have swallowed you. You would have starved to death like the son I couldn't raise. Today, you are accusing me, but have you ever thought where you would be, where Champui would be if I hadn't been around?' Her chest was heaving as she finished speaking in one breath, her words dissecting the man she never had any respect for.

An uneasy calm settled on the house. Champui returned to her room quietly, leaving the floor to mutual animus between her parents. Her mind tried to block the unsavoury sight of them unleashing spite on each other. But the impact of the unholy war was spreading into her nervous system like slow venom. Surjakanta sat on his chair, drinking to forget. And Amala locked herself into her room to forgive.

The next morning, Champui found the door to Amala's room ajar. She craned her head in to find her bed empty. Only, the crumpled bed sheet and a dent in the pillow held the outlines of her mother's body, an image that would stay embedded in her subconscious forever.

Champui's intense search for her mother found no passage into any discoveries. Amala had vanished without a trace, remaining in Champui's fond memories as an intrigue.

✣✣✣

The old lady always woke up at 6 am to drink a cup of tea that would be left on a stool by her bed. Two hours later, the attendant who brought it to her, found the tea untouched. She was still sleeping. This shouldn't be. All these years, the old lady never missed her morning cup. The attendant looked at the bed. She had a strange calmness on her face that she hadn't noticed before, as if a little girl had raised her face to receive the first summer showers. There would no more be another cup of tea for this bed.

Sheets of paper and a few pencils were found under the mattress near the area where her head used to be on the pillow. Each sheet of paper was filled with her random thoughts in beautiful handwriting. And two words kept appearing unfailingly in the writings: 'Champui Hills.'

ACKNOWLEDGEMENTS

What started from a chance conversation with an abandoned woman from the Sunderbans has finally found fruition. The spark that set me off to write this collection of short stories based on real-life circumstances found meaning, substance and direction because of the Editorial Director of Niyogi Books, Dr. Nirmal Kanti Bhattacharjee. This book wouldn't have seen light of the day had it not been for his support, inspiration and guidance. But, above all, I offer my undying gratitude to those individuals who took a leaf out of their lifetimes to share their ordeals with me, telling me true stories of their lives that defy logic and reasoning. Their agony and triumph that I have presented in a fictionalised form in this collection mirror the humankind's greatest discovery—hope.